D1524090

MURDER IN MARSEILLE

BOOK 14 OF THE MAGGIE NEWBERRY
MYSTERIES

SUSAN KIERNAN-LEWIS

SAN MARCO PRESS

Carried Away
Stolen Away

The French Women's Diet

1

The afternoon sun filtered through the thick haze of clouds overhead. It wasn't supposed to rain today, for which Maggie was grateful. But it did promise to be hot and humid.

Not unusual for August in the south of France.

But still not pleasant.

She engaged the auto drive on her Peugeot sedan as she drove the A7 south to the Marseille Provence Airport. Today of all days she didn't want to be late. With her thoughts boomeranging around her brain all morning, it was safer to let the car regulate a consistent speed.

At seventeen miles northwest of the coast, the Marseille International Airport was actually nowhere near downtown Marseille but was convenient for Maggie who lived near the small Provençal village of St-Buvard.

With so many other unique recreational opportunities in Provence she rarely found a reason to visit Marseille. While it had long since shrugged off its reputation as a treacherous town, a palpable patina of menace stubbornly remained.

Maggie tried to remember the last time anyone visiting

from the States had suggested a tour of Marseille. Her husband Laurent insisted the city's Old Port was imminently worth visiting, especially the fish markets which he frequented often. But there were so many other charming and more accessible tourist venues near their village that Marseille had never really ranked high on Maggie's go-to list.

She glanced at the dashboard clock. Three o'clock. Nicole's flight would be arriving within the hour. She leaned forward in expectation just thinking about seeing her niece again.

It had been ten months since Maggie's father's memorial service—the last time Maggie had seen Nicole—and she'd been startled then at how grown up the girl had become.

Maggie bumped the air conditioning up a notch to combat the intense summer heat attempting to claw its way into the car. She noticed her phone vibrating on the dashboard.

It was Laurent.

With his work at the monastery *l'Abbaye de Sainte-Trinité* involving a new influx of refugees from all over Europe and the Middle East, Maggie hadn't had to lobby too hard to be the one to collect Nicole from the Marseille Airport today. Laurent also had the upcoming harvest of their vineyard at Domaine St-Buvard to get ready for, not to mention his insistence on cooking most meals for the family and orchestrating most of the activities of their two children.

Three children now, Maggie reminded herself.

They'd unofficially adopted a homeless teenager last fall. The experience had proved challenging on several levels.

Maggie picked up the phone.

"Hey," she said. "What's up? I've only been gone thirty minutes."

The exit for the airport was coming up. She put her turn signal on.

"Mila cannot find her favorite whisk," Laurent said, referring to their nine-year-old daughter. His voice was low and nearly guttural. When Maggie first came to France and was trying to learn the language, she'd had the most trouble understanding Laurent of all people. He seemed to breathe his words rather than speak them. Plus half the time he communicated only in shrugs and grunts. She used to tease him: *"How am I ever going to learn to speak French if you don't use actual words?"*

Somehow, after thirteen years and in spite of that, she'd managed to learn.

"Tell her to look in the bottom kitchen drawer by the dog bowls," she said.

Mila had a passion for making pastry and dreamed of being a world-famous pastry chef someday. She was constantly whipping up dessert souffles and *gâteaux* in the Domaine St-Buvard kitchen as Laurent looked on with pride.

"Will you be going near a *boulangerie*?" Laurent asked.

"I can if you need me to."

Maggie maneuvered toward the sweeping arc of triple lanes leading to the airport off the A7. She felt her pulse quicken at the thought of seeing Nicole again—and of bringing her home to Domaine St-Buvard.

"Une baguette. C'est tout."

"Got it. See you soon. Love you." She disconnected before he could respond because another call was coming in. A photo of Maggie's mother materialized on the phone screen.

"Hey, Mom. What time is it there in Atlanta?"

"It's nine o'clock. Is she there yet?"

Maggie could hear the tension in her mother's voice. It seemed to be there all the time lately but more often when she was talking about Maggie's niece.

Thirteen years ago when Maggie's sister Elise was presumed dead and little Nicole orphaned, Maggie had brought the child to the US from the south of France to be raised by Maggie's parents.

As Maggie's parents had aged, that arrangement became

more and more difficult. Three years earlier, her parents sold the Atlanta house they'd lived in for nearly fifty years so that Maggie's father could move to a memory care facility. Maggie's mother and Nicole had relocated to a condo in Midtown.

Even so, Elspeth Newberry had become less able to keep up with Nicole as the months went by. Now that Nicole had graduated from high school, the time had come to change the original arrangement.

At least *Maggie* believed it was time.

"No, Mom. Her plane doesn't get in for another twenty minutes. I told you I'd call you but there's no reason for you to stay up past your normal bedtime."

"You don't need to worry about my bedtime, Margaret. Just let me know when she arrives safely."

Maggie fought back a splinter of irritation. There had been plenty of times in the last two years when her mother had no idea where Nicole was and hadn't seemed bothered by that at all.

Now that she saw Nicole poised to leave the nest for good, Elspeth was frantically attempting to hold on.

"So is she excited about the visit?" Maggie asked.

Originally Maggie had arranged for Nicole to spend the entire summer with her and Laurent at Domaine St-Buvard, but Nicole's busy summer social calendar had reduced the visit to the month of August.

"I don't want you to get your hopes up. I'm sure Nikki is very excited to see all of you…"

"But?"

"But frankly she doesn't want to move to France. Can you blame her? She doesn't know a soul there."

"You mean aside from me and Laurent and her two cousins and Grace and Zouzou and Danielle—who by the way she used to call *Mamère*?"

"Please don't get defensive, darling. I'm not saying Nikki won't be delighted to see you all but her friends are here."

"You're on Ben's side, aren't you?"

Maggie knew her words sounded childish and now that she'd said them she wished she hadn't. But it was so aggravating to hear her mother siding with Maggie's older brother. *Again.*

"I'm on nobody's side. I just don't want to see you disappointed."

"Ben didn't spend five minutes with Nicole while she was growing up," Maggie said in frustration. "And now he wants her to move in with him?"

"The place I'm going to does not allow children."

Elspeth had already put down a deposit at the assisted living center where she planned to move to at the end of summer. "Honestly I think it will be good for both of them."

"It's not Nicole's job to get Ben through an emotional rough patch."

"That is not what this is," her mother said, vexation creeping into her voice. "The two of them have gotten close in the months since your father passed. I truly believe her moving in with your brother is the best thing for Nikki too."

It infuriated Maggie that her mother and Ben both called Nicole *Nikki*. It was like they wanted to erase her Frenchness.

And make no mistake, Nicole was French.

Way more French than Ben or Maggie's mother knew.

Maggie pulled into the lane for the thirty-minute airport parking lot and collected the ticket from the automated parking machine.

"Look, Mom, I'm about to lose our connection when I drive into the underground parking. I promise I'll have Nicole call you as soon as I get her."

"Thank you, darling. Be sure and—"

The call dropped as soon as Maggie drove into the parking

garage. She gave a sigh of relief followed by a quick spasm of guilt as she tossed her phone onto the passenger's seat.

It was all just so maddening!

Ben had literally not paid any attention to Nicole in thirteen years! He'd not gone to a single drama presentation at her school or attended any of her soccer games. Nor had he shown up at even one of her many equestrian competitions over the years.

And now he wants to be Father of the Year?

Maggie drove past a bank of elevators and headed to the far corner of the garage where there were usually vacant parking spots. It was a Tuesday and, except for business travel, the garage would be relatively uncrowded. After twelve years of marriage to Laurent she was in the habit of parking as far as possible from the terminal entrance to lessen the chance of car doors dinging her vehicle.

She pulled into the inside lane facing a cement wall and parked. She was right to park this far from the elevators. There was only a single other car in the section, and it was parked behind her around twenty feet away.

Even on a bright summer afternoon, the garage was dark and cool. The overhead lighting fixtures were positioned every six feet and gave off a sickening yellow light. The bulb directly over Maggie's parking spot was out.

She grabbed her purse and swung out of the car, careful to keep her keys in her hand. She'd already succeeded in locking them inside the car twice this year when her mind had been focused on other things.

Does Mom really think Ben will be a better parent to Nicole than I would?

Her mother had always been in the habit of excusing any and all less than admirable behavior from Ben. Maggie knew for a fact that her father had been disappointed in his only son. Maggie felt a flinch of sadness when she thought of her father.

While he'd only died last year, his mind had started unraveling two years earlier. Maggie missed him. Missed his words of wisdom. His laughter. His voice.

But it had been a long time since her father had indicated his feelings about anything—disappointment or otherwise.

Maggie shook off her melancholy and thought back to the last time she'd seen her brother at their father's service in Atlanta eighteen months ago. Ben had come alone. Although technically still married to Haley he didn't even visit her any more.

Maggie remembered Ben had looked depressed and downcast although, to be fair, she probably had too. After all, their father had just died.

But still! Could she conjure up even one single solitary memory of Ben interacting with Nicole during that whole visit?

No. Because as usual, it had all about Ben and how Dad's passing was affecting *him*.

They'd all lost a loving father, husband and grandfather. But somehow Maggie still managed to thank everyone for coming and had played hostess to the crowd of over two hundred of her parents' friends. Granted, while Laurent had been the one to arrange all the food, Maggie still had to manage her mourning sufficiently to be able to look after her mother as well as Jemmy and Mila.

And what had Ben done except drink too much and sit in the corner of the room looking at his cell phone? Nothing.

And now he wants to be responsible for another human being?
Shouldn't he start with a dog first?

Maggie's annoyance rippled through her as she stepped across the dark expanse of the parking garage. A couple was heading toward her, dragging their rolling luggage behind them, the sound of it reverberated loudly on the cement surface. Unlike in the States—and specifically the south where

Maggie was from—Maggie knew better than to make eye contact with the couple as they passed.

Or, God forbid, smile.

Besides, she had worked herself up into a mood. And that was *not* the state of mind she wanted to be in when she greeted her darling, much missed niece.

She paused for a moment, putting a hand against the wall, closing her eyes, and breathing in and out before turning and hurrying toward the elevator which would take her to the main terminal and arrival gates.

The last thing she wanted was to be late for Nicole's first visit back to France in five years!

Everything needed to be perfect.

In fact things needed to be better than perfect if Maggie was going to convince Nicole that moving to France to live with her and Laurent was what Nicole should do.

2

L aurent put the beginnings of his mushroom risotto in the fridge, setting it aside for tonight's dinner.

The kitchen was painted in a pale ochre yellow. The Provençal sunlight infused the kitchen through the wide oak-framed window over the sink that faced the front driveway. The space was designed for utilitarian use. The look was clean, airy, and masculine. It was definitely Laurent's room.

"Are you going to *Dormir* today?" Mila asked.

Laurent turned to regard his daughter. Blonde and blue-eyed, there was never a moment when he wasn't struck by her beauty, her innocence, her sweetness.

"Only briefly," he said. "I'm going to *l'Abbaye de Sainte-Trinité*. Can I trust you to stay home alone without burning down the house?"

Mila wrinkled her nose. "Is Jemmy in charge?" she asked, referring to her older brother. "That's not fair. He's only two years older than me. Luc can be in charge of us."

Laurent knew she had a point. Their foster son Luc Thayer was seventeen and certainly old enough to watch a ten-year-old and twelve-year-old without parental supervision.

"I am taking Luc to *Dormir*," Laurent said. "Is your bed made?"

"Yes, Papa."

"Why not go pick some sunflowers from the garden for Nicole's bedroom?"

Mila's eyes lit up at the suggestion and she turned to fish out a pair of scissors from one of the kitchen drawers.

Laurent ran a cloth over the countertops of the kitchen and spotted Jemmy with his remote control helicopter in the gravel drive out front. Beside him stood Luc.

A tall boy for his age, Luc had only been with them ten months—ten relatively quiet months until recently. Laurent frowned as he watched the teen through the kitchen window.

In the space of a few weeks, Luc had gone from being helpful and outwardly grateful for his good fortune to border-line surly and disruptive.

Just as he was before he came to live with us.

Just as Laurent's brother Gerard had been every day of his life.

Gerard.

Luc's biological father.

Laurent grimaced when he remembered the altercation with Luc last night which had ended in Luc's yelling "You're not my father!"—*as if that had anything to do with anything*—and slamming the door to his bedroom.

A bedroom door I provided him, Laurent thought. *Attached to a private room I gave him. Complete with three meals a day and a sense of belonging—if the ungrateful pup even cared—to a family.*

Gerard certainly hadn't.

Laurent's brother Gerard had hated every moment of his life when he and Laurent were living with their grandmother in Paris. Right up to the moment at age fifteen—two years younger than Luc now—when he packed his bags, stole a thousand francs from his grandmother and left in the middle of the night.

Like the thief he was.

"Papa?" Mila said breathlessly as she returned to the kitchen with a fistful of sunflowers. "Pretty?"

"Mm-mm," Laurent said, reaching for a vase from the upper cabinets. At six-foot-four—tall for a Frenchman—he often used his height to his advantage like now. Height also helped in the line of work he'd once had on the *Côte d'Azur* when intimidation and showmanship meant more than money or status.

He handed his daughter the vase.

"Mind your brother while I'm gone," he said before giving her a quick kiss. "*Maman* will be back with Nicole before I am home. Keep an eye on the roasting tomatoes, *oui*? But don't take them out. The pan is too heavy for you."

"It's not," Mila said with a pout. "I put heavy pans of cake batter in the oven at *Dormir* all the time."

Dormir was the bed and breakfast Laurent had created on property he'd bought a couple of years ago. Their good friend Grace Van Sant and her daughter Zouzou managed it with another dear friend, Danielle Alexandre. Grace and Danielle often had Mila over to help make the pastries and desserts served to their guests.

"Just turn the oven off if it looks like it is cooking too quickly," Laurent said with an arched eyebrow. He was used to pushback from Luc and even Jemmy but had hoped that Mila would continue to be sweet and compliant. For at least a little bit longer.

"Yes, Papa."

He would have preferred not to leave at all this afternoon—especially with Nicole coming in from the US—but it couldn't be helped. Frère Jean couldn't meet with him any other time and he needed to sort out the incoming flux of seasonal workers.

He picked up his keys and cell phone from the foyer hall table.

If Grace hadn't asked to borrow Luc today Laurent would have been forced to make up a reason to bring the boy with him.

As he walked out front where Luc and Jemmy stood talking, Laurent realized that for whatever reason he didn't trust Luc alone at Domaine St-Buvard.

3

The recently remodeled *Aéroport de Marseille Provence* sported a stunning twenty-two meter high glazed hall with a dramatic inverted beam roof and continuous overhead grids formed into dozens of glass skylights.

A panoramic terrace overlooking the main terminal had been designed to capture the bright Provençal sunlight while paying homage to the spirit of the airport's earlier 1960s design.

A little bit old, a lot of bit new, Maggie thought as she hurried through the terminal toward the arrivals lounge. Without doubt it was a beautiful airport and a brilliant introduction to the South of France.

While the Nice airport seemed to announce one had arrived on the Côte d'Azur in all its glamour and blue brilliance, the Marseille Airport was content to depict a rustic elegance that evoked the essence of Provence.

"*Pardonnez-moi, excusez-moi,*" she said as she maneuvered her way through the crowded food court until she reached the greeting area of the arrivals terminal beyond which no non-ticketed person could pass.

A flood of weary travelers pushed past her as she strained to catch sight of her niece. Like Maggie, Nicole had dark hair and was not very tall.

When she didn't see Nicole in the crowd at the arrivals gate, Maggie felt a knot of anxiety begin to pulse in her chest.

Had Nicole missed her flight?

Maggie her cell phone out of her purse to double check she hadn't gotten the arrival time wrong. She immediately saw two texts from Nicole.

<where R you>

<this place sucks! did you forget about me?>

Maggie quickly dialed Nicole's phone number and started to move away from the arrivals gate.

Nicole didn't answer.

Frustrated, Maggie, leaned against a wide stainless steel pillar that shot dramatically to the ceiling and texted Nicole.

<Im here where are you>

Almost immediately, Maggie felt her phone vibrate and glanced down to see the incoming text message.

<bag claim>

Because of the crowds it took Maggie nearly five minutes to make her way down the escalator and across the main food court to the baggage claim area. She scanned the luggage carrousels and saw her niece standing off to the side, her wheeled bag already collected and at her feet.

Nicole's hair was cropped short around her face. She was wearing a tight singlet, obviously no bra, and a pair of shorts. When Nicole turned to look at the giant plexiglass clock hanging overhead, Maggie could see half her *derrière* was hanging out.

Fighting her initial reaction of horror, Maggie called Nicole's name but Nicole had her ear buds firmly in her ears.

Maggie hurried over to her and as Nicole looked up, she threw her arms around the girl.

"Oh my gosh, you look so adult!" Maggie said. "I'm so sorry I wasn't at the gate to greet you."

Nicole rolled her eyes. "Fine. Can we go, please?"

Surprised at Nicole's manner, Maggie glanced around at the other passengers waiting for their bags.

"Is everything—?" Maggie started to say.

"Yes!" Nicole said sharply, grabbing the handle of her rolling bag. "Everything is just peachy, okay? I've only been waiting for an hour and meanwhile every suck-all French weirdo in this stupid country has come over to smack his lips at me, that's all!"

Maggie felt a knot forming in her stomach. "Your flight got in an hour early?'

"*No*, Aunt Maggie," Nicole said with sarcasm. "You caught me. I'm exaggerating. Now can we go?"

Pulling her bag behind her, Nicole lurched off in the direction of a big orange sign announcing the way toward Parking.

4

"Why do I need to go to *Dormir?*" Luc said from the passenger seat of Laurent's aging Citroën coupe. "I was just there yesterday."

Laurent didn't answer him. Luc couldn't see Laurent's eyes behind the sunglasses he wore but knew that he wouldn't have been able to interpret Laurent's expression or mood even if Laurent hadn't been wearing sunglasses.

Luc felt his body tensing.

During the time he had been living at Domaine St-Buvard he'd been forced to go to school in Aix—every day! And when he wasn't sitting in a classroom like some simpleton being forced to learn something he'd never in a million years ever need, he was being worked like a field hand at Domaine St-Buvard.

And when there wasn't something for him to do there, Laurent loaned him out to work at *Dormir!*

One of the kids at the monastery who Luc had known from the summer he'd lived there himself said everyone knew that the only reason Laurent had brought him into his home was so he didn't have pay the going rate for day laborers.

Luc glanced at Laurent and felt an irrational frustration and anger filter through himself. He gripped the armrest of the car, digging his fingers into the leather.

"Stop that," Laurent said without looking at him.

"Why do I have to go to *Dormir*?" Luc said again, hearing the whine in his own voice and hating himself for it. "I worked in the garden all day yesterday."

"The job is not finished."

The job will never be finished, Luc thought angrily. *Not while this slave driver has a three hundred hectare vineyard and a bed and breakfast that needs constant work.*

And a helpless laborer at his beck and call.

Lum stared out at the passing scenery and tried to bite his tongue. It wasn't Laurent's habit to talk about things that were bothering him or to pick up on anything that might be bothering anyone else. He was the most selfish bastard on the planet.

At least he didn't hit me.

Yet.

Luc had to admit there had been a few good moments here and there over the winter and spring. Maggie was always kind to him and she smiled a lot. Once he got used to that it wasn't terrible. Maybe even nice. And Jemmy and Mila actually treated him like a brother.

But of course, they could afford to be gracious since it was *their* house that he was just a guest in.

Nobody needed to tell him that as bad as things were now they were only going to get worse. Last summer he'd worked Laurent's fields in the grape harvest and he knew Laurent was an exacting taskmaster. But at least then Luc had been getting paid for it! Now he'd work every day until he dropped and they expected him to be glad for a hot meal at the end of the day!

He began to grind his teeth as he glanced at Laurent.

And it's not like he even notices what I do. He never tells me I did a good job. Never!

Luc crossed his arms and glowered at the road ahead as Laurent turned down the village road toward *Dormir.*

It's because nobody ever says no to him.

Because of his height and his money—nobody can stand up to Laurent and expect to be standing for long.

Which is why I have only one option, Luc thought with bitter conviction.

I need to get the hell out of here as soon as I can.

Laurent didn't expect Luc to do anything except get out of the car and slam the door behind him. So he wasn't disappointed when that was exactly what he did. He'd already called Grace so he knew she would be nearby to steer Luc to the job she needed him to do in the *Dormir* garden.

He backed out of the gravel drive and pointed the car in the direction of the *l'Abbaye de Sainte-Trinité.*

He would call Danielle later to confirm that Luc's attitude in the car hadn't carried over to them. It was one thing to be a *dégénéré* with Laurent, but a different matter altogether to act that way with Grace and Danielle. Grace would likely tell Laurent that Luc behaved well even if he'd thrown a tantrum and broken private property.

Danielle would tell him the truth. He knew she was fond of the boy but when asked directly if he'd behaved himself she wouldn't lie to him.

Forcing himself to at least temporarily shelve thoughts of Luc and whether the current situation was or wasn't working out, Laurent focused on the task ahead at the monastery.

For the past five years he'd hired as much of the steady stream of refugees that came through the monastery as he could manage to work his harvest. If they were good workers and showed conscientiousness, he would often keep some of them on to do other jobs in the vineyard through the fall and winter. To this end, he had built a series of four mini-houses on the perimeter of his property to house them.

The young women and teenage boys needing the work tended to stay in dormitories at the monastery, leaving the mini-houses for couples and small families.

So far it had worked out well. Two of the mini-houses had been inhabited by the same couples for the last two years while the other two houses had changed over from year to year.

Thinking of the mini-houses made Laurent frown. Currently one of the mini-house couples—Gigi and Bernard— was showing signs of wear.

When they first arrived, Gigi had been heavily pregnant so only Bernard worked Laurent's fields. Later when Gigi miscarried, Laurent agreed to have them stay on until they could find work elsewhere. That was over a year ago. Gigi never did find any other form of employment and her allergies made it impossible for her to work in Laurent's fields.

Bernard had been drunk and disorderly twice during last summer's six-day harvest.

Laurent would have evicted them before now but then Luc had come to live with them at Domaine St-Buvard and Laurent had gotten distracted.

He pulled into the parking lot of the church and stared up at the imposing stone rectory.

Situated on the far side of the village, *l'Abbaye de Sainte-Trinité* was bordered to the north by what used to be Eduard Marceau's vineyard. With its cylindrical turrets and towers, the monastery looked like a medieval castle. Not for the first time, Laurent wondered at the monastery's history.

His working arrangement with the monastery was a good one for all concerned. Frère Jean—the monk who ran the refugee program at *l'Abbaye de Sainte-Trinité* —had more people needing shelter, food and work than he could provide. And Laurent needed dependable workers year after year. Taking some of the people from the dormitories to live in Laurent's mini-houses allowed Frère Jean to help more families every year.

As Laurent walked toward the rectory, he nodded at two monks who appeared on the front gravel walk, their hands tucked into the sleeves of their robes. He thought he remembered they were Polish. They nodded at him but didn't speak.

Laurent went to the rectory door and knocked. The door was opened by a monk easily as tall as Laurent and one whom Laurent had never seen before.

"Is that Laurent?" Frère Jean called from inside. "Come in! Come in!"

A volley of harsh coughing erupted and when Laurent walked into the room, he saw Frère Jean bent over, red in the face, trying to catch his breath.

"*Mon frère?*" Laurent asked.

Frère Jean waved away his concern. "It is nothing. I'm fighting a bug. Come sit down."

Laurent took a seat opposite Frère Jean. The other monk remained standing as though not sure he would be staying.

"Laurent, this is Frère Dominic. He is a Benedictine and new to us."

Laurent nodded at the monk. He immediately was aware of registering an instinctive dislike of the man. From years of learning to pay attention to his gut for a line of work he no longer did, he did not dismiss the feeling as irrational.

"First things first," Frère Jean said, rifling through a stack of file folders on his desk. "We have many more possible workers this year. Do you think you can use them all?"

"How many?"

Frère Jean flipped through the folders, stifling another wet cough. "Maybe thirty?"

Laurent did not need thirty people to harvest his vineyard. He would be happy with half that number. But thirty people needed work and for that he would take them.

"That is fine."

"And what about accommodations?" Frère Dominic said, stepping forward. "We need the dormitories for the women and children here at the monastery."

"Yes, thank you, Frère Dominic, I was just getting to that," Frère Jean said. He turned to Laurent. "Are all your houses full?"

Laurent knew that Frère Jean was well aware that they were. Laurent had plans to construct another four houses later in the year, but right now he only had four.

"Unfortunately, yes," Laurent said. "We had talked about possibly setting up tents."

Frère Dominic again interrupted. "These people deserve better than tents! That is no more than they would get in a state-run detention camp!"

Although far better than a ditch at the side of the road, Laurent nearly said.

"Yes, well," Frère Jean said before he began coughing again. "We will have to give this more thought. Meanwhile, I have a dozen young men from last year." He pushed the folder across the table to Laurent. "And another dozen men and women. And the ones who are living in your houses now will work the harvest, I assume?"

"I am not sure," Laurent said with a frown.

"I thought it was a condition of them living in the houses," Dominic said with an acid tone of voice. "If they don't work, they should be made to leave."

"As they are my houses," Laurent said, "I decide who leaves and for what reason."

"How fair is that?" Dominic said, looking at Frère Jean. "You have people there not working yet they are living rent-free?"

"Is that not what we do here too, Frère Dominic?" Frère Jean said calmly, one eye on Laurent to gauge how angry he might be getting.

"Well, of course, if you have enough money you may do what you want," Frère Dominic said with a shrug. "Always that has been the way of the world."

Laurent swallowed down his building anger. He'd never easily worn the mantle of a wealthy man with status and to have it spat in his face so baldly was hard to endure. He flexed his fist and then released it to pick up the file folder.

"We have three young men," Frère Dominic continued, "who are nearing the age where they are too old to remain here at *l'Abbaye de Sainte-Trinité* unless married. You said that yourself, Frère Jean."

"This is true," Frère Jean said but shrugged as if to say, *but what is to be done about that?*

"And they are white, true Frenchmen," Dominic said, raising his voice. "Do they not deserve the best chance to succeed?"

Laurent had heard enough. He stood up with the folder in his hand and bowed to Frère Jean.

"Get that cough checked out," he said. "It does not sound like you are winning the battle with it."

"Oh, it is nothing. Let me know, Laurent, if the population of your houses changes, yes?"

"Of course."

"Meanwhile, when do you think you will begin the harvest?"

"It is still too soon to say. I would say if the rains hold off, we are looking at the first two weeks of next month."

"Very good. *Au revoir*, Laurent! Say hello to Luc for me, yes?"

Laurent smiled briefly and left the room, happy to have kept his temper under wraps.

It certainly would not do to punch the new monk in the nose on his first day on the job.

Laurent's phone buzzed and he fished it out of his pocket as he got into the driver seat of his car.

It was Danielle.

"*Allo*, Laurent," she said. "Is this a bad time?"

"No time is bad for you, Danielle. Is everything all right?"

"Oh, yes! But of course! Absolutely. There is just one small question."

"Yes?" Laurent said, impatiently. "And what is that?"

"Did you drop Luc off? Because we have yet to see him."

5

Maggie knew Nicole must be exhausted and she kicked herself for not being there when Nicole got off the plane. She hurried to catch up with her niece.

"Are you hungry? Uncle Laurent has something special planned for tonight but we can definitely stop and get a snack if you're peckish."

"Yeah, about that," Nicole said with exaggerated weariness. "None of my friends call their relations *aunt* or *uncle* like they're five years old or something. So if you don't mind, *Maggie*."

Maggie forced herself to smile. "Oh. Sure. No problem."

"What about Laurent?"

"I don't know, sweetie. Your uncle is very old school. I'm afraid you'll have to ask him."

Nicole groaned as if even the *thought* of doing that was too much to be endured.

As they walked out of the terminal the heat and steam of the day clung to Maggie's hair. It felt like a weight settling on her shoulders as she guided Nicole to her parked car.

"We're this way, down two levels," Maggie said. "How was

the flight?"

"Oh, dear God. It was a flight, okay? It stayed up in the air. Nobody died."

Is this just jet lag? Maggie wondered in bewilderment. At the memorial service Nicole had been her usual sweet and pleasant self. Whoever this doppelgänger was who'd gotten off the transatlantic flight from Atlanta, she was *not* her niece.

"Do people just piss in the streets over here?" Nicole blurted out in disgust as they walked past a particularly malodorous corner wall near the escalators.

Maggie didn't smell anything but it was entirely possible she was so used to the smell she couldn't detect it any more. Some French men, especially the older ones, often thought nothing of unloading wherever they happened to be as long as there was at least a bare minimum of privacy.

And sometimes when there wasn't.

"I think there's a *fête* in Avignon this weekend," Maggie said brightly. "It's music and also *faience* and artwork. And of course food! Should be a lot of fun. I'm trying to remember if we ever took you to Avignon when you were younger."

"Do I look like someone trying to decorate a house? And whatever the hell *faience* is, just give me a break."

Nicole produced the word "fay-yance" like she had no idea of what the word meant.

"How's your French?" Maggie asked with a slight frown as she pulled out her car fob and unlocked the car as they approached. The car chirped and its parking lights flashed at them.

"I don't know. How's your Swahili? You seriously don't think I know a word of this stupid language, do you?"

Maggie reminded herself that Nicole had just gotten off a long flight and was not herself. But the thought still shocked her.

She doesn't speak French?

"I thought you took it in school," Maggie said as she pulled the passenger car door open for her.

Nicole let go of her luggage handle and the bag tipped over and banged into the car door. She tossed her purse in the car.

"I switched to Spanish instead. Uncle Ben said it made more sense."

Him you call uncle?

Maggie reminded herself that Nicole was young and she'd be able to pick up the language in no time.

Maggie unlocked the passenger door and opened it for Nicole, who got in and looked up at Maggie.

"How long do I have to stay?" Nicole said with a grimace.

Maggie smiled through the nausea forming in her stomach. "Well, it looks like we've got you for the month, *chérie.*"

As I know you already know.

"Oh puh-leeze. God. I'm sorry, Maggie. I just never thought *you* would be the kind of person who sprinkled French words in their sentences. So pretentious."

Maggie felt her ears starting to burn. Turning away to hide her embarrassment and her mounting annoyance, she jerked Nicole's bag around to the back of the car and instantly spotted that the trunk lid was not shut all the way.

She clenched her hands and felt a stiffness form in her jaw. The lock had been broken for at least two month and Laurent had promised he would fix it before Nicole's trip. She felt a blast of annoyance—with Laurent and Nicole and her mother and Ben and basically the world at large.

She grabbed the trunk handle and jerked it upward, then balanced Nicole's bag on her hip to angle it into the back— snagging a hole in her favorite silk cardigan in the process.

And then she stopped.

She stood there, the bag resting on the rim of the trunk.

And stared.

Inside the trunk two glassy eyes stared back at her.

6

D ead. A man. Cold. No blood.

Maggie dropped Nicole's bag to the ground with a loud echoing thud.

A leather briefcase was on the man's chest. His eyes were open. So was his mouth. Flecks of foam dotted his lips.

"Hey! I have valuable stuff in there!" Nicole shouted as she got out of the car.

"Nicole, no!" Maggie said, turning to her. "Don't come back here!"

"What are you talking about?"

Nicole looked angrily at her bag on its side on the dirty car park floor and then at the interior of Maggie's trunk.

With the dead body in it.

And she started to scream.

Maggie slammed the trunk shut, but it bounced back open. She whirled around and grabbed Nicole by the shoulders and walked her away from the car. Nicole was shaking, her eyes glazed and unseeing.

"What is...who...?"

"It's okay," Maggie said, her mind racing as took out her

phone from her purse while keeping one hand on Nicole. "It's just a...misunderstanding."

Nicole's knees gave way and Maggie let her slip slowly to the ground as she held up her phone.

No reception.

She looked at Nicole. She couldn't leave her here.

A young woman walked across the parking lot forty yards away. She was looking down focused on her own phone.

"*Excusez-moi!*" Maggie called to her. The woman didn't look up.

"I think I'm going to throw up," Nicole said.

Maggie knelt beside her. Nicole's face was white, her lips trembling.

"Can you stay here while I get you a bottle of water out of the car?" Maggie asked.

Nicole's eyes went to the car. The trunk lid was still poised obscenely in the air. She swallowed hard and nodded.

Maggie gave her a brief squeeze and walked away until she finally got reception. From there she could see Nicole and the car. She dialed a number in her phone's contacts.

"You said you would lose this number," a groggy voice said on the line.

"There's been a murder. At the Marseille airport. In the short-term parking lot. You need to come. *Now.*"

Before he could respond, Maggie disconnected and rang Laurent.

It took the police thirty minutes to get there and when they did, the first one out of the patrol car was Jean-Baptiste Moreau, the young detective who Maggie had worked with the year before when he was based in Arles. She'd heard he'd been transferred to Marseille and she had spent the better part of the last half hour flushed with gratitude that he had.

While she and Nicole waited for the police Maggie gave Nicole the water and sat with her on the cold cement floor. Nicole had taken enough deep breaths to stop threatening to vomit. But she still wasn't ready to stand up.

"I want to go home," Nicole said softly, her eyes riveted on the open trunk lid.

"We'll be home soon."

Maggie knew she'd been gone from the parking lot no more than thirty minutes from the moment she'd parked and walked into the airport to the moment she and Nicole returned. She knew that whoever had done this had likely been watching her and waiting to her to leave. And because she had no idea who was the dead man in her trunk, she had to believe his being there was just a random circumstance.

I was just a clueless traveler with a dodgy trunk lid announcing to the world that the vehicle was unlocked.

As soon as the first police car showed up, Maggie stood and helped Nicole to her feet. By the time she'd helped dust Nicole's clothes off, Laurent was getting out of his car and striding toward them.

The Marseille police department was seventeen miles away. Laurent had been nearly thirty.

But they both got here at the same time.

Nicole whimpered when she saw Laurent and launched herself into his arms. He caught Maggie's eye over Nicole's shoulder and Maggie registered his annoyed indictment.

Are you kidding me? How is this my fault?

She turned to greet Jean-Baptiste Moreau as he approached from around the back of her car where a team of medical examiners in white lab coats were setting up a work perimeter.

"*Bonjour,* Jean-Baptiste," Maggie said. "You made good time."

With curly chestnut hair and large brown eyes, Jean-Baptiste's angelic appearance belied his usually serious demeanor. Two years earlier when he and Maggie had worked together on the Arles Amphitheater murder, he'd been an eager and naive rookie.

She could see he'd grown up since then. Unfortunately, like most detectives Maggie had known who'd had a little bit of success, he appeared no longer eager or amicable.

"Tell me how the body came to be here," he said as Laurent joined them.

Maggie could see Nicole sitting in the front seat of Laurent's car with her head bowed over her cell phone.

"I would be interested to hear as well," Laurent said, narrowing his eyes at Maggie and putting his hands on his hips.

"I came to pick up my niece from a flight from Atlanta," Maggie said to Jean-Baptiste. "I parked where you see my car is now. When I left my house two hours ago I promise you it did not have a dead body in the trunk."

Damn. And she'd been *so* close to making a completely snark-free statement.

"You do not know the man?" Jean-Baptiste asked her.

"What are the odds I would know a random dead body stuffed in my trunk? Stupid question."

"Maggie," Laurent said, the edge in his voice low but unmistakable. "Just tell him what happened. Detective Moreau is not accusing you of putting the body there."

"Do you or do you not know who—" Jean-Baptiste said again.

"No, I don't know him!"

"I will need you to make a statement to the effect."

Over Laurent's shoulder Maggie saw that Nicole still appeared to be engrossed in her cell phone.

Maggie hated that Nicole's first impression of France since her last visit five years earlier was going to be poisoned by this terrible event.

"Are you arresting her?" Laurent asked, his hand moving to

lightly grip Maggie's arm. She knew he was trying to ground her, to prod her to take a breath and remain calm.

"No," Jean-Baptiste said, reluctantly it seemed to Maggie. He glanced at his team working in the cordoned off area at the back of Maggie's car. "But I'll need to take a statement from her at the station."

Maggie felt a sudden heaviness invade her body. She wasn't surprised of course but she couldn't help the disappointment of knowing that she wouldn't be there to welcome Nicole to her new home. She wouldn't be there to see her reaction to the fresh flowers, the garden in full bloom, the zinnias and roses in her room.

That was all ruined now.

Maggie turned to Laurent. "Go on and take her home. I'll come as soon as I can."

"Your car will need to be impounded," Jean-Baptiste said. "Needless to say."

Maggie felt her eyes fill with tears and she angrily brushed them away. Laurent's hand was still on her arm. As Jean-Baptiste walked away, Laurent pulled her into his arms and she buried her face in his chest, feeling the solidity and security of him.

"It will be fine, *chérie*," he said softly. "Children are resilient."

"I wanted everything to be perfect," she said before pulling back to look into his face. "And now it's all horrible."

"*Oui*, particularly for the poor man in the trunk of our Peugeot."

Maggie knew he was trying to break the tension but she couldn't manage a smile.

"Everything will be fine, *chérie*," he said again, rubbing a hand down her back.

Laurent was not given to public displays of affection of any kind. Maggie was tempted to give him a kiss but didn't want to push his comfort limits.

"I'll call as soon as I can," she said as she felt him pull away.

"*Bon*," he said and then surprised her by giving her a quick kiss on the cheek. As he walked back to his car, she felt a sickening combination of depression and determination.

Whoever was dead in the back of her car—and however he got there—she would get to the bottom of it.

She'd get Nicole's summer back on track if it killed her.

7

W hen they arrived home, Laurent parked next to
Danielle's car in front of Domaine St-Buvard.
Danielle had left a voice message on his phone
saying that Luc had finally turned up and she was giving him a
lift back to Domaine St-Buvard.

It is just as well, Laurent thought. If he hadn't gotten the call
from Maggie when he had, he probably would have driven to
Dormir, found the boy and killed him.

Nicole put her hand on the door but made no move to get
out of the car. She had spoken very little on the ride from the
airport.

"You are hungry, *chérie?*" Laurent knew she was of course
upset. *What sane person wouldn't be?* He also knew that food
could soothe most woes.

"I just want to lie down," Nicole said, staring out the
window at the looming stone facade of the *mas*. "Do you think
they'll catch who did it?"

"I am sure of it."

Nicole waited for him on the driveway as he pulled her bag

out of the trunk when Mila flung open the front door and squealed, "Nicole! You're here!"

Mila bolted out of the house and threw her arms around Nicole but then pulled back, her enthusiasm muted by Nicole's nonresponse.

"Nicole is weary from her trip," Laurent said. "Show her to her bedroom, *chérie*. Where are Luc and Jemmy?"

"In the garden," Mila said, gently taking Nicole's arm and walking with her into the house.

Danielle met them in the foyer and greeted Nicole with a hug. This time, Laurent noticed that Nicole managed to hug back.

"Nicole has had a hard trip," he said to Danielle. "She is going to lie down for a bit."

"Oh, I'm sorry, *chérie*," Danielle said to Nicole. "No matter. We will visit later. You go on."

Nicole nodded mutely and let Mila lead her up the wide stone staircase to the upstairs bedrooms. Laurent set Nicole's bag at the foot of the stairs. He watched her go and then turned to Danielle.

"Where is he?" he asked gruffly.

Danielle's face hardened at his tone and she crossed her arms. "Luc is not in trouble," she said.

"I'm not sure that is for you to decide," Laurent said as he moved to the French doors where he could see both boys digging in the flower bed.

"I've set them both to work. I would appreciate it if you did not countermand me."

Laurent snorted and glanced at her. "I know what you're doing, Danielle."

"I'm not surprised. Unlike you, Laurent, I do not make a secret of my intentions."

"Where did you find him?"

"Apparently he was never lost. He just went for a walk. I myself can often see the merit of a walk on a nice day."

"He knows I know what he did," Laurent said, still watching both boys. "He can't be allowed to believe I would let this behavior go unpunished."

Mila came downstairs, her shoulders drooping.

"*Chérie*," Danielle said and opened her arms so that Mila came into them. "Why don't you get the *profiteroles* I brought?" She looked over at Laurent. "Mila and Zouzou made them earlier this week. They are perfection. *Bechards* could not have made them as well."

Heartened, Mila turned and disappeared into the kitchen.

"So," Danielle said as she settled into a chair in the living room. "A coffee, perhaps? And then you can tell me what happened at the airport."

Laurent sighed and turned away from the sight of the two boys. It was just agitating him, anyway. He sat down beside Danielle.

"Mila," he called. "Can you start the coffee, please?"

"Of course, Papa!" Mila said, clearly excited about the idea of being entrusted with the task.

"She is a big help to us at *Dormir*," Danielle said. "But she is growing up fast."

"Too fast."

"So where is Maggie? And why was a healthy seventeen-year-old girl somehow done in by a mere transatlantic airplane ride?"

Laurent ran a hand through this hair. "Maggie found a body in her car trunk at the airport."

Danielle sucked in a quick intake of breath and then shook her head. "Typical Maggie," she said with a small smile. "These things only happen to her."

"Notice that, did you?"

"When did the body get there?"

"At the airport, presumably," Laurent said.

"Well, that explains why Nicole is upset," Danielle said with a glance at the stairs. "Did you talk to the police?"

"Briefly. That's where Maggie is now—at the police station."

Danielle arched an eyebrow at him. "She really does make a habit of this."

Mila came into the room with a tray holding a plate of *profiteroles*, two cups and a French Press.

"Thank you, *chérie*," Laurent said.

"Did *Mamère* tell you about the picnic tomorrow?" Mila asked looking from Laurent to Danielle.

Because Maggie's parents were not often in France and Laurent's parents were dead, Danielle and her late husband Jean-Luc had served as de facto grandparents for both Jemmy and Mila. Laurent knew the relationship between Danielle and Mila was especially strong.

"Mila and Zouzou are planning on making *éclairs au chocolat*," Danielle said, smiling proudly at the girl.

"Philippe loves *éclairs*," Mila said.

Grace's three-year-old grandson Philippe had come to live with Grace at *Dormir* after being unceremoniously dropped off two years earlier when Grace's problem daughter Taylor had tired of him. Grace's ex-husband Windsor and his new wife regretted that the baby they were expecting would take too much of their time to allow them to take care of Taylor's child too.

It was an adjustment on everyone's part to incorporate an active toddler into the middle of trying to run a business but Grace and Zouzou had managed—with Danielle's love and help as well as Maggie and Laurent's support. Grace had found a girl from the village to help.

"Who is watching him today?" Laurent asked.

"Colette is there with Zouzou," Danielle said. "She has the

necessary energy. He is a tornado on two legs. But we adore him, *bien sûr.*"

"Papa, can I go watch Luc and Jem work in the garden?" Mila asked.

"Don't get dirty," he said as she bounced up and out the French doors. He watched her go.

"How is the work at the monastery coming?" Danielle said as she leaned over to plunge the coffee and pour it into their cups. "Frère Jean is still involved I trust?"

A couple of years ago an unfortunate travesty involving Frère Jean at the monastery had resulted in him losing his monkhood as well as his position at the monastery. Because Laurent had spoken up for him, once he was free to return to the area he had immediately resumed his managerial duties at *l'Abbaye de Sainte-Trinité*. However, the title *frère* was now honorary only.

"Of course. Although I do not like the sound of a new cough of his."

Danielle nodded sympathetically. "How many refugees this time?"

"Thirty."

"Laurent, how can you accommodate so many?"

"I will manage."

Laurent heard the French doors open and all the children came inside. He stood up.

"Laurent," Danielle said in a low voice. "Patience, yes?"

Jemmy and Luc appeared in the doorway. It looked like they'd rolled in the muddy flower bed they'd been digging. The family's two big hunting dogs came in with them, their large feet tracking thick clods of mud into the house.

"Turn around," Laurent said to them. "And strip down on the terrace."

"But Papa!" Jemmy said, his eyes glowing with indignation. "Mila will see us!"

"Out! And take the dogs with you."

"Come on, Jem," Luc said. "I told you it was no use."

Laurent stood up. "What did you say?"

"Laurent, *please!*" Danielle said.

Laurent's eyes drilled a hole into Luc but the boy only shrugged insolently and went back out to the garden.

"Laurent, you don't have to call him on every single insubordination no matter how slight."

Laurent looked at Danielle with mild surprise. "Of course I do."

Danielle's cell phone began vibrating and she pulled it out and then fumbled for her glasses before handing the phone to Laurent.

"I think the message is from Grace," she said. "What does she say?"

Laurent picked up her phone and read the text.

"She says she is dropping off two of her guests at the airport and will swing by the police station in Marseille and pick up Maggie and bring her home."

"Oh, very good. Now at least we have Maggie sorted."

An hour later after the boys had showered and gone to their separate rooms until dinner time. Mila was busy making a *tarte Tatin* in the kitchen and Danielle was preparing to leave. Laurent followed her down the front steps to the driveway.

"I know Colette and Zouzou are perfectly capable of handling young Philippe by themselves," she said as she climbed into her car. "But they are both just children themselves. I will feel better if I go home."

Laurent turned to glance back at the house. He could see Luc's bedroom window and the flashes of changing light in the room told him Luc was watching television.

"Laurent," Danielle said, "please remember that you yourself were a teenager once."

Laurent snorted in reply.

"Promise me you'll be patient with him. He's had a difficult childhood."

"I promise."

"You are just saying that to get rid of me."

He grinned. "I will try," he said. But as he stood in the driveway watching her drive away, the last thing he felt was patient.

He pulled out his phone and checked to see if he'd received word yet from Maggie but there was nothing.

Aware of a nagging premonition in the form of a prickling sensation across his scalp, he sent her a text.

<is everything okay?>

He looked at the message box and saw the little dots bubbling away that told him she had received his message and was composing a reply. But then the little dots stopped moving and no message appeared.

Sighing, he turned to go back into the kitchen to start stuffing the *foie gras* into the tomatoes for dinner.

8

Compared to the incessant, discordant noise of the open bullpen at the Marseille police station, the interview room where Maggie now sat was quiet as a graveyard.

She picked up her cup of coffee from the bare metal table in front of her and glanced at the handcuff rings that jutted from its underside.

For someone who is not a suspect I certainly do feel like I'm in trouble. She glanced at the one-way mirror on the wall.

Is there anyone living who does not know that there are people watching on the other side of that mirror?

Within moments the door to the interview room opened and Jean-Baptiste stepped inside.

"I have had a shock," Maggie said. "Why am I being made to feel like a suspect?"

Jean-Baptiste made a face and sat down opposite her.

"You have *not* had a shock. You find dead bodies more often than my grandmother finds snails on her pepper plants."

"Is that why you're treating me like a suspect?"

"I am not treating you like a suspect."

He turned on the recording device. "Jean-Baptiste Moreau entered the interview room to take a statement from Madame Margaret Newberry Dernier, an American, living at Domaine St-Buvard, who discovered the body of Leon Boucher today, the tenth of August. Now, Madame Dernier, tell me what happened."

Maggie had of course already told him no fewer than six times.

"I found a dead body in the trunk of my car where it was parked at the Marseille airport."

"Can you elucidate, please?"

"I was there to pick up my niece who had just flown in from the United States. I parked in the short-term parking lot around fourteen hundred hours. I didn't look around because I had something on my mind. I locked my car and left the parking lot to go to the arrivals terminal."

"You locked your car?"

"I did, yes. But the trunk lock is broken so it didn't shut properly."

"And could anyone see this by looking at your vehicle?"

"You know very well they could, Jean-Baptiste," Maggie said, rubbing the space between her eyes where the start of a headache was forming. "Who was the victim?"

Jean-Baptiste ignored her question.

"Did you see anyone in the area around your car?"

"No."

"No one at all?"

"I saw a couple enter the parking area with luggage, but as I said I was distracted so I didn't get a look at them."

"A couple. Male and female?"

"I think so."

"But you didn't look at them?"

"*As I said*, I was upset about something and was not really

aware of my surroundings. I noticed two people walk past me
and I didn't look at them."

Jean-Baptiste pursed his lips for a moment.

"Interview terminated at seventeen hundred hours." He
leaned over and turned off the recording device. "The department secretary will print out a copy of your statement for you
to sign. The victim's name was Leon Boucher." Jean-Baptiste
cocked his head at Maggie. "Ever heard of him?"

"Is he famous?"

"He is a somewhat unpopular figure running for the office
of mayor here in Marseille."

"Why was he unpopular?"

"That is all I need from you at this time, Madame Dernier."

Maggie felt the weariness of the day and its events creep
into her shoulders. Her phone vibrated on the table and she
saw a text from Grace appear. <I'll be out front in twenty>

"Where was he killed?" Maggie asked.

"You know I can't tell you that."

The door to the room opened and a small man with a bad
comb-over and a blotchy complexion stuck his head in the
room. He looked first at Maggie's breasts and then his eyes raked
down her body to her legs. He was wearing a white lab coat.

"What is it, Chevalier?" Jean-Baptiste said.

"Beachre said to catch you before she left," Chevalier said,
his eyes devouring Maggie although still yet to focus anywhere
near her face. "We'll need her prints. We pulled a partial thumb
off the trunk handle. Nothing in the system matches so far."

"Yes, yes," Jean-Baptiste said irritably. "Now leave us and
close the door!"

The man shrugged, finally looked Maggie in the face,
winked and then retreated.

Maggie turned to Jean-Baptiste. "You've really come up in
the world, Jean-Baptiste. Last time we worked together you

were just a junior detective. Now you're yelling at poor forensic techs like they answer to you."

"They do answer to me," he said with a scowl. "And I've earned the position I have."

"That would sound better to someone who didn't know the truth."

Jean-Baptiste's face darkened and Maggie told herself not to needle the man any further.

"This isn't like the last time," Jean-Baptiste said pointedly. "This victim was a valued member of the Marseillais community. Do I have your word you'll let us do our jobs without interference from you?"

"I can assure you I have no intention of involving myself in your case."

Jean-Baptiste gathered up the folders on the desk in front of him.

"As long as you promise you'll keep me informed," Maggie added.

"I promise I'll arrest you if I think you're interfering."

"Did you or did you not get a promotion to Lieutenant Detective Inspector from Detective Sergeant as the result of the Arles Amphitheater case? A case that *I* solved for you?"

Jean-Baptiste's nostrils flared indignantly. "I got the promotion, Madame Dernier," he said, biting off his words, "based on detective work and perseverance on a case that was solved by the Gendarmerie d'Arles."

"Well, then I guess it's just as well you *don't* update me since your memory is so faulty the Intel obviously wouldn't be worth much." She flushed angrily. "Who was it who faced down the killer in the bowels of the Arles amphitheater?"

"And who was it who trespassed in the Arles Amphitheater in the first place after being warned not to?"

"If I hadn't trespassed," Maggie said, standing up, her eyes flashing, "you'd never have found the killer! No, wait. That's right. Finding the killer wasn't your priority, was it?"

"We're finished here, Madame Dernier." Jean-Baptiste walked stiffly to the door and held it open for her. "Do not think I won't put you in a jail cell if you attempt to interfere with my work."

Furious but too tired to think of a good comeback, Maggie lifted her chin and with as much dignity as possible walked out the door of the interview room.

9

This part of Marseille wasn't the prettiest, Maggie thought as she stood waiting for Grace outside the *Commissariat de Police*. Ugly midrise buildings hemmed in the street and blocked any possible view of the Old Port with its picturesque bobbing sailboats or the gleaming statue of Mary atop the iconic basilica *Notre-Dame de la Garde*.

The police headquarters was however close enough to the harbor that Maggie could smell the fish and the sea. She rubbed the goosebumps from her arms which were chilled in spite of the summer heat and took out her vibrating phone. A picture of her mother appeared on the screen.

Maggie's heart sank. She glanced at her watch. It was after midnight back in Atlanta.

"Hey, Mom. I was just about to call you."

"I just got off the phone with Nikki."

Maggie thought she detected a slur in her mother's words and assumed she'd probably calmed herself ahead of the phone call with a few glasses of Merlot.

"So I guess you already know—"

"I know my granddaughter is begging to come back home to Atlanta."

"She's just upset."

"Wouldn't anyone be? *A dead body? In your trunk?* What in the world is going on over there?"

"Nothing, Mom, that doesn't go on in Atlanta every night of the week. Nicole is just upset."

"Who was he? Did you know him? Why was he in your trunk?"

"Nobody knows anything yet."

"How was he killed?"

"Again, nobody knows anything yet. I didn't see any blood but that doesn't mean—"

"Oh, my Lord! Poor Nikki! I wish you could have heard her, Maggie. She was absolutely begging me to let her come back."

"I hope you didn't tell her she could," Maggie said as she spotted Grace driving down the Canebière, the wide boulevard that stretched all the way to the Old Port. She lifted a hand to wave.

"Of course I told her she could! I don't understand how you can minimize what happened to her today. She's been traumatized, Maggie!"

"Yes. I know," Maggie said, stepping off the curb as Grace pulled up. "I have to go now, Mom. Please try to get some sleep. We're all safe and sound over here. I'll call you when and if I know anything. Love you."

Maggie hung up and tossed her phone in her purse before sliding into the passenger's seat of Grace's BMW.

"Darling, you look a fright," Grace said. "I cannot even believe this has happened to you. And on Nicole's first day here!"

"I know, it's horrible. Thanks for the ride."

"So who was he? Do you know?"

"His name is Leon Boucher. Have you ever heard of him?"

Grace shook her head. Blonde with classic cool looks, she had taken the time to make up her face and curl her shoulder length hair.

"I don't get out much, as you know," Grace said.

Two years ago, in an effort to get her life together—and her relationship with at least one of her daughters back on track—Grace had begun managing the bed and breakfast owned by Laurent and located one village over from St-Buvard.

Dormir was run by Grace but owned by Laurent who had bought it from Danielle who had lived there for twenty years since she was a young bride.

Twenty very unhappy years.

"I guess things are pretty crazy at *Dormir*?" Maggie asked.

"It's summer," Grace said. "So things are off the charts crazy. I just dropped off one American couple at the airport and was supposed to pick up another but they texted me that they decided to come by way of Paris instead so that gives me at least a little breathing room. Luc has been such a help. I hope you know that. I couldn't have gotten ready in time without him."

"I'm glad. I know Laurent is a big believer in keeping boys busy so they don't have time to get into trouble."

"Luc is not a problem boy."

"He has his moments."

"He's so good with little Philippe too. He's practically the only one who can get the child to settle down long enough to eat his lunch or go down for a nap."

"That's good," Maggie said absentmindedly as she pulled her phone out to see if there were any texts from Jean-Baptiste yet.

"I just hope Laurent is listening to him," Grace said. "A boy like Luc—who can be quite sensitive, you know—is just no match for the steam roller that is often your husband."

"Uh huh," Maggie said, scrolling through her email messages to see if Jean-Baptiste might have sent her something there instead. She tossed her phone back into her purse in frustration.

"Problem, darling?"

"Did I ever tell you that Jean-Baptiste Moreau got transferred to Marseille? He's the lead homicide detective here."

"Is that good?"

"I'm not sure. Honestly, I hope he's not going to be a problem."

"What are you talking about?"

"I really need this murder to be solved quickly," Maggie said, turning in her seat to face Grace. "It's imperative for Nicole to see this wrapped up as fast as possible."

"Well, I'm sure Detective Moreau will do everything in his power to do that."

Maggie sighed. "I hate to break it to you, Grace, but Jean-Baptiste is seriously incompetent."

"Darling, really? I thought he was perfectly adequate last time."

"Are you kidding? I had to hand him every lead he got and even then half the time he didn't follow up. But this time it's even more important."

"Why is that?"

"Grace, you should have seen Nicole's face! I can't have her thinking France is a dangerous country!"

"So are you going to help investigate this murder?"

"I told Jean-Baptiste I wouldn't."

"My question still stands."

"No, absolutely not. I have enough on my plate. It's just that I keep seeing Nicole's face, you know? She went absolutely white."

"Well, she would, since she's normal," Grace said dryly.

"When she was a little girl, it used to take her forever to warm up to people," Maggie said. "I know she was popular in school but underneath all that teenage bluster is still a scared, insecure child."

"Are you sure, darling? We are talking almost a dozen years ago now since you first brought her to the States. People do change. Especially children."

"Trust me. I know her."

"I'm sure you do but one thing I've learned—and as usual I've learned it the hard way—is that assumptions we make that are rooted in the past are usually wrong."

Maggie groaned and smiled at Grace. "Seriously, Grace?"

"Yeah, that sounded corny even to me," Grace said with a grin.

"In any case, I have my work cut out for me. Some welcome! She hasn't been to Domaine St-Buvard in five years."

"Why not?"

"She's a very busy, very popular girl back home."

"If she's so popular I'm surprised she's willing to give up her social scene back in Atlanta to immigrate to France," Grace said and then turned to scrutinize Maggie. "Or does she know she's immigrating?"

10

———

Oleander and ivy clustered in thick tangles of dark green against the fieldstone walls of Maggie and Laurent's farmhouse. A black wrought iron railing framed a second-story Juliette balcony that jutted out over the front door giving the house an upscale elegance not typically seen in the area.

As Grace pulled into the half-circle gravel drive Maggie felt a familiar tug of pride at the sight of the *mas*.

"I can't come in," Grace said. "I've got a family of three coming tomorrow although why a couple would want to go on vacation with their two-year-old I have no idea."

"Maybe you can do a play date with them and Philippe." Maggie smiled at her friend and gave her a quick kiss. She knew Philippe wore Grace out. Grace had only had daughters before Philippe and she was discovering that raising a boy required a whole different set of skills.

"I'm sorry I can't dash in and see Nicole," Grace said. "But I'll see her sometime this week when you bring her over. Give her a hug from me."

"Will do," Maggie said as she climbed out of the car.

She waved Grace off and then hurried into the *mas*. She already knew through a text exchange with Laurent that Danielle had stopped by for a brief visit and that Nicole had retreated to her bedroom.

She paused in the foyer to drop off her handbag. Not surprisingly she heard sounds coming from the kitchen.

"*Maman!*" Mila called out to her. "Nikki is here!"

Maggie fought down annoyance at the use of Nicole's nickname and hurried into the kitchen where Laurent stood facing his stove with his back to her. He looked over his shoulder and smiled in greeting. Their son Jemmy—short for Jean-Michel— stood beside his father holding a plate of raw veal chops.

"Hey, Mom. We're grilling out."

"Smells lovely," Maggie said, moving into the kitchen to give Mila a kiss where she perched on one of the stools at the kitchen counter. "Where is she?"

"She has a headache," Mila said.

"And Luc and I are digging a trench out back," Jemmy said.

"You are?" Maggie frowned and glanced through the French doors that led to the terrace and the back garden.

"A glass of wine wouldn't go amiss," she said, feeling the weariness of the day begin to settle into her shoulders.

An hour later the meal was cooked and the table set in the garden but Nicole still hadn't made an appearance downstairs. Maggie carried a plate of tomatoes stuffed with *foie gras* outside and wondered if she should let the girl sleep. She could always make her a sandwich later if she woke up hungry.

Maggie glanced at Laurent. He wasn't a fan of people not sitting down to a meal when there was one arranged. Before she could decide whether or not to go upstairs and knock on Nicole's bedroom door, she saw her at the open French doors leading to the terrace.

"Nikki!" Mila sang out when she saw her cousin, then ran to her and threw her arms around her. Maggie was relieved to see Nicole return the hug.

"You are sitting here, *mon chou*," Laurent said to Nicole as he pointed to a chair at the table. "Luc? The candles?"

Luc was staring at Nicole as if he'd never seen a teenage girl before. Maggie was sure he probably hadn't seen too many like Nicole. She had dark hair with an olive complexion. Her eyes were chocolate brown. But if she looked much like most of the refugee girls Luc had known in his earlier life at the monastery, that was where the similarities abruptly ended.

Nicole wore tight jeans and a midriff-baring eyelet top. Her teeth were straight and her skin clear and glowing. Diamond studs adorned her ears. She glanced around the table with the confidence of one who'd never gone hungry—or not since she could remember—and who'd been raised to believe she was loved and valued.

Not at all the sort of thing found in Luc's usual set of friends.

"Luc?" Laurent said again, jarring the boy out of his trance.

Luc blushed as soon as Nicole noticed him. He turned to pick up the box of matches and knocked over Mila's water glass.

In the midst of Luc's frantic mopping up of the spill, Nicole went to Jemmy and hugged him.

"Hey, handsome," she said. "Now I know why old people always comment on how much I've grown. You look at least eighteen."

Maggie saw the delight on Jemmy's face at her words and he stood a bit taller.

By the time Luc got the candles lit and had taken his seat— as far away as possible from Nicole—Maggie was beginning to feel a pleasant lightness in her chest, so welcome after her trying day.

Fairy lights bobbed on drooping wires in the early evening

breeze overhead. Laurent had strung them from the roof of latticework he'd recently erected over the main dining area of the terrace.

"Were you able to nap?" Maggie asked when Nicole sat down.

Instantly, the expression on Nicole's face soured.

She's connecting me with what happened today, Maggie realized unhappily. *Well, of course she would.*

The family's two hunting dogs Izzy and Buddy stayed nearby hoping for a handout.

"What's this we're eating?" Nicole asked Laurent. "It looks like stuffed peppers. Only without the peppers."

"Elbows, Jemmy," Laurent said.

Maggie noticed that before Laurent was able to look at him, Luc snatched his elbows off the table.

Laurent passed a bowl of mushroom risotto to Mila and kept his eye on her while she served herself and passed it along.

"Are we not supposed to talk about what happened today in front of the kids?" Nicole said as she cut into her veal chop.

"What happened?" Jemmy asked, looking first at Nicole and then his father.

"Nothing," Laurent said to him.

Now Luc was looking around the table and frowning. "Was it something bad?" he asked in French.

Maggie sighed. Jemmy and Mila were of course fluent in French. Talking about it in either French or English would in no way insulate them.

"We might as well tell them," Maggie said, turning to see Laurent's astonished look.

"And ruin the meal?" Laurent said.

"It won't ruin it if we don't let it," Maggie said, turning back to Jemmy. "Nicole and I had a terrible experience today. We found a man's body at the airport."

"You found a *dead* body?" Jemmy asked in French, his eyes big with surprise.

Mila sucked in a gasp and looked at Laurent. He reached over and patted her hand.

"At the airport?" Luc asked, also in French. "On the tarmac? Where?"

"Will somebody tell me what everyone is saying?" Nicole said, slamming down her fork.

"We do not raise our voices at the dinner table," Laurent said to Nicole.

Maggie hoped Nicole could hear the steel in Laurent's voice. She resisted the urge to remind her husband that Nicole was jet-lagged and had just had a traumatic experience.

Neither of course carried much weight with Laurent as far as an excuse for bad table manners.

"Yes," Maggie said in English. "When we came back to the car in the parking lot, someone had placed a dead body in the trunk..."

"In *our* trunk?" Jemmy said and then quickly turned to Luc and translated it although Maggie could tell Luc already understood. He'd been steadily picking up more and more English ever since he moved in with them.

"Who did it to him?" Mila asked, her eyes wide.

"We don't know," Laurent said.

"It was very upsetting for everyone, of course," Maggie said.

"Was there blood?" Jemmy asked.

"Are you interested in finishing your dinner or the trench you started at the end of the garden?" Laurent said to him in French.

"Sorry," Jemmy said, looking down at his plate.

"What kills me," Nicole said crossing her arms and clearly no longer hungry, "is how everyone is always going on about how much more dangerous the US is."

"Well, statistically," Maggie said, "that is true. I read somewhere that there are two homicides a day in Atlanta and that's just—"

"I'm just saying!" Nicole said, glancing at Laurent and quickly lowering her voice. "Dead bodies in trunks don't happen to me in America nearly as much as they do here."

"It was a once-in-a-million situation," Maggie said. "Statistically, France is much safer than the US."

Nicole tossed her napkin on the table and stood up.

"Well, I don't give a damn about statistics, Maggie. I give a damn about not seeing the image of a dead man in the back of your trunk every time I close my eyes! I give a damn about feeling safe when I walk to a parked car in a public airport! I give a damn—"

"Sit back down or leave the table," Laurent said to her.

Nicole hesitated, her eyes brimming with tears before turning on her heel and bolting for the house. She slammed the door behind her.

Maggie watched her through the French doors as she headed for the staircase and her bedroom.

Laurent refilled Maggie's wine glass and then his own before tossing a piece of bread to one of the dogs and turning back to her.

"Did she just call you *Maggie*?"

11

T hat night after the children had turned in, Maggie showered and slathered her favorite lavender lotion onto her arms and knees before climbing into bed. She picked up the novel she'd been reading and held it on her lap while she waited for Laurent to finish locking up the house for the night.

When he brought the dogs inside, they bounded up the stairs and pushed open her bedroom door. One by one they went to her and licked her hand before finding their beds underneath the window overlooking the garden.

Laurent came in and closed the bedroom door. She saw him check that the dogs were in place before going into the bathroom for his shower.

She hated that Nicole's first night at Domaine St-Buvard had ended the way it had. But even she could see that tapping on Nicole's door and trying to get her to talk about it was probably better left for the next day.

Sometimes no matter how many words of wisdom you had or soothing phrases you were sure would help ease or defuse a situation—sometimes you just needed a reboot.

Laurent came out of the bathroom drying his hair before tossing the towel aside and climbing into bed with her.

"Well, that went well," he said.

"I see you're well on your way to mastering American sarcasm."

"Americans did not invent sarcasm, *chérie*. The light?"

"I just thought that talking about it might help take some of the horror out of it for her."

"Except you didn't talk about it. You allowed her to relive it." Laurent leaned across Maggie to turn out her bedside light, then kissed her.

"What a mess," she said.

"So don't make it worse."

Maggie sat up, stung by his words. "How am I making it worse?"

Laurent sighed. "She is not like Jemmy or Mila. Nicole does not need you to guide her."

"She's only seventeen! Of course she needs me to guide her."

"You must let her work it out herself. Wait for her to come to you if she wants your help."

"Some people have trouble asking for help."

"You must assume that Nicole is not one of those people until she shows she is."

"She acts so angry. Don't you think?"

"She is a teenager. They are all angry."

"I wasn't."

Laurent laughed and then sat up and reached for her.

"Tell me what happened at the police station."

Maggie sighed and snuggled up beside him. "I found out that they pulled a partial print from our trunk handle. They took my prints to rule me out. I assume your prints are in the system so the cops can eliminate you?"

He raised an eyebrow at her. "What are you up to, *chérie*?"

"What? Nothing. I'm just telling you what I heard. I swear I am totally leaving all of this to the police."

"Why do I not believe you?"

"I'm serious, Laurent. There's no reason for Jean-Baptiste not to find this guy's killer. I mean the victim's not a pedophile or a junkie. He's a somewhat respected member of the community. They don't need my help."

"Where is my wife? What have you done with her?"

Laurent leaned over and kissed her deeply. Maggie felt herself melt in his arms. Just when his hand dropped to cup her hip and draw her closer to him, she heard the unmistakable sound of a phone vibrating against a wooden surface.

Cursing under his breath, Laurent pulled away and grabbed his phone from the nightstand. "*Allo?*"

Maggie turned on the bedside lamp and watched his face. She knew it couldn't be news about her mother because *she* would have been the one who got that call.

"Who is it?" she whispered.

Laurent spoke a few words before hanging up. He was already out of bed and pulling on his jeans before Maggie realized he was leaving.

"What is it?" she asked. "Who was that? Where are you going?

"That was Frère Patrick," Laurent said as he pulled on a cotton sweatshirt and picked up his wallet from the dresser.

"Frère Jean has been rushed to the hospital in Aix."

12

L aurent returned home some time during the night but by the time Maggie was awake the next morning, he was gone again.

He texted her before he left saying that Frère Jean had experienced what the doctors were calling a "cardiac incident" and would not be returning to *l'Abbaye de Sainte-Trinité* for the foreseeable future. Laurent was at the hospital again this morning and would spend the remainder of the day at the monastery working with the refugees and the interim director Frère Dominic.

Mila sat now at the kitchen counter as Maggie stood at the stove flipping pancakes.

"Where are the boys?" Maggie asked her.

"Jemmy said Papa told him and Luc to fix the break in the *potager* wall today."

Maggie felt a fissure of annoyance at Laurent's compulsive need to keep both boys—but particularly Luc—constantly working or engaged.

"Did they not have breakfast?" She squinted through the French doors to see if she could catch a glimpse of them.

Before Mila answered, Maggie heard Nicole coming down the stairs. The girl was already talking to someone on her phone.

"But all you have to do, Nana," Nicole said, "is give me your credit card number. I'll do the rest."

Nicole sat down next to Mila at the breakfast bar, giving the girl a brief smile.

"Is that my mother?" Maggie asked her.

Nicole gave her a long-suffering look.

"Oh, for crying out loud," Nicole said into the phone. "I'm practically being held prisoner here. Did you tell Uncle Ben what happened? He isn't returning my calls."

Mila looked at Maggie with dismay.

"Does Nikki want to leave?"

"Okay, Nana," Nicole said. "I will. You tell him I said so. Yeah, okay. Bye." She disconnected and looked at Maggie as if to say *Happy now?*

"Nicole, I'm so—" Maggie started to say.

"Just stop. Please," Nicole said. "I need coffee. I don't need useless platitudes. If you really cared how I felt you'd book my flight back home."

"That seems a little drastic," Maggie said before smelling that she was burning the pancakes. She turned back to the stove.

"I don't want you to go, Nikki," Mila said.

"I know, sugar," Nicole said. "Why don't you come visit me in Atlanta? Remember how much fun we had at the Coke museum last time you came?"

Maggie turned around to see that Nicole had put her arm around Mila's shoulders.

The idea that this whole rotten situation could somehow be solved—needed to be solved—came once more searing into Maggie's brain. There was one thing and only one thing that was going to fix what had happened and that was solving the murder.

Maggie needed to show Nicole that yes, bad things happen. But most of them can be tidied up quickly, if not even remedied. That's what Maggie wanted Nicole to know.

To do that she needed Jean-Baptiste to find Leon Boucher's killer. *Now.*

She picked up her phone from the counter to check her text messages.

Still nothing from Jean-Baptiste.

Why am I surprised?

Everyone knew the first few hours of a murder investigation were the most critical. She remembered his less than enthusiastic approach to the last case they had worked together.

It was becoming very clear that just like last time, if she wanted to see results before the next ice age—or before Nicole began to spiral into a depression or a conviction that France truly was a terrible place—Maggie was going to need to do something about this murder herself.

For the rest of the morning Nicole and Mila sunned themselves in the garden while the boys filled in crevasses in the *potager's* broken stone wall. The children came into the house periodically for lemonade and water. Maggie saw little of them which was just as well since she had a full morning of work to knock out before she could think about putting together a plan for going back to Marseille.

She had woefully neglected her newsletter of late. She had started the newsletter as a result of a blog she'd begun writing a few years earlier about life in Provence as an expat. Using her skills as a writer to paint a picture of rural village life, she quickly found a following around the world.

More important than the international subscribers she'd

started to rake in was the fact that the blog was a hit in France and the UK, whose residents were interested in ordering the many local products Maggie advertised in her blog. Soon her monthly blog had morphed into a newsletter with over twenty thousand subscribers and was connected to all the major travel websites. Local artisans who advertised in her newsletter quickly began to see substantial boosts in their sales.

Because her relationships with vendors and advertisers were so important—and because they were French so also somewhat mercurial—Maggie devoted at least half the morning to returning emails and making phone calls to her more difficult clients.

Her next newsletter would focus on the nearly ten thousand gypsies from all over Europe who were expected to attend the annual celebration of their patron saint Black Sara.

As soon as she sat down at her desk Maggie found an email from the Women's Guild of Arles waiting for her. She had worked closely with these ladies in the past and there wasn't anyone within a hundred miles who had better access to Arles artisans than she did. Her working relationship with the Guild was very nearly the backbone of her newsletter.

She didn't want to piss them off.

Maggie opened the email and as expected, saw an annoyed message from the president of the guild, Cosette Villeneuve, asking *when* Maggie was going to bother attending one of their upcoming chapter meetings?

The date of the next meeting—a date that Maggie knew would be worth her career if she missed it—was the following week. Citing family issues, she quickly wrote back apologizing for the lack of contact—she'd already pushed them off nearly a month and broken two dates to meet—and promised she would be there for the meeting next week.

Her phone rang and she saw it was Ben. She'd been expecting his call all morning.

"Hello, Ben."

"Did you really tell Nikki that there are two homicides a day in Atlanta? What is *wrong* with you?"

"I was trying to calm down a very upset teenager," Maggie said, flushing uncomfortably at the realization that her brother's accusation was completely accurate.

"I'm just wondering about your sudden interest in being Nicole's uncle," she said defensively. "I mean is there a new girlfriend on the scene who has kids you're trying to impress?"

"Can you *be* any more offensive?"

"That is rich coming from you. Or have you forgotten trying to extort money from my husband eight years ago?"

"Laurent forgave me for that!"

"Ask me if *I* have!"

"Look, Maggie. You aren't the only one who cares for Nikki. And your assumption that her living in France with you and Monsieur Perfect is the only path for her is just downright arrogant!"

"She's *not* going back to Atlanta. She just got here!"

"Even if she's afraid there? Do her feelings not matter to you?"

"Of course they matter! I'm doing this for her!"

"I've heard of some self-deceiving BS before..."

"I don't know what you've said to her or why she now thinks she only wants to live in the US. But she is *French*, and I—"

"*Half* French! She's *half* French and she has the right to make up her own mind!"

"No, she doesn't. She's a child and she needs guidance. If she had a weight problem would you allow her to eat Snickers bars all day?"

"What the hell are you talking about? Nicole is as thin as a rail!"

"It's an analogy, you moron!" Maggie shouted and felt like

she'd transported back in time to when she and Ben were still bickering children.

He always could get under her skin.

"I'm telling you that what you're doing is disrespectful to Nikki and to me and to Mom," Ben said. "We want the best for Nikki and you're too self-absorbed to see anything but what *you* want."

"I see well enough to know she's not leaving here until she's had a chance to discover this country—*her country*—and decide for herself. And now if you'll excuse me, Ben, I still have work to do and I really don't want to begin my day by hanging up on you."

"Then allow me," he said and disconnected.

Maggie sat back in her desk chair and forced herself to calm down. She got up and refilled her coffee, glancing outside to see that Nicole and Mila were laughing and talking animatedly on their lounge chairs.

Maggie took a long breath and willed herself not to overreact. Once Nicole saw that this terrible situation with the car trunk was just a bizarre one-off, Maggie was sure she would relax and put things into perspective.

Not to mention the one thing that Maggie knew that Ben didn't know: Nicole wasn't half French at all.

She is fully French.

Thirty minutes later after researching some photographs of lavender fields she was thinking of using in her newsletter, Maggie found herself typing *Leon Boucher* into her browser window.

What came up was not at all what she'd expected.

A handsome man with a cruel mouth and sharp feral eyes, Boucher was prominently represented on the campaign website *Le Façade Nationale*. Maggie scanned the website pages.

Below the black reversed out box of type that announced Monsieur Boucher's recent tragic and senseless death was a bulleted list of campaign promises.

Maggie read them with growing astonishment.

"Immigration today is an organized attempt to replace our French population! Mosques will swamp our cities, tearing down our culture, even our history! Soon our very language will be lost!"

Sound bites from rally appearances were reproduced proudly on the website to highlight Boucher's uber-conservative views.

"The EU is killing France!"

"Burkas will be the death of France!"

"Homosexuals are killing France!"

Although Maggie didn't see any swastikas on the *Le Façade Nationale* website—the word *neo-Nazi* came to mind as she clicked through the navigation tabs.

* *Who is Leon Boucher?*

* *What We Stand For—and Against!*

* *Keeping Marseille Safe from Invaders*

It all made sense now after what Jean-Baptiste had told her about Boucher being unpopular.

At least with most civil, decent people.

The link under the tab *Recent Media* took her to a YouTube video of Boucher speaking at a rally. Maggie quickly put her headphones on so none of the children would hear what she was listening to if they happened to walk in.

She was pretty sure it wasn't meant for tender ears.

After a few minutes of listening, Maggie pulled her headphones off and turned off the video. There were more videos but she'd heard enough.

The man was even further to the right than Marine Le Pen, the conservative politician who was head of the National Rally.

Leon Boucher wasn't just conservative. He was an anarchist.

After what Maggie had seen on the website it was hardly a

surprise that somebody wanted to kill him and stuff him in the first available car trunk they could find.

At one point in the video she saw Boucher throw his arm around a beautiful young woman standing in the front row of the audience. He kissed her and then turned away to continue his hate-filled anti-Semitic, anti-everything-decent spiel. Whoever had produced the video had helpfully added the caption under the woman's glowing face: *Angeline Sauvage.*

His wife? Surely not. Much too young.

Maggie opened another browser window and typed in *Angeline Sauvage.* She was quickly able to find Sauvage's Facebook page where she scrolled through page after page of posts. Clearly Mademoiselle Sauvage cared about her clothes and being photographed. There were several photos of her and Leon Boucher together, hugging and kissing.

While Sauvage didn't have her own Wikipedia page like Boucher, because of her association with him she was nonetheless well documented on the Internet, including an address in the heart of Marseille.

"*Maman?*"

Maggie looked up and blushed guiltily. Mila and Nicole stood in the doorway to her office.

"We're hungry," Mila said. "Is lunch ready?"

13

L aurent stood in front of the line of refugees in the monastery forecourt. He introduced himself and shook their hands. But in the end, making friends was not the order of business today. And he thought they should know that.

The first row of workers—hand-selected by Frère Jean before he became ill—were in their twenties, male and female. Usually there were entire families but not this year. That was just as well, he thought, since he had no vacant mini-houses available this season.

"It is hard work," he told the young people, "but it is not lengthy. A harvest does not usually last more than seven days."

"Are we paid by the day?" one of the women asked.

"By the basket. I won't pay you just to show up. Who has picked grapes before?"

He was encouraged to see several people raise their hands.

He'd already notified a few other local vintners to see if they needed help picking their fields. Most of them used machines but with labor this ready and cheap, it made sense for them to consider hand-picking this year.

"Who has experience with construction?" he asked.

No hands went up.

He hadn't expected anything different.

"Will we live offsite?" one of the young men asked.

"That is being arranged," Laurent said evasively. From behind the crowd he saw Frère Dominic's bulky form. Laurent wasn't surprised to see him or to realize that the man had been there listening all along. Frère Dominic had been put in charge of the new refugees as well as interfacing with Laurent in Frère Jean's absence.

Laurent was fairly sure he'd never met Dominic before. But he was also just as sure that the man had a problem with him. Why, he would undoubtedly discover as they went along.

"That is all," Laurent said. "You'll all get work if you want it. I'll meet with you again to walk the vineyard with you and give you your final instructions."

"It's like being in the army!" one young man said.

"Exactly," Laurent said, locking eyes with him. The boy reddened and turned away with the others.

Frère Dominic approached Laurent. He watched the dispersing young people until he was alone with Laurent.

"I take it you have all the workers you need?" he said with a sneering grimace.

Instead of answering Laurent waited for the rest of the monk's message. He didn't have to wait long.

"I noticed from the files I found in Frère Jean's office that Luc Thayer is staying with you."

Laurent felt a sudden restlessness. "Why is that of interest to you?"

"Only because I know you do not want the monastery to be tainted in any way by its association with you. And as I understand it, the boy is with you illegally. Unless I am mistaken and you have the appropriate papers of adoption?"

Laurent narrowed his eyes. "What is it you want?"

"Only for all of us to be on the same page, legally speaking. If it were to become known that you had the boy without the proper papers, I would be obligated to report it."

He turned and looked at the monastery behind him. "Of course, he could not return here to the monastery but the state has refugee camps set up for people like him."

People like him.

Laurent's muscles tensed. He wouldn't honor this man's argument by telling him that Luc was born in France to French nationals. Besides he didn't have the papers to support those facts. And what Laurent knew about Luc's origins, he was not willing to reveal to anyone.

At least not before he told Luc himself.

"Luc is legally fostered by my family," Laurent said stiffly and turned away.

"Except that we both know that he is not," Dominic called to him. "But if he is, it can be easily proven with the correct documentation."

Laurent kept walking. It didn't matter what papers Luc did or didn't have or what documentation Laurent lacked to prove he was fostering the boy. It was clear that none of that mattered to Dominic.

Dominic had an agenda that had nothing to do with Luc.

And Laurent needed to discover what that was.

Dominic watched Dernier get in his car and drive away.

It was all he could do not to pick up a handful of gravel and hurl it after the big Frenchman. But he forced himself to remain calm, to watch and wait.

It had been years since he'd seen Dernier and clearly the man had no memory of the encounter.

He felt his body tensing at the thought.

Even in those days Dernier had treated his associates like servants. It was hardly a surprise he didn't remember him. Naturally he wouldn't remember the Cannes heist with five other men that had gone so badly wrong that all but two had ended their criminal careers that night and gone to prison for the next fourteen years.

Yes, he'd found God in Meaux-Chauconin penitentiary and he would be forever grateful that he had. His life had changed the day he became a brother of the Benedictine order.

But even such a life-changing experience as that could not blot out a man's memory.

And Dominic's memory would always hold that warm summer evening seared in his brain forever when the police descended upon them in the still darkness of a beautiful residential boulevard off the Promenade de la Croisette.

As he'd raised his hands in surrender, knowing he was going to prison, he'd seen the tall shadow of Laurent Dernier silently disappear behind a tall sculpted garden hedge.

14

The sun was high and baking the terrace pavers of Domaine St-Buvard by late morning. Deciding there could be no midday meal on the patio today, Maggie called all four kids in for lunch. They trooped in silently from their rooms and sat down to the *pot au feu* Laurent had prepared before he left.

As the children ate their lunch Maggie tried to determine if she could leave for an hour to go into Marseille. The children had been quiet all morning, but that didn't mean the afternoon would prove as uneventful.

"Is everyone okay if I run a quick errand after lunch?" she asked. She knew Mila, who might normally beg to come with her, wouldn't be interested with Nicole here. And it wouldn't occur to Jem or Luc to come along.

Fortunately—at least for now—Nicole showed no interest in going anywhere.

Mila glanced at Nicole who merely shrugged, and the boys didn't respond at all.

"Great," Maggie said. "I won't be long. Jemmy, you and Luc

clear the table after lunch and Mila, please load the dishwasher."

Without waiting for a reply, Maggie turned to go back to her office where she pulled out her phone and put in a quick call to Danielle.

Even though Luc and Nicole were both seventeen, Maggie felt uneasy about leaving them on their own for the afternoon. She had no idea when Laurent was coming back.

"Hi, Danielle," she said into the phone when Danielle picked up. "Any chance you can swing by here for an hour or so?"

"Oh, I am sorry, *chérie*. I am in Aix at the hairdressers. Do you need something?"

"No, I just needed to run out and was hoping you could watch the kids."

"My goodness, *chérie*," Danielle said with a laugh. "Luc and Nicole are old enough to be parents themselves!"

"Ha, ha. Very amusing, Danielle."

After disconnecting, Maggie called Laurent to find out his itinerary for the day.

She hadn't really talked with him about how important she felt it was to resolve the murder as quickly as possible. In any case she had a pretty good idea of what he would say about that.

"How is Frère Jean?" she asked when he picked up

"They are doing tests. The doctors are confident it is not too serious."

"That's good. Are you still at the monastery?"

"*Non*," he said. "I am headed home to pick up Luc and Jemmy to take them to *Dormir*. Grace needs help in the garden."

Perfect.

"Take the girls too," Maggie said. "I have to run to Arles for a women's guild thing." She felt a flinch of discomfort at the lie.

Maybe she'd have time to truly run by Arles so it wouldn't be a lie?

"*Bon.* We'll see you at home tonight."

Maggie disconnected and called for an Uber.

As it turned out, since Uber drivers were hardly overflowing the streets in provincial little villages like St-Buvard Maggie was still home when Laurent came home shortly after lunch. She overheard Nicole on the phone with Grace's daughter Zouzou, planning a late afternoon picnic for their day at *Dormir*.

After waiting nearly an hour for her ride to show up, Maggie settled back in her seat for the thirty-minute ride to Marseille and collected her thoughts about what she would say to Angeline Sauvage.

There was a very real possibility that Jean-Baptiste had not yet interviewed the woman. It wouldn't surprise Maggie at all if the detective had restricted his investigation to the victim's immediate family.

He's so lazy!

In any case, she felt confident that Jean-Baptiste would not find out that she had talked to Angeline Sauvage.

She gave the driver Sauvage's address and wasn't surprised when he drove to La Corniche, a very upscale residential neighborhood in Marseille.

If Sauvage was Boucher's mistress—and from the woman's social media presence what else could she be?—it stood to reason she would be well taken care of.

Maggie stepped out of the car in front of the Haussmann style apartment building. She recognized the familiar stonework, quintessential decorative flourishes, wrought iron balconies, and mansard roof.

Because Leon Boucher was a public figure and, from what Maggie could discern from the Internet, very well off, it made sense his mistress would live some place like this. Besides, what self-respecting French mistress wasn't going to live in a neighborhood at least as nice as her lover's wife?

Maggie noticed that there was a café on the corner in easy walking distance to the apartment. She wondered if Angeline and Leon had spent much time there. She made a mental note to go there after her visit with Angeline to ask around.

Maggie rang the outdoor bell and was surprised to be immediately buzzed in. She pushed the heavy outer door open and felt a brief chill from the blast of air conditioning against her skin. She shut the door against the thick heat of the day— too late in the afternoon to be mitigated by any harbor breezes.

Checking her phone for the apartment number, she made her way up the ornate spiral stairs and wondered who had let her in.

She found the apartment, paused to take a deep breath, and knocked.

The door was instantly opened by Angeline Sauvage herself. Elegantly beautiful and taller than Maggie, her hair was curled in what must have taken the entire morning to style.

"Madame Sauvage?" Maggie said. "I am Margaret Newberry from the *International Tribune*."

"*Oui*?" Angeline wrinkled her nose as if something didn't smell right and Maggie was briefly impressed by the woman's instincts.

"I was told by Leon Boucher's campaign headquarters that you would allow me a few words on this terrible tragedy?" Maggie said.

Maggie had had enough time on the ride to Marseille to frame exactly how she would get Angeline Sauvage to talk with her. Most people loved being interviewed and none more than beautiful women.

"They did?" Angeline said. A small smile appeared on her face and then vanished. "Yes, of course. Please come in."

Angeline led Maggie into the salon, which was everything Maggie would have expected from the promise of the building's façade. High ceilings with dramatic floor-to-ceiling windows let the Provençal sunlight pour across the herringbone parquet before abutting an ornate white marble fireplace.

The walls and ceilings had the signature Haussmann ornate molding. In the center of the room, a large antique chandelier sparkled in the morning sun.

Maggie tried to imagine what Angeline had been doing before she knocked on her door. The place was immaculate. If she'd been doing anything—laundry, watching TV, putting a puzzle together—there was absolutely no hint of it.

"Our readers are very interested in Leon Boucher's life," Maggie said. "And I was assured that you were one of the best resources for that."

"What would you like to know?"

"Well, before I drill into the back story of who Leon Boucher was *and who helped him rise to his lofty position*, my editor needs the facts of his recent death. Do you know if there is someone I might go to for that?"

Maggie watched the woman flush and she knew she'd struck just the right chord. To suggest that anyone *else* knew him as well as Angeline did—or knew facts that she didn't—was definitely going to trigger Angeline into proving her position with Boucher was unassailable.

"That would be me," Angeline said.

"Oh! Very good," Maggie said, pulling out a small spiral notebook that she kept in her handbag for grocery lists. She poised a pen over the pad. "I know how difficult this must be for you but if you could tell me what you know—if anything— about how Monsieur Boucher died."

Again, goaded by the suggestion that she might not have insider knowledge, Angeline was quick to respond.

"Leon was murdered in his vehicle at the Marseille Airport after he returned from a short trip to Paris."

"I see." That was two pieces of information Maggie hadn't had before she walked through Sauvage's door. Where he was murdered and where he'd been before that.

"How is it you know that he was killed in his car?" Maggie asked.

Angeline made a surprisingly ladylike snort. "The police told me last night."

Maggie was surprised that not only had Jean-Baptiste questioned Angeline but he'd done it so soon. It was just possible she had misjudged him.

"My sources indicated that Monsieur Boucher was found in the trunk of another car," Maggie said carefully.

"That is correct. The detective I talked with suggested it was done in order to delay the discovery of the body."

"Okay. So Monsieur Boucher was killed inside his own car and then moved to another. I don't suppose the police told you *how* he was killed?"

Angeline frowned. "Do you not have a media liaison with the Marseille police? Surely your paper has that connection?"

That is a very good question, Maggie thought, trying to think quickly.

"We do, of course. This would only be to fact-check our sources from within the Marseille police department."

Angeline nodded. "I am sorry. I don't mean to be rude. This has been a terrible time for me."

"I'm sure it has and on behalf of the *International Tribune*, we would like to extend our deepest condolences at your loss."

"Thank you. I suppose it would be all right to reveal that Leon and I were to be married soon."

"Married?" Maggie was positive the Internet had said Boucher was already married.

"As soon as his divorce came through."

"He was in the process of divorcing?" Maggie asked, pretending to write that down.

"We are expecting a child together."

Maggie looked at Angeline's flat stomach.

"We only just found out."

"Congratulations," Maggie said. "This must be truly heartbreaking for you." She nodded sympathetically at the woman. "You said you knew how Monsieur Boucher was killed?"

Angeline began to flex her fingers. "I do. And I also know who killed him."

Maggie held her pen over the pad expectedly and held her breath.

"He was killed by his son, Gaston," Angeline said.

"Why do you say that?" Maggie asked, trying to remember if she had seen anything on the Internet about Leon Boucher having a son.

"For several reasons," Angeline said, leaning back into the sofa, her hands lightly massaging her stomach. "First, Gaston hated his father."

That always helps as a motive for murder.

"And secondly?" Maggie prompted.

"Gaston Boucher is a nurse."

Maggie blinked in confusion.

"He is a nurse," Angeline repeated as if that would make things clearer. "So he is familiar with drugs."

"Was Boucher poisoned?"

"You could say that. He was killed by lethal injection."

15

L *ethal injection!*
    Did that mean that Boucher's murder was an execution? Was the murder connected to Boucher's politics or was a hypodermic needle in an underground parking lot just the fastest way to dispatch him?

"You do not even know this very basic fact of how he died?" Angeline said, arching an eyebrow at Maggie. "May I see your press pass, please?"

"Ah. I think I left it in my other purse."

Angeline stood up abruptly. "I will show you out."

As Maggie was escorted out the apartment door, she was pretty sure the next time she bumped into Angeline Sauvage, the woman would not be quite as forthcoming as she had been this time. But perhaps that wouldn't be necessary.

Once outside, Maggie walked to the café on the corner and ordered a coffee in order to better digest everything she'd learned.

One thing Angeline was not wrong about was the fact that a nurse would be high on the list of people who could get their hands on the kind of drug that could do this and of course be comfortable in the delivery method.

Maggie drummed her nails on the café table. She needed to find out the exact drug cocktail that had been injected into Leon Boucher.

Would Jean-Baptiste tell her? If she revealed that she already knew that Boucher had been killed by lethal injection, perhaps he'd decide that divulging a little more wouldn't matter.

It also occurred to her that if Angeline told the police of her suspicion about Gaston—and even Jean-Baptiste had to figure Gaston was a prime suspect—then Maggie had better talk to the son as soon as possible.

What were everyone's alibis? It was so frustrating for Jean-Baptiste not to share what he knew. It meant that Maggie was going to have to interview the same people he did in order to get the same information.

She pulled out her phone and scrolled through the *Le Façade Nationale* website. After leapfrogging through all the usual fear-mongering propaganda, she narrowed in on the campaign offices for Boucher's efforts to become mayor of one of the eight arrondissement *secteurs* of Marseille.

His rival in the mayoral race was a Muslim named Mohammed Olivier.

With the election only a month away, Monsieur Olivier looked like a shoe-in to win. Maggie assumed that Olivier—unless he had a particularly airtight alibi—would have been the first person Jean-Baptiste spoke to about Boucher's murder. Since that was likely the case, she decided to approach Boucher's campaign manager Joelle Mercier instead.

First, Mercier wasn't family so again Maggie stood a better chance of slipping through the cracks and not showing up on the police's radar.

Second, Madame Mercier would know better than anyone the truth about Boucher's marital status. And because Mercier obviously believed in Boucher's platform, she would know the victim better than anyone—possibly even better than his wife or mistress.

Maggie made a note of the campaign headquarters address in downtown Marseille, paid for her coffee, and hit her Uber app for a ride into town.

Although she desperately wanted to talk to Boucher's son, Maggie had to believe that he was too visible right now—both to the cops and the press—to do that easily. She would need to work on the perimeter of the suspect pool for now and ease her way in.

Using the same lie that got her into Angeline Sauvage's apartment, Maggie called *Le Façade Nationale* Campaign Headquarters and made an appointment with Joelle Mercier.

"Madame Mercier can give the press five minutes of her time," the secretary told Maggie.

"That will be fine," Maggie said, grateful just to get her foot in the door.

As she rode up the elevator to the tenth floor and the location of the headquarters, Maggie ran through her questions—and her strategy. She knew that Mercier would be watching the clock and ready to toss her out as soon as her five minutes were up, which was why she had to provoke her in such a way that the woman would be inclined to talk longer.

And Maggie thought she knew exactly what that might be.

When the elevator opened up on a plain hallway of threadbare carpet and peeling wall paint, Maggie followed the signs that directed her to the double glass doors of the headquarters.

Inside she came to stand before a desk that she recognized as classic Ikea. The woman behind the desk was young, tattooed, with her nose, ears and lip piercings and a sullen expression.

Maggie glanced around to see if anything about the place indicated that the staff was in mourning.

Was it possible they had a back-up candidate to take Boucher's place?

Because things did not at all look as if they were shutting down due to the loss of their candidate.

The girl at the desk looked up. "What?"

"I have an appointment with Joelle Mercier. I'm from the *International Tribune.*"

The girl's eyes fluttered at Maggie's clothes in appraisal—and found the result wanting. "You need to wait."

Maggie turned and sat in one of three plastic chairs in the waiting room as the girl got up from her desk and left. Not unlike most grassroots campaign offices, Maggie assumed that everyone did a little bit of everything. Surely with money so tight for most election campaigns, they couldn't afford a dedicated receptionist.

The waiting room was windowless and smelled of cigarettes and rotten food. Maggie glanced at her watch. She'd made her appointment for four o'clock and it was four now.

Maggie waited thirty minutes but the receptionist never returned. Finally Maggie got up and walked to the door through which the receptionist had disappeared.

In the dozen years Maggie had lived in France she had used her alien status to advantage whenever she could. Usually that meant doing something she knew was illegal or wrong and claiming ignorance due to her being a foreigner.

Today was one of those days.

Following the sound of conversation, Maggie tiptoed down the hall. However much money Leon Boucher did or didn't personally have, his campaign headquarters was a shabby affair. Maggie could understand why nobody wanted to spend money to fix up their offices but on the other hand, any and all attempts to get donors to support their cause could only be weakened by such a poor presentation.

Or was that not the case with neo-Nazis?

Was there a perverse benefit in presenting a squalid, run-down operation? Did it somehow go hand in glove with the platform promises of protecting the citizens of Marseille against the evil designs of incoming refugees?

Or was Boucher just a cheapskate?

"What are you doing back here?"

Maggie jumped and turned to see the surly receptionist standing in the doorway of an office, a bottle of beer in one hand.

"Oh!" Maggie said apologetically. "I thought you had forgotten about me. I'm sorry. My French isn't very good."

The receptionist narrowed her eyes at Maggie and for a minute Maggie was sure she was going to call her on that. After twelve years, Maggie would have to say her French was not bad at all.

"Is that her, Babette?" someone said from behind the girl.

A petite woman with alabaster skin and blonde-white hair appeared in the doorway. She smiled at Maggie.

"You are the reporter from the *Tribune*?" she said.

"That's right. Maggie Newberry."

"Yes, all right," Joelle Mercier said, ushering Maggie into her office. "Five minutes."

Maggie smiled at Babette but the girl scowled back at her.

"Leave the door open," Joelle said to Babette as she walked away.

Mercier sat down behind another cheap desk—this one battered and even more decrepit than the ones in the outer office.

Maggie took a seat opposite her. "Thank you very much, Madame Mercier for—"

"Yes, yes. The clock is clicking, Madame."

Maggie whipped out her notepad. "First, my paper wants to extend our deepest condolences, Madame Mercier for your loss."

When Joelle didn't respond, Maggie looked up and was shocked to see the woman was staring at her with tears in her eyes.

"Do you know you are the first person—the *only* person—to say that to me?"

"I am so sorry," Maggie said, her mind racing to see how she could pivot on this obvious weak spot to buy her extra time.

"Leon wasn't just my boss. We were in school together. We were friends."

"Where did you go to school?"

"Montpellier."

"Is that where Monsieur Boucher began his interest in his political beliefs?"

"That's where we developed *Le Façade Nationale*, yes."

"You developed it together?"

"We did. We were partners in this." Joelle waved her hand to encompass her dilapidated office. "Our greatest passion."

That makes three women who think they and they alone hold the key to Boucher and his great passion.

"Now that Monsieur Boucher has joined the ages, my editor at the *Trib* believes there will follow an interest in what triggered his somewhat more polarizing views."

"You are referring to Leon's latest treatise?"

I'm just spitballing here but sure.

Maggie poised her pen over her pad. "Exactly."

"As I'm sure you are aware, Leon felt strongly about keeping aliens out of Marseille and out of France. He was developing a strong and resolute plan to accomplish just that. It is a tragedy for all of France that he died before being able to enact his master plan."

Gosh. Who does that sound like?

"Are there plans to front another candidate in his place?" Maggie asked. Again, she noticed Joelle's eyes misting.

"I will likely be forced to run myself.".

Maggie controlled herself so as not to show her excitement. This was definitely a motive. She was pretty sure Jean-Baptiste hadn't unearthed *this* little jewel in his canvassing.

From the antique brass clock on the windowsill over Joelle's shoulder, Maggie could already tell that her five minutes had come and gone. And yet Joelle continued to look at her expectedly.

"When will you make that announcement?" Maggie asked while she tried to think how to get Joelle back on the subject of Leon Boucher's specifically alienating politics.

"Soon obviously."

"Do you have any reason to believe that Monsieur Boucher's politics might have triggered this attack?"

Maggie held her breath. Since Joelle clearly endorsed the same platform of fear-mongering and racism, she would likely be only too eager to lay his death at the feet of his opponents.

"Leon was a restorative character," Joelle said, tears still in her eyes. "But his truth was hard for some people to hear."

Especially if you weren't white.

"If it was anybody else I might be tempted to agree with you. It takes moral courage to stand up to the liberal left and their calls for reform and opening France's borders. Nobody likes to be seen as the bad guy."

Maggie nodded eagerly. "So you do think it was his politics that got him killed?"

"Not at all. It was that bitch Angeline Sauvage that got him killed."

16

The outdoor dining table at *Dormir* sat in the middle of Grace's garden surrounded by dahlias, peonies and sunflowers—a lush setting for the late afternoon picnic. Grace had set up the meal buffet style so that her bed and breakfast guests—if they were around—could just help themselves and then settle into lounge chairs or go off to spend their day in the surrounding countryside as they liked.

Laurent had made suggestions for the menu which he could see Grace had considered. Plates of salmon *rillettes* sitting on a bed of crushed ice sat beside bowls of lentil salad and platters of baguettes, cheese and paté. He'd also suggested *tête de veau* but wasn't surprised not to see it.

The children were playing some sort of net and ball game in the adjoining lawn and Nicole and Zouzou were keeping a careful eye on little Philippe. Grace and Danielle were in the kitchen organizing drinks and putting the final touches on a dessert.

Laurent himself had spent much of the last hour working on the bathroom sink in Grace's main cottage and mulling over his conversation with Frère Dominic, wondering if there wasn't something familiar about the monk. In the end he decided that there *was* something vaguely familiar about the man's brutish features but he could not nail down what or from where.

Dominic was like many men Laurent had known in his previous line of work—hungry, desperate and violent. They were the kind of men he had known but had never spent much time really getting to know.

If Dominic truly was from back then, the memories or associations that would have helped Laurent identify him were unfortunately gone now.

Only direct confrontation would reveal the truth and Dominic's ultimate goal.

Laurent walked around the house and pulled out his phone before calling a contact he knew in the city government in Nice. Luc had never lived in Nice but this woman would be able to tell Laurent what he needed to know about the likely repercussions of Luc's not having the correct papers.

Fifteen minutes later, Laurent ended the call and lit a cigarette. He usually tended not to smoke until the evening and he preferred not to do it around Mila or young Philippe. He took a long drag of tobacco into his lungs.

From the call he had learned that in order to legally foster Luc, Laurent needed the boy's birth certificate. That wasn't possible, because Luc had come to *l'Abbaye de Sainte-Trinité* with fewer documents than most refugees. While Laurent could have a birth certificate forged for Luc, his Nice contact told him he would also need signed depositions from at least three people who had known Luc's parents.

Again, an impossibility unless fabricated by Laurent. Luc's mother and stepfather had been transient, never settling in one place long enough before the car accident that killed them, leaving behind an orphaned twelve-year-old boy.

Laurent rubbed a hand across his face. Even if he had the

falsified birth certificate created, he'd need a national number for Luc and that could not be as easily acquired.

His attention was captured by Luc jumping down from the big black alder in front of the main house, a long pole in his hand and his face flushed with the success of knocking down a wasp nest. As Grace's handyman Gabriel appeared with a gas can, Laurent resisted the urge to supervise the job.

At seventeen, Luc only had another year before he would be old enough to stay at Domaine-St-Buvard without any documents at all.

But a year was a long time when one person appeared determined to make sure Luc did not remain at Domaine St-Buvard.

Why did the monk care so much? Why did it matter to him where Luc lived?

But Laurent knew the answer.

The monk's concerns had nothing to do with Luc. They had to do with Laurent.

"Oh, there you are!" Grace called to Laurent and waved.

Laurent tossed down his half-smoked cigarette against the garden pavers.

"Darling Laurent," Grace said as she walked over to him. She was wearing a cotton sundress and a wide-brim straw hat that she held on to against the afternoon breeze.

"I haven't had a chance to ask about poor Frère Jean," she said. "Is he on the mend, I hope?"

"The doctors believe so, yes," Laurent said as they walked back to the others who were picking at the food on the outdoor tables.

"Thank God for that," Grace said. She stopped and Laurent stopped too, turning to look at her with a frown.

"I just wanted to thank you, darling Laurent, for all your help with the plumbing problems. And for Luc, who has been a treasure. I honestly don't know what I would have done without him this spring."

Laurent grunted and scanned the scenery until he spotted Mila and Zouzou. They were coming from the house, each holding a freshly baked cake.

"But I did want to warn you," Grace said conspiratorially, "in case you weren't seeing it, that Luc and Nicole appear to be getting along a little too well. Have you noticed?"

Laurent frowned and looked around. The two young people were talking but were not standing close together. Laurent was an excellent interpreter of people's body language—in his old business he'd had to be. It was clear by the way Luc and Nicole were standing that they were not comfortable with each other. Luc appeared to actually be in pain the way he shifted from foot to foot and looked down at the ground.

Nicole on the other hand hardly to be even aware that Luc was there. She stood staring out over the garden, scanning the hedgerows as if looking for an escape.

"They look fine," Laurent said.

"They look like one of them is about to ask the other to the prom. I should have known you couldn't see it. I should have mentioned it to Maggie first."

"Do that," Laurent said, thinking this was exactly the sort of nonsense he expected Grace to engage Maggie in. He was not sorry to be left out of it up to now.

"What I'm *saying*, Laurent, is that you need to do a better job of keeping those two apart."

When he looked at her in frustration, she grabbed his arm and put her mouth close to his ear.

"You know," she said in a low whisper, "because of the fact that they're really half brother and sister?"

Laurent groaned internally. Since Grace was Maggie's best friend, she would of course know about their belief that Luc was Laurent's brother Gerard's son. But what she *didn't* know—

because that particular secret had been forged long before Maggie met her—was the other part of the dark mystery.

And that part effectively made Grace's worry about incest null and void.

"Just keep an eye on them, is all I'm saying," Grace said. "Nicole has really grown into a beauty and if you don't think Luc hasn't noticed, just look at him. I know you're holding off telling him the truth about who he is so unless you want to tell him sooner than you'd planned."

Laurent put a hand on her arm. "Yes, thank you, Grace. I will take it under advisement."

Grace looked hurt. "Well, I'm just trying to be helpful. People don't think this sort of thing is a problem until it is."

"Yes, I agree. *Merci.*"

"Why do I feel like I'm getting the brush off?" Grace said with a frown before turning to scoop up Philippe as he ran to her.

As she walked off, Laurent felt his eyes drawn again to the sight of Luc and Nicole standing in the garden. This time when he did, he felt his heart sink at the sight of them.

17

Maggie's hand was still poised above her writing pad but all pretense at writing had ceased with Joelle's words.

"Excuse me?" she said.

"You heard me. That whore Angeline Sauvage stood up at the Café Disco two nights ago with everyone listening and swore she would kill Leon if he didn't marry her."

"That sounds like the sort of thing people say when they're upset but don't act on."

"And then he's killed the next day? That's too much of a coincidence for me. Why aren't you writing that down?"

Maggie obediently scribbled on her pad.

"What can you tell me about Angeline and Leon?" Maggie asked. "How long had they been together?"

Joelle snorted dismissively. "Less than a year."

"She shows up on your website. It looked like she was a part of the campaign. More so than his wife even."

"Well, that's true. Marie-France was barely speaking to him."

"Marie-France is his wife?"

"Shouldn't you know that sort of basic information? Which paper did you say you wrote for?"

"The *International Tribune*."

Joelle stood up, her hands on her hips. "I thought the *International Tribune* had been bought by the *New York Times*."

Uh oh.

Maggie stood up. "Er, yes, now that you mention it, it has."

"Then why did you tell me you were a reporter for the *Trib*?"

Before Maggie could respond, Babette appeared in the doorway.

"Who are you really?" Joelle asked, her eyes flashing.

"I'm a reporter for *UK Cosmo*," Maggie said, stuffing her pad in her purse and backing out of the room. "And again please accept my deepest condolences."

Pushing past Babette, Maggie hurried down the hall and out the door to the elevators. Breathing heavily as she waited, Maggie tried to think what she'd learned from Joelle beyond the fact that she was just as racist and xenophobic as her boss Leon.

Well, that and the fact that she has a significant motive for wanting Leon dead: so she could take his place on the ticket.

Maggie was tempted to ignore Joelle's accusation against Angeline. Not that she didn't think Angeline wasn't capable of murder—in her experience most people were—but because she didn't have enough information to make a determination about it one way or the other.

Not yet anyway.

The late afternoon sun crept across Maggie's café table where she sat on the rue Sainte Francoise a few blocks from the Old Port. She'd already exchanged two texts with Grace so she knew her family was enjoying their day at *Dormir*—or at least Nicole and Mila were.

Laurent had taken off for someplace else and Luc and Jemmy were spending the rest of the day digging in Grace's vegetable patch.

She glanced at her watch. It was a little before five o'clock. It would take her thirty minutes to get home. And nobody was wondering where she was.

Which meant she had time for one more visit.

She signaled for her bill to the waiter standing in the doorway of the café and glanced at her phone again.

Still no calls or messages from Jean-Baptiste and now she was pretty sure they weren't coming.

Pushing her annoyance away, Maggie reviewed what she felt she knew at this point. She had at least two viable suspects for Leon Boucher's murder, with a third that was at least mildly possible.

Gaston Boucher and Joelle Mercier, with Angeline Sauvage bringing up the rear.

The son had means and, if Joelle and Angeline could be believed, motive as well. The other two both had motive in varying degrees. With a little more digging Maggie was confident she could determine whether any or all of them could qualify for the grand trifecta of Means, Motive and Opportunity.

She opened up a Notes app on her cell phone where she'd jotted down the address of Mohammed Olivier's campaign offices. She couldn't help but wonder if Mohammed Olivier was his real name. If so, without even opening his mouth he could count on the votes of any and all Muslims living in Marseille— and by Wikipedia tallies that was significant—and with such a French last name he could comfortably collect the rest of his future constituents' votes too.

Maggie had no doubt that Monsieur Olivier's family had

probably come to France generations ago—ergo the French last name—but would do everything he could to benefit from the association with his first name.

Leon Boucher, on the other hand, had a ready-made political affiliation with his name alone. Maggie couldn't help but wonder if he'd made it up.

Leon was Greek and meant lion. So far so good for a political candidate. *Boucher* on the other hand was French for "butcher."

Maggie wondered whether Monsieur Boucher might have renamed himself in the process of getting ready for public office.

The waiter dropped off her bill, which she quickly paid and then left the café. Olivier's campaign office was only six blocks away. Easily walking distance.

This time she decided not to call ahead but to take her chances that Olivier would be interested in a little free publicity. She couldn't believe she'd made that stupid mistake with *The International Herald Tribune*.

As she walked she thought of Nicole and how upset she'd been last night. She didn't blame her a bit—anyone would be devastated by what she'd seen. With every step Maggie felt a deepening conviction to do what she could to erase this terrible beginning to Nicole's visit. And quickly.

One thing Maggie knew about Jean-Baptiste was that he didn't do anything quickly.

Oh, he'd get the right answers eventually as to who killed Leon Boucher but by then Nicole would have dug in her heels about France.

Maggie had to reverse course on Nicole's budding antipathy *now*.

The first thing Maggie was struck by when she walked into

Mohammed Olivier's campaign offices was that he must have very good donors. Wall-to-wall carpeting, muted pastel walls that looked freshly painted, and subtle recessed lighting gave the office an updated, sophisticated feel. The employees were on their cell phones at their desks—still from Ikea but new— and looked young and well dressed.

The receptionist smiled when she approached and Maggie assumed she'd been trained to treat everyone like a potential donor.

"I'm here to see Mohammed Olivier," Maggie said. "I'm a stringer for an American newspaper covering his campaign."

"Oh!" the girl said, momentarily taken by surprise.

Maggie repeated herself slowly and then added, "I just need a statement from Monsieur Olivier for our readers back home."

"Of course," the girl said, punching in a number on her landline and speaking into the phone in low tones that Maggie couldn't hear. After a moment, the young woman looked up, still smiling. "He'll be right out."

And he was. Maggie had barely had time to thank the woman when Mohammed Olivier was striding through the waiting room, his hand outstretched to her. Maggie got to her feet and shook his hand.

"Thank you so much for seeing me without an appointment, Monsieur Olivier."

"Not at all, not at all."

Dark with rugged good looks, Olivier reminded Maggie of a young Omar Sharif. He smiled broadly, revealing a set of straight, very white teeth.

He looked around the waiting room as if there might be more in Maggie's party and she realized he was looking for her photographer.

She tapped her handbag. "I have my own camera," she said.

"*Bien, bien,*" he said and led the way back down the hall to a set of double doors. Behind the doors was a spacious office. A petite blonde woman was standing by a large oak desk in the center of the room and looked up as if startled to see Maggie and Olivier enter.

"Everything all right, Cayenne?" Olivier said to her.

"I was just checking something," the woman said softly before leaving the room.

"Sit, sit," Olivier said expansively to Maggie, waving to a large upholstered chair in front of the desk as he took his seat behind the desk. His computer terminal was set up so that the screen was visible from the door—or to any guest in the chair facing the desk.

On the screen a video was playing on a repeating loop. It showed clips of Olivier at a rally, listening attentively to people at a *fête* and then waving from a podium, his arm around the very same woman who had just been in his office a moment earlier.

"Now, what can I help you with?" Olivier said, rubbing his hands together.

"Well, I'm sure you're not surprised that my visit today was triggered by the sudden death of your opponent in the mayoral race."

"Ah, yes. Such a tragedy. Our prayers go out to his wife and son."

"Did you know Leon Boucher personally?"

"Thank God, no," Olivier grimaced. "The man was a pig. Don't write that. He would have been a disaster for Marseille had anyone taken him seriously."

Or had he lived.

"I understand your platform positions were quite...opposite," Maggie said. She really didn't think their political differences were that crucial but she was hoping that talking about them might make this consummate politician a little less careful with his words.

"Leon Boucher was a bastard and the worst thing possible

for a place like Marseille," Boucher said. "Marseille! Can you imagine? With its strong immigrant base? What was he thinking?"

"Good point."

"Ah, but do not be deceived, Madame. There are plenty in Marseille who hold the same vile beliefs Boucher was spewing." He sighed. "But he was I suppose a human being and so I am sorry for his family."

"Had he been in Marseille politics long?"

"That is something you will need to ask his campaign manager. Or perhaps his family."

"How do you think his demise will affect the election now?"

"How do you think?" Olivier narrowed his eyes at her. "Unless they come up with another candidate in the next two weeks and can campaign him or her in Boucher's stead, I believe you are looking at the new Mayor of the 14th and 15th *arrondissements*. Don't write that."

"Of course," Maggie said. "One last question. Can you tell me where you were two days ago at midday?"

Olivier frowned at her. "The time of Boucher's murder? Are you serious?"

"It's just a routine question. My editor will fuss if I don't ask."

"I was in the middle of a very public rally. You can find it on YouTube, time and date stamped. My wife was there too."

Before Maggie could respond, a young man came to the door and cleared his throat.

Maggie knew an exit prompt when it was delivered. And besides, Olivier was looking much less hospitable now.

"Well, I know how busy you must be," she said, standing up.

"When will the piece come out? And will my staff be able to vet it before it publishes?"

"Sure," Maggie said and shook his hand.

As she walked down the long marble stairs to the lobby,

Maggie felt a sadness drag on her shoulders. She was pretty sure she had found out precisely nothing from her meeting with Mohammed Olivier.

She pushed the Uber app notification and stepped outside to wait for her ride home.

At least Nicole had had a lovely day at *Dormir*, she thought. Perhaps the ugly start to her visit could be managed on more than a few fronts.

As she waited for her Uber to show up Maggie felt her phone vibrate where she'd tucked it in her pocket.

She glanced down to see she'd received a text from Nicole.

<when can i book my flight back home??!>

18

By some miracle Maggie made it home to Domaine St-Buvard before Laurent and the children. She was able to let the dogs out, put on some music, start dinner and generally look as if she'd been home for hours. She'd even had time to jump on her computer to find out who Mohammad Olivier's wife was—*Cayenne, didn't he say?*—and discovered there was very little about her on the Internet.

Guess I'm going to have to do this the old-fashioned way.

Just before seven Jemmy and Mila came running into the house, as usual starving although they'd eaten just a few hours ago, followed by Luc and Nicole. Maggie greeted each of them and on impulse poured a glass of wine for Nicole.

On the one hand Maggie knew that Nicole was old enough to drink a glass of wine—at least in France—but also knew she was offering it largely to pander to her disgruntled niece. When Laurent came in and saw the three wine glasses, he arched an eyebrow at her.

I don't care. Right now I'm desperate.

"Everyone have a nice picnic at *Dormir*?" she asked as Jemmy and Mila washed their hands in the kitchen. Luc was already heading outside and Maggie felt a flash of annoyance at the thought that Laurent had put him to work yet again.

Is he trying to make him think he's the hired hand?

"Oh, it was so much fun!" Mila gushed. "Wasn't it, Nikki? Philippe is so cute! He knows his complete alphabet already. And I'm teaching him some English words. *Mamère* says he's very smart. Oh, and *Maman*, Luc and Jemmy found a garden snake!"

"You mean garter snake," Jemmy said.

"How about you, Nicole?" Maggie said. "Fun day?"

"I hate picnics," Nicole said as she sat down at the kitchen counter. "Ants and bugs everywhere, but Grace wanted us all outside."

"You mean Madame Van Sant," Maggie said, and then bit her tongue. She should have just let it go.

"Whatever."

Laurent came into the kitchen and began looking under pot lids. Maggie knew he would take over making dinner.

"Who are my helpers today?" he asked as he washed his hands.

"Me!" Mila said. "And Nikki!"

"I have to do that thing on my laptop," Nicole said. "Remember I told you about it, Mila?"

Mila's eyes lit up and she turned to her father. "I have to do something with Nikki," she said.

Laurent shrugged. "Jemmy?"

"I want to see what Luc's doing," Jemmy said.

"I want to know what Luc's doing too," Maggie said. "Are we finally putting in that swimming pool? And are you making a seventeen-year-old boy dig it single-handedly?"

"A pool? Really, Papa?" Mila said excitedly.

"Your *Maman* is being funny," Laurent said. "If no one is helping, then everybody out of the kitchen."

Nicole and Mila left the kitchen and Maggie picked up her

wine glass and realized she had never actually offered Nicole her glass of wine.

"How was your day?" she asked as she sat on a counter stool facing into the kitchen. From there she could see Nicole and Mila in the living room with Nicole's laptop open in front of them.

"*Bon.*"

"What is it you're making Luc do?"

"Nothing that social services needs to know about. Hand me that jar of honey, *chérie.*"

It occurred to Maggie that she hadn't really talked to Luc in a few days and had barely even looked at him since Nicole came. She was about to ask Laurent if he was having a problem with Luc when she heard Mila squeal with delight.

Maggie could see a flash of color on Nicole's computer screen and the words "Creative tattoos."

What in the world was Nicole showing Mila?

Dinner was a quiet affair—much more so than one would expect, Maggie thought, considering it was summer and they had four children at the outdoor table. Laurent, although taciturn at the best of times, appeared embroiled in his own thoughts. Maggie noticed he didn't even react when Jemmy fed a piece of his honey-braised pork to one of the dogs.

Luc ate his food mechanically without looking up—another change from how he'd been all winter when he'd made such great strides in fitting into the family. Now he was acting like an unwelcome outsider invited to sit at the family table.

Maggie tried several times to ask Luc what he was working on outside but got only grunts until Laurent, finally roused from his own thoughts, growled at Luc to stop feeding the dog. Maggie noticed that Jem had the good form to at least blush guiltily as Luc took the blame.

Before Maggie could confront Laurent with whatever his problem was, Nicole spoke up.

"I have a million things to do back home," she said in a whiny voice. "Nana wants to move into her new place and I'm afraid she's going to throw my stuff out in the street."

"You know very well she would never do that," Maggie said. "And she's not moving until September. You have plenty of time."

"Why can't I go home? I hate it here." She glanced over at Mila. "No offense, Mila. It's not you."

Maggie saw Mila's eyes fill with tears.

"I need you to give this visit a chance," Maggie said. "You're supposed to be here for the full month of—"

"I'll kill myself if you make me stay the full month," Nicole said, her eyes going to Laurent to see if her tone would elicit a response from him.

"We don't discuss serious matters at the dinner table," Maggie said. "The French believe it ruins the digestion. And they have a point. Plenty of studies have shown—"

"Oh, stop," Nicole said, holding up a hand. "What a weird country. *Un*-believable. Come on, Mila. I want to show you my friend Parker's website. He does amazing work."

Nicole and Mila stood up, their dinner plates in their hands.

"Oh?" Maggie asked. "Is he a painter or a sculptor?"

"What? No," Nicole said. "Come on, Mila."

Jemmy and Luc stood up too and grabbed their plates.

So much for the family dinner table, Maggie thought as they excused themselves.

Laurent was still staring off into space—clearly somewhere far away from his body's location.

"Earth to Laurent."

He turned to her as if seeing her for the first time all evening.

"How is Frère Jean?" Maggie asked.

He shrugged. "Tests. More tests."

"But the doctors are optimistic he'll make a full recovery?"

"If you can believe such things."

"Laurent, is everything okay?"

Laurent stood up and whistled to the dogs who both came bounding over to him.

"Of course. I will take a little walk around the vineyard."

Maggie watched him walk down the terrace path, stopping briefly at the stone wall Luc had been working on before disappearing at the end of the garden into the vineyard.

What is going on with him?

An hour later, Laurent was back in the kitchen. Maggie knew he enjoyed cleaning the kitchen, putting every pan and casserole pot back in its place. He usually required one or both of the children to help him, but tonight he worked alone.

Jemmy and Luc were watching television in the living room. Nicole and Mila had disappeared upstairs to Nicole's bedroom. Maggie was very curious about the websites that Nicole was showing Mila. She knew they couldn't be anything inappropriate, for Nicole was very protective of Mila.

With everyone settled, Maggie took her glass of wine to her study and sat down at her computer. She'd tried to contact Jean-Baptiste earlier but he had not responded to her texts.

That was just as well. She decided she wasn't ready to share with him what she'd discovered.

Not that I've discovered very much.

She opened up a browser window on her computer and typed in *property sales for Marseille*. As soon as the web page came up, she typed *Leon Boucher* into the search window and immediately got the date that his house was purchased—four years ago—as well as the amount he purchased it for—one point six million euros—and, most importantly, the address.

Joelle had said that Boucher's wife was divorcing him. Did that mean she didn't live at this address any more? What about the son?

His son, the nurse.

Who has easy access to toxic drugs.

She typed in *Gaston Boucher* on the same web page but nothing came up. That probably meant he didn't own property of his own. There was a good chance that even if he had his own apartment, now that his father was dead, he might have moved back in with his mother.

Assuming his mother lived at the address Maggie was looking at.

Maggie sighed. All she could do was drive over and see for herself. If Marie-France or Gaston didn't live there, she'd look for the next lead that told her where to find them.

As she opened up another browser window to map out Boucher's address she wasn't surprised to see that Angeline Sauvage didn't live far away.

At the thought of her visit with Angeline today, Maggie also thought of how the woman hadn't mentioned threatening Leon's life two days before he was killed. Maggie would have to talk with her again.

A peal of laughter made Maggie look up to see Nicole in the kitchen with Mila and Laurent. Nicole was barefoot and laughing at something Laurent had said. The laughter was a balm to Maggie's agitated nerves.

As she watched Nicole, Maggie couldn't help but think, *Just as soon as I solve this murder, she is going to be perfectly fine again.*

The next morning before Maggie was awake, Laurent was gone again. So were the dogs. As Maggie swung her legs out of bed and rubbed the sleep from her eyes, she seemed to remember him saying something about meeting a contractor or service repair person at one of the mini-houses this morning.

Laurent's mini-houses were his answer to the need to house some of the refugee families staying at the nearby monastery during his harvest. Each of the little cottages was simply furnished with a bedroom, kitchen, shower and toilet.

All night long Maggie's brain had been buzzing with the information she'd found out yesterday about Angeline and Joelle, as well as her impressions of Mohammad Olivier.

Unfortunately, no pieces of the puzzle were falling into place. From past experience, Maggie knew she just didn't have enough pieces yet.

She was hoping to remedy that today.

Downstairs she saw that before leaving Laurent had begun breakfast and made a fresh pot of coffee. If it were up to Maggie, she'd just dash to the *boulangerie* in the village and pick up a baguette for *pain beurre* for breakfast.

But she'd gotten up too late to do any of that and she could already hear the children descending the long marble staircase to the kitchen.

Luc and Jemmy greeted her with as few words as possible. Luc poured himself a coffee and grabbed a slice of *brioche*. Then he and Jemmy went outside where the two big dogs jumped excitedly in anticipation of getting a few bites of bread.

Mila and Nicole seated themselves at the breakfast counter. Nicole's cell phone was on the counter, screen up, as if she was expecting a call.

"Good morning," Maggie said. "Sleep well, I hope?"

Nicole ignored her but Mila proceeded to tell Maggie about a dream she had. Meanwhile, Maggie poured coffee for Nicole and an orange juice for Mila and slipped two croissants on saucers across the counter to them.

"Where's Laurent?" Nicole asked, still staring at her phone.

Maggie noticed that Nicole didn't dare address Laurent without his avuncular title when he was present to hear it.

"He had to check on something at one of the mini-houses," Maggie said. "I was thinking of going in to Arles today. Are you interested?"

"Oh, *Maman*, I can't!" Mila said. "*Mamère* is coming to take me to *Dormir* this morning. We're making *cannelés*." She turned to Nicole. "Want to come? It's so fun!"

"No, thanks," Nicole said before turning back to Maggie. "I've been to Arles before, you know."

"You were just a child then," Maggie said. "Each time you see Arles it has new wonders to reveal."

"Ugh. Did you really just say that?"

Why do teenagers always make you feel like the biggest idiot on the planet?

But Maggie kept her smile in place.

"Maybe another day then," she said, pouring herself a coffee. "I'm going to need to dash out as soon as Danielle comes to pick up Mila. Will you be all right here by yourself?"

Nicole looked up, a sliver of panic in her eyes. "Will Luc and Jemmy be here?"

"Yes, I think Laurent has them fixing a fence or something in the vineyard."

Nicole's posture seemed to relax. "Okay good. Not that it matters." She took her coffee and walked into the living room.

Watching her go, Maggie felt a heaviness creep into her bones.

An hour later Maggie was in the back of another Uber that again took nearly forty minutes to arrive in Marseille. Before she left Nicole had made it clear that she was not open to any more conversation and had finally taken her laptop out to the terrace. Luc and Jemmy and the dogs were visible from the garden where they worked on the *potager* wall.

Maggie revisited that moment of fear she'd seen in Nicole's face when she thought for a moment she would be alone at Domaine St-Buvard.

It was a look that sliced right into Maggie's heart.

She would give anything to wipe it away—to erase the core event that had put it there.

She straightened her shoulders. And wrapping up this case was the first step to doing exactly that.

She looked again at the map on her cell phone and glanced out the window as her driver pulled up to a curb.

It was a nice neighborhood. Very nice. Even nicer than Angeline's and as Maggie had already discovered, not far away either.

Once on the sidewalk, Maggie looked down the street to the

front of Leon Boucher's apartment building. She'd debated for the whole drive to Marseille whether she should just go up and knock on the door as she had with Angeline or take a more indirect approach.

On the one hand, taking people by surprise—although not always pleasant—generally tended to yield better results. People taken off guard without time to prepare tended to blurt out information closer to the truth.

On the other hand, this was the family of the victim. If there was anything that was going to unhinge Jean-Baptiste— possibly even test him on his promise to arrest Maggie for interfering—knocking on that door would be it.

Maggie glanced at her watch and saw that it was already past lunchtime. Looking up, she noticed a wrought iron bench nearly hidden by a line of beech trees facing the apartment building.

Perfect.

She might still go and knock on the front door but she could afford to wait an hour first to see who came in or out.

She had barely sat down and gotten comfortable when the front door opened and a young man wearing nursing scrubs walked out. Immediately Maggie was on her feet, hurrying toward him.

"Excuse me, Monsieur?" she called. He turned and waited for her to catch up to him on the sidewalk. Gaston Boucher was a slim man with sandy blond hair and blue eyes. He had a weak chin but full lips and was overall pleasant looking.

"I'm sorry to bother you. My name is Margaret Newberry and I wanted to tell you how sorry I was about your loss."

"American?"

"Yes. How could you tell?"

He smiled. "I went to school in Florida."

Gratified that he seemed willing to talk to her, Maggie

slowed her pace hoping that would force him to slow too. It must have because he nodded at the bench she'd just left.

"I would suggest a coffee," he said, "but I'm on my way to work."

"No problem," Maggie said as they walked over to the bench she'd just left. "I wanted to tell you how sorry I was. I lost my father last year."

Gaston grimaced. "I am sorry for that, Madame. But I'm sure you did not loathe your father as I did mine."

"I'm sorry to hear that," Maggie said, although she was actually delighted to hear him say it. In her experience, anger got people talking even more than grief.

"Where in Florida did you go to school?"

She knew she needed to reinforce the connection she had with him. Most French—if they didn't outright abhor Americans—rather enjoyed them.

"The University of Central Florida. Do you know Orlando?"

"Not really, but I'm from Atlanta and so annual jaunts down to Disney World were sort of *de rigueur*."

"I love Disney World! I know it's embarrassing to say that—especially for a Frenchman."

"Not at all. I've dragged my husband there at least four times with the kids and I know he's enjoyed himself."

"You married a Frenchman?"

"I did."

Maggie knew Gaston didn't have a lot of time before he would have to leave. She looked over at the apartment building.

"So your father didn't live here?" she asked.

"He used to. And I'm only here at the moment for my mother. Not that she's mourning him either. She was in the process of divorcing the bastard."

So that part is true.

"I don't know why anybody is surprised that someone

would want my father dead. The man was despicable. Do you know anything about him?"

"Not really."

"He had a mistress. She lives just down the street. He moved her into an apartment there while my mother and I lived here. Can you imagine?" Gaston's eyes filled with tears as if relieving the humiliation.

Maggie tried to imagine someone as sensitive and emotionally tentative as Gaston appeared capable of killing his own father in cold blood.

It was hard to believe.

"How awful," she said. "Do you have any idea of who might want have wanted to hurt your father?"

"Only everybody. Everybody in Marseille. The cops said he was stabbed in the neck with a needle in his own car. They said that meant the killer was someone my father knew well enough to invite into his car."

"A friend?"

Gaston snorted. "My father had no friends. Just people he could use until they figured it out and became enemies." He looked away. "I hated him." Then he looked back at Maggie. "But I couldn't have killed him."

"Of course not."

"The police think I did."

"Surely not."

"I don't have an alibi and I...it's well documented how I felt about him. I once posted a tweet about what a pig he was and it got ten thousand hits. Plus just last week he was over here screaming at my mother while I was here and we...I called the cops."

So Jean-Baptiste knows there was a domestic violence charge against Leon Boucher.

"Add that to the fact that I have no alibi and I have a history of hating my father *and* I made a recent police call for domestic abuse and you have a class A prime suspect."

"I'm sure the evidence will exonerate you," Maggie said, knowing that was not at all how things always worked out.

"Why are the police looking at me? I can name five people off the top of my head who wanted the bastard dead!"

But were they skilled with a hypodermic needle with access to dangerous drugs?

"You mean like your father's mistress?" Maggie asked innocently.

Gaston huffed in disgust.

"She could have done it, to be sure, but as bad as she is, she isn't as bad as that *putain* Danon."

"Who?"

"Danon Chastain. My father's boyfriend."

eon Boucher was gay?

Maggie shook her head in wonder.

How did that work? A neo-Nazi who hates anyone different has a secret boyfriend?

"Well, that's a surprise," she said.

"Isn't it? Imagine what his would-be constituents would make of that, huh?" Gaston glanced at his watch and stood up. "I must go or I'll be late for work. Thank you again for your condolences, Madame."

"Before you go," Maggie said as she stood up, "I would love to extend my condolences to your mother too."

He hesitated only briefly before taking her phone to input his mother's phone number.

"It's her private cell phone. Although she doesn't usually answer. While I'm at it I'll give you Danon's number, too. I didn't even tell the police about him," he said, handing her phone back to her. "And now I really must go."

He shook Maggie's hand and then turned and hurried down the street.

Maggie sat back down on the bench in front of his house. She looked at her cell phone screen to see that Gaston had punched in Danon Chastain's phone number *and address*. Just looking at it gave her a thrill of accomplishment.

If it was true that Gaston hadn't told the police about the secret relationship, then Jean-Baptiste probably didn't even know Danon existed.

He can't be mad at me for talking to someone he doesn't even knows exists!

She glanced at Marie-France Boucher's private cell phone number above Danon's.

Pretty good for one twenty-minute interview that she hadn't even had to lie to set up!

As soon as Maggie located Danon's address on her phone map she realized it was too far to walk, so she called up another Uber driver and gave Gaston's mother's number a call.

It rang until it went to voicemail. Maggie disconnected without leaving a message. Now that she had access to Marie-France's direct line, sooner or later she was sure to connect with her.

As Maggie waited for her ride, she reflected back on her conversation with Gaston. He seemed very vulnerable—as if he was constantly on the verge of tears—and while he was definitely angry at his father, Maggie could also detect a deep sadness under the surface of his anger.

You can't lose a father and not have it be a gut punch. Even one you think you hate.

Maggie looked at the phone number she'd found for Angeline Sauvage last night. She debated calling and confronting her about the threat she'd made against Leon, but decided to hold off for now.

She could keep that little nugget in her back pocket in case she needed it to unsettle Angeline the next time she interviewed her.

She saw her Uber weaving its way down the long street toward her and stood up and waved to him.

A neo-Nazi with a male lover?

Things were definitely starting to get interesting.

Danon Chastain's apartment was located in the sixth district just a few blocks from the Old Port, the famed Marseille harbor.

It was the sort of neighborhood that was difficult to say whether it was self-consciously bohemian—in which case it was hardly poor—or leaning toward actual poverty. The surrounding art galleries, speakeasies and *brasseries* increased the likelihood of the former description.

Opting to break with tradition and encouraged by her approach with Gaston, Maggie decided to make this as easy as possible on both her and Chastain. She called him from one of the busy cafés on the corner of his block.

"*Bonjour,* Monsieur Chastain," she said, making her voice friendly but efficient. "I was directed to your number by a friend of Leon Boucher's. Do you have time to talk and answer a few questions?"

"Who are you?" His voice was hesitant but not unfriendly.

"I am a distant cousin of Leon's in town on vacation and hoping to bring some answers back to my mother—Leon's mother's second cousin once removed."

There was a pause on the line. "Are you in Marseille?"

"I am in fact," Maggie said, trying to rein in her excitement. "I'm at the Café Pepé. Do you have time right now to meet me?"

"I'll be there in five minutes."

Maggie hoped that interviewing Chastain in a public place would make him less defensive. A café was always a social, convivial place. Besides, how could anyone be defensive over *Kir Royal*?

Maggie positioned herself at a table that backed up to an interior wall with a good view of the street. She wanted Chastain to feel free to talk and she had an idea that confessing that he was a neo-Nazi's lover might be something he'd prefer not to broadcast to the whole neighborhood.

She spotted him immediately striding down the street and wasn't surprised to see he was handsome. He had thick blond hair and a square jaw. His blue eyes narrowed when he saw her but he lifted a hand in a wave—as though they were old friends.

The second part of her plan to make Chastain relax involved revealing a few personal nuggets about herself. That always tended to work and worked even better if they had the ring of truth about them.

She stood up and they shook hands.

"Thank you for meeting me," Maggie said.

"No problem. Your French is very good but do you mind if we speak English? I'm always trying to practice."

"Not at all."

They sat. Although it was just past lunchtime, Maggie had ordered a *Kir* with a small dish of peanuts. Danon caught the waiter's eye and ordered the same.

"How did you know that I knew Leon?" he asked once the waiter left.

"Gaston told me." Again, the truth was always best until she came to that moment when she couldn't use it any more.

"I'm surprised. I think he hates me."

"He's pretty upset right now as you can imagine."

"Not over the death of his father, surely?" Danon cocked his head at Maggie and she thought she detected a profound sadness in his face.

"He says not. But you know how that is. You can hate your father right up to the moment you realize you're losing him."

"How well did you know Leon?" Danon asked.

"Not at all. He was just a line on an ancestral tree. But I was in Marseille on vacation..."

"Alone? Surely not?"

Maggie saw him glance at her wedding band and she cursed the fact that she hadn't thought to remove it.

"No, I'm here with my husband. He's down by the Old Port checking things out."

"No kids?"

"No, but we're traveling with our niece. She's seventeen."

Danon laughed. "That sounds frightening."

"Trust me, it is. Nicole lives on her lap top or cell phone and is horrified any time my husband or I suggest she might join in a conversation."

"Where are you from?"

"Atlanta. We're only in France for a couple of weeks."

"What do you want to know about Leon?"

"Well, I was upset to discover he'd been murdered this week. I was told that Marseille was no longer a dangerous city."

Danon snorted. "Who told you that?"

"Is it not true?"

"I don't think Marseille is any more dangerous than any other large city."

"I told Nicole that. She was pretty upset to hear about Leon's death. I mean we didn't know him but still, what were the odds he'd be murdered? So now she thinks all of France is dangerous."

"Well, not compared to the US."

Maggie tried to mesh the image she'd had of Leon up to

today with the man sitting across the café table from her. Danon was intelligent, gentle, and candid. What in the world was he doing with Leon Boucher?

"You're not the first person I've talked to in Marseille about Leon," she said.

"You said you talked with Gaston."

"Right. I also talked with Leon's campaign manager Joelle Mercier."

She figured she'd hold off on any mention of Angeline in case Leon's mistress was a sore subject with Danon.

"I'd be interested to hear your take on Joelle," he said.

"Just that she...well, honestly, if I had to say I'd say she was in love with him."

"You are very intuitive! That is exactly what she is." Danon's eyes hardened. "Only not in the same sense that most normal people would define the emotion."

"What do you mean?"

Danon took a sip of his drink and hesitated as if making up his mind as to how much to tell Maggie. She held her breath. She knew not to hurry the process by talking.

"Joelle was obsessed with Leon," Danon finally said. "She has been since university."

"Did they have a sexual relationship?"

Danon shook his head. "She always wanted to. That was obvious but Leon swore he never took her up on it."

Having met Joelle, Maggie could easily imagine that Danon was correct. Joelle was definitely heartbroken over the loss of her partner.

"Plus there was always the little matter of Michel," Danon said with a frown.

"Michel?"

"Joelle's brother. A handsome bastard, *absolument*! It was hardly a surprise to anyone who knew Leon that, well, you know."

"Leon had an affair with Joelle's brother?"

"*Oui.* Long before my time of course."

Maggie tried to make sense of what she was hearing. "So would you say that Leon was bisexual?"

"You mean because of his relationship with Angeline Sauvage?"

"And his wife."

"His marriage had been dead for decades. But yes, I suppose Leon could be considered bi."

"I can only imagine what a catastrophe that would be to his campaign if it ever got out."

"He was not ashamed of me."

"But nobody knew about you. I mean, I've been all over his website and there's not a breath of a whisper that you exist."

"Of course not. How could he tell the world about me? He was running on an anti-gay platform! My very existence would sink his candidacy."

"I think that's kind of my point. That must have been hard on you."

"I understood why we needed to be covert. I think what mattered, at least to me, was that I never felt ashamed or disrespected by him. The need for secrecy was just a part of our relationship I had to accept if I wanted to be with him."

"I'm just saying that must have been hard."

"I hope you're not suggesting I might have wanted to alter the terms of my relationship with him by killing him?"

Maggie blushed. She'd gone too far.

"I wasn't suggesting that."

"Because if anybody wanted Leon dead it was Joelle."

"You mean because of unrequited love?"

He drained his drink and tossed a few coins down on the table.

"No. Because when Leon ended his dalliance with Michel

five years ago he did it in a most humiliating fashion at a popular gay bar."

"Well, that's horrible but not much of a motive."

"And I would agree with you, Madame, if not for the fact that Joelle's brother went home that night and slashed his wrists."

21

M aggie's mouth fell open.

Joelle Mercier's brother killed himself after being dumped by Leon Boucher?

"That's...that's terrible," she said as Danon stood up. She looked up and saw the moment his face relaxed.

"I'm sorry to have said it like that," he said wearily. "I know Leon could be a bastard but he had many wonderful qualities too. I'm not saying Joelle killed him. But when I heard he'd been murdered, she was the first person I thought of. Don't you think that says something?"

Maggie lifted her hands in a helpless gesture.

"I have to run," Danon said. "I'm sorry you came to beautiful Marseille to meet your cousin and found this instead but I hope you and your husband are able to enjoy the rest of your time here. Marseille really is an amazing city like no other in all of France."

"Thank you, Monsieur Chastain," Maggie said as they shook hands. "And I'm sorry for your loss."

Immediately his eyes filled with tears.

"*Merci*," he said hoarsely, giving her hand a small squeeze before turning and walking down the sidewalk toward the center of town.

Maggie sat staring into space for a moment.

Joelle Mercier had just jumped to the top of her suspect list. Did Jean-Baptiste know about this? Did he know Leon was bisexual? Did he know about Michel Mercier or Danon Chastain?

She paid for her drinks and was about to push the app for another Uber when she saw a text message appear on her screen from Jean-Baptiste Morceau.

<call me>

Maggie looked at her recent calls but there was nothing there from him. She quickly called him and settled back into her seat at the café.

Jean-Baptiste picked up without saying hello. "I've just gotten off the phone with Mohammad Olivier. You told me you wouldn't interfere."

"And you told me you'd keep me informed."

"I told you nothing of the sort and besides I have nothing to inform you of!"

"Well, then I'm not doing anything."

"Look, Maggie. Let's start over, yes?"

"I'm happy to start over, Jean-Baptiste. Because I've found some amazing info that I'm almost positive you don't have."

"I won't ask you how you came by this info. What is it?"

"Not so fast. I'm not telling you anything until you answer a few of *my* questions."

"This is obstruction of an investigation. I could have you arrested."

"Go ahead and do that and then get out the water boards because that's the only way you'll find out what I've learned."

There was a pause on the line and Maggie signaled to the waiter for another *Kir*.

"We believe the body was moved postmortem," Jean-

Baptiste said slowly. "And we do not believe we are looking at a woman for this."

"Even though Boucher was poisoned? And poison is a woman's weapon?"

"Thank you, Agatha Christie. Police forensics have advanced considerably since the 1920s. Men use poison now just as much as women. I will refer you to the poisoning of Sergei Skripal and his daughter not too long ago and before that Charlie Rowley and his girlfriend."

"Fine, fine, I get it. Men use poison too. Anything else?"

"Not until you tell me what *you* know."

Maggie took a sip of her drink and mentally ran through everything she'd recently learned. She didn't want to tell him anything that would close the door for future investigations for her but on the other hand she needed to tell him something worth hearing.

She knew the information that Angeline had been heard threatening Leon was soft. That could just be emotional ranting. Just because she shrieked "I'll kill you!" didn't mean she'd really do it.

Likewise the fact that Danon appeared tired of being a dirty little secret kept by Leon also felt weak as a motive. As far as telling Jean-Baptiste about Danon, she would keep that in her back pocket for now.

As for Gaston, Maggie had learned little to nothing to implicate him. If anything, her gut instinct told her he didn't do it.

All she really had was Joelle Mercier.

"I recently found out that Joelle Mercier's brother had an affair with Leon Boucher which ended in Mercier's suicide."

"You're joking."

"It's easily confirmable. Look it up. His name was Michel Mercier. My source told me that Leon publicly humiliated

Michel when he broke up with him and then Michel killed himself. That gives Joelle a strong motive for killing Leon."

"This is all you have? Do you not even *know* who Leon Boucher was?"

"Yes, Jean-Baptiste, I do know. My source is another man who is widely known to have been Leon's lover at the time of his murder. So if you're ready to dismiss this information out of hand because you think there's no way Leon would have had a sexual relationship with a man, then get ready to be made a fool of when all the facts come to light."

There was another pause on the line. "I will check it out."

"You're welcome," Maggie said.

"And now you will stop talking to people in connection with this investigation."

"I'm happy to let you get on with your job. Under one condition."

"I don't deal with terrorists."

"Very funny. I'll back off if you promise to keep me informed. That's all I ask. I have a personal stake in this case as you know since it's *my* niece who's having a nervous breakdown over what she saw at the airport that day and the sooner this is wrapped up the better."

"I will keep you updated."

"Thank you. By the way, did you ever get a match for the partial print on the door handle of my trunk?"

Jean-Baptiste sighed. "We got no matches."

"So the killer isn't in the system."

"You are assuming the partial was left by the killer. Could it not just as easily be one of your husband's friends or the grocer helping put bags in your trunk?"

Maggie had to admit the partial was too circumstantial to hang a murder case on.

"What else can you tell me?" she asked.

"We pulled several sets of fingerprints off the victim's car.

They were Leon's, his son, Gaston's and two others not in the database."

"That's pretty crappy Intel. *Anyone* would assume Leon and his son's prints would be on his car!"

"Well, if that doesn't impress you, how about the fact that Gaston Boucher is on probation for possible drug use?"

Maggie felt her skin tingle. "Why is he still allowed to work at the hospital then?"

"I said *possible*."

"Okay, Jean-Baptiste, either the drug test came back positive or it didn't. Why are you playing games with me?"

"There is no official record of the drug test. We only heard about it through his colleagues."

"Gossip, you mean. So basically the test came back positive but Gaston was able to pay to expunge it. Is that what you're saying?"

"That's possibly what I'm saying."

"Is it enough to make an arrest?"

"I'm bringing him in for questioning this afternoon. I expect the interview to end in an arrest. Happy?"

Actually she wasn't. Maggie tried to feel what she might expect to feel at the near wrap-up of a case—and especially one that had some personal ramifications for her—but something bothered her. She got a quick image of Gaston's face, his brows knit in frustration and his eyes sad beyond measure at the loss of his father.

"I'm happy if he really did it," she said.

"You talk in riddles. In any case, you can stop harassing the good citizens of Marseille. As of eighteen hundred hours today we will have our prime suspect in custody."

"Great."

"I mean it, Maggie. I'm officially closing this case with an arrest this afternoon. And it's not Joelle Mercier or whoever else you may have drummed up."

"I'm happy, Jean-Baptiste. Beyond happy."

You are arresting the wrong man.

The feeling was as strong and indelible as anything Maggie had ever felt.

"Meanwhile," Jean-Baptiste said, "if you hear of anything else you think I should know about, you have my number."

He hung up and Maggie was left holding the disconnected phone to her ear.

"Oh, trust me I do," she said.

22

Nicole sat at the outdoor stone table on the terrace of Domaine St-Buvard, a glass of iced tea in front of her. She knew she probably shouldn't drink it. Her nerves were already so jangled she couldn't sleep at night but the water from the tap here tasted weird.

It was too hot to sit outside but she felt too cooped up inside. A faint breeze was doing little to mitigate the strong southern sun. Nicole looked out over the vineyards which began at the back of the garden and seemed to go on forever.

They looked so bushy and green and she tried to remember if she'd ever visited this close to harvest before. Normally when she came, it was winter and the vineyard looked like so many blackened match sticks jammed into the ground.

As she looked at the fields, she could see Luc and Jemmy walking toward her. Luc carried a shovel over his shoulder.

She couldn't imagine what Maggie and Laurent were thinking when they let that kid come and move in with them!

They must be desperate for company or wanting more kids or something!

She turned and glanced at the façade of Domaine St-

Buvard. It looked so old, with its pockmarked stone walls and purple flowers draping all over it like they'd probably done before the beginning of time. It was totally believable to her that this place had been here during the time of Charlemagne.

She pulled out her phone and scrolled through her recent text exchanges with her Uncle Ben. She was getting pretty tired of platitudes from both him and Maggie. She sent him another text.

<I want to come home!!!! Please talk to your sister!!>

She set her phone on the table and watched the bubbles beneath her text as Ben wrote his reply.

She could hear Jem and Luc talking now. They were speaking in French so she couldn't understand what they were saying.

It was impossible for her to believe that at one point when she was little she knew French. Sometimes she tried to remember back to those days—when Aunt Maggie had brought her from France after Elise had died—but she honestly had no memory of that time at all.

Why was Maggie going on and on like this was her home? She'd been in France a total of two weeks over the last thirteen years! And it was horrible! The bathrooms were terrifying, the food took forever to get to you, there was no easy way to get any fast food and when you did your burger tasted like the cow had eaten a field of grass! She made a face and glanced at her phone.

Still nothing.

Why can't I just go home? What is the point of torturing me like this?

"Hey, Nikki," Jemmy said as he and Luc stepped onto the terrace.

Nicole looked up and made a face. Luc had taken his shirt off and she could actually smell the sweat on him.

"Please stand down wind of me," she said to him.

Jemmy laughed and translated for Luc, who did not laugh. Instead, he said something to Jem in French which didn't sound very nice at all.

"What did he say?" she asked Jem, lifting her chin high.

"Nothing," Jemmy said uneasily, still smiling but clearly uncomfortable.

"You know you don't belong here," Nicole said to Luc, suddenly furious.

She was furious that he dared to stand there half naked in front of her and make snarky comments about her, and furious that he dared prance around Maggie and Laurent's vineyard like he owned the place.

"I'm not translating that," Jemmy said.

"I understood it," Luc said in English, his face a thundercloud as he regarded Nicole.

Nicole didn't know why she suddenly felt so angry but it was all she could do to sit there so she stood up and grabbed her phone.

"You're not really family, you know," she said to him, watching him blush with anger. "You're just their pet of the month!"

Before he could respond, Nicole turned and ran back to the house. She had no idea why her eyes were full of tears. She jerked open the French doors and nearly tripped over the two dogs waiting inside.

She ran up the broad staircase to her bedroom and slammed the door before flinging herself on the bed.

Her heart was pounding as she clutched the bed's duvet tightly with both fists.

Why are they doing this to me? she thought, her jaw clenching painfully.

She looked at her phone but there was still no message from Ben.

Feeling she had to do *something*—she couldn't just sit here and endure this!—she grabbed her laptop from the desk. The first thing she did was go to her Facebook page. All her friends had been very sympathetic about her being trapped over here in France.

Right now she could use a little support.

She wrote on her timeline.

<I would check in except Domaine St-Buvard is in the middle of effing NO place so Facebook doesn't even recognize it! #Stillstuckhere #rescueme #francesucks>

She published the post and sat back, feeling a little better. After a moment, she noticed that a private message had appeared. She clicked on the icon and read the message and as she did she felt the bile in her gut creeping up into her throat.

<Not enjoying your stay Nicole? Maybe we could meet and I'll change your mind>

Fear prickled across her scalp as she stared at the words.

At first her thoughts wouldn't come together.

It wasn't possible. It can't be.

She slammed the laptop shut, her hands trembling on the lid.

And then she got up and walked calmly to the bathroom where she threw up her lunch.

23

L aurent drove down the A7, his thoughts crisscrossing around his brain and ending in disappointment and defeat.

After this morning's meeting at *l'Abbaye de Sainte-Trinité* to consider the possibility of taking on even more refugee workers, he'd made an impulsive detour to Aix and the mayor's office to inquire into the exact requirements for his formal fostering of an underage child.

The officious and tip-lipped woman behind the counter told him precisely what he'd already learned from his contact in Nice.

A birth certificate. Three depositions from people who knew Luc's parents. Luc's national number.

None of which Laurent had or could easily get. At least not legally.

How much trouble was Dominic willing to make? Did he want money? That didn't seem likely. He didn't appear to be just going through the motions of his brotherhood and most monks disdained money or possessions.

Then what?

Laurent had known many different situations with desperate or venal people. While most involved greed, a few were motivated to do evil just for the pleasure of it. An image of his brother Gerard came to mind.

But in Laurent's estimation that was not Brother Dominic's goal.

Unfortunately it appeared that whatever Frère Dominic's motivation was it would remain secret at least for now.

With Luc's future in the balance.

Laurent had nearly driven past the exit to Domaine St-Buvard when he decided to swing by and bring Jem and Luc with him to the mini-houses. He'd been meaning to involve Luc in the houses especially since he intended to build more.

The mini-house in question today was the one Bernard and Gigi lived in. Normally he would insist that the couple help with the repair work on the house. But he had every expectation that Bernard would be drunk and Gigi useless.

None of which would get Laurent's property repaired.

He called Luc's cell phone.

"I need you and Jem to be out front," Laurent said. "I'm nearly home."

"Where are we going?" Luc asked.

Laurent ignored his question. "Is Nicole nearby?"

A muffled conversation ensued and then Nicole came on the line.

"Hello?"

"I am taking the boys off for the afternoon unless you—"

"Yes! I want to come," Nicole said quickly.

Laurent hesitated. She didn't ask where she was going. But he decided that was all to the good. Not that a visit to the mini-houses would rank very high on anyone's summer vacation but perhaps she was already bored sitting around the house.

"Very good. Five minutes. Out front," he said and disconnected.

. . .

By the time Laurent had picked up the teens and driven to the mini-houses on the far side of the Domaine St-Buvard property, a fine haze had begun to bleach the hot summer sky, turning it nearly white.

Laurent had built the four houses on the back twenty hectares of the property that had once belonged to Danielle and her first husband Eduard Morceau. The houses were close but not too near each other, affording each inhabitant at least some privacy.

Laurent had learned a great deal about construction in the making of these four houses and he planned to use that knowledge to improve the next four.

While he didn't need an army of pickers every year living on his property, the monastery could not house all the refugees they gathered in. Laurent felt strongly that it was his responsibility as one of the leading landowners in the area to do what he could to help.

Often, those inhabiting his houses spent full winters doing nothing but enjoying the fresh vegetables they harvested from the monastery gardens and their own little plots. They also enjoyed taking long walks around the vineyards. There was very little work to do during the off season. And in support of Laurent's belief that nobody whole and capable should remain idle for long, the houses tended to clear out every few months as inhabitants found reasons to leave.

As he drove to the first house in the line of four, it occurred to him that all three teens in the car had been unnaturally quiet. He smiled at the thought that if Mila had been with them, that would not have been the case. The child took after her mother in that way and her upbeat gregarious personality was one in which Laurent particularly delighted.

Both Luc and Jemmy tended to be reticent.

And because of her current state of chronic pouting, Nicole also spoke less than she might normally.

Laurent pulled up to the first mini-house and parked. A bicycle was leaning against the porch. It had no chains on it.

"Luc, grab the tool box," Laurent said as he got out of the car. "It's in the trunk. Jemmy, help him."

"I don't need any help," Luc said truculently.

Nicole opened her car door and looked around at the bleak scenery but did not get out.

Suddenly the front door of the house flew open. Bernard staggered out and glared at Laurent from the small raised porch.

"We are not taking visitors today!" he said. "Go home!"

The man was unsteady on his feet and obviously drunk.

"I'm here to repair the back window," Laurent said. "One of the neighbors reported it broken. Where is Gigi?"

"None of your business!" Bernard said loudly and nearly lost his balance with the exertion. "You don't own me! Get out!"

Laurent didn't know if it was the alcohol making Bernard behave so aggressively or if drugs were also involved. He waved Luc and Jemmy back to the car.

He should have dealt with this sooner. And he was not going to do it now with the children here.

He turned and walked toward the porch.

"I am just going to check that Gigi is all right," Laurent said firmly.

Without warning, Bernard rushed him. Laurent easily dodged the charge and Bernard went flying off the porch. Laurent stepped across to the front door.

The smell of the place—rank and fetid—hit him before he even entered. Standing in the doorway, he could see ragged holes in the walls, broken plaster around the sink and gaping spaces where the appliances had been. He took a step inside and saw the pipes had been pulled apart and scattered on the floor.

The floor had been gouged and pried up.

"Stay away from my stuff!" Bernard shouted and ran up the porch steps.

Laurent turned and shot out one arm, catching Bernard solidly on the chest. Bernard grunted on impact with Laurent and his legs buckled. He knelt on the porch, breathing heavily.

"Where is Gigi?" Laurent asked, keeping his voice steady and trying to avoid giving in to the nearly overwhelming urge to pick the man up and fling him into the nearby oleander bushes.

"She left," Bernard mumbled. "Went home to *Maman.*"

Laurent didn't know there had been any family to go home to. He observed Bernard for a moment where he sat on the porch, rubbing his face. The odor was coming off the man in sickening waves. Laurent glanced over his head to the car where all three children were watching in rapt attention.

"I'm locking this door," Laurent said, pulling the front door closed. "You are out."

Bernard snapped his head up. "My stuff is in there!"

"It's my stuff now. Get off the porch."

"You can't throw me out!" Bernard shouted, climbing to his feet. "I have rights!"

"You have nothing," Laurent said. He turned and nodded toward the road as he pulled his cell phone out. "I'll give you a head start on the police if you leave now."

"But my stuff," Bernard said weakly now, looking at the closed door. "You can't just throw me out."

Laurent could see that doors had opened at some of the other mini-houses and concerned faces were poking out. One woman who had worked Laurent's fields the year before but who now had a job at the village bakery shouted, "It's about time!"

"You'll pay for this," Bernard said, stumbling down the steps of the porch.

Laurent's mind was occupied with the repairs necessary to make the house habitable again. He couldn't imagine it would be ready for new residents before the end of summer which was too bad.

Standing at the bottom of the porch steps, Bernard looked around at the people from the other houses who were now openly staring at him from their front yards.

"The hell with all of you!" he shouted.

"Go on now," Laurent said.

"Yeah, piss off!" a man at the nearest house shouted. "Wife beater!"

Laurent flinched when he heard that and turned to look at Bernard. If he'd truly been so distracted by whatever he was doing last winter that he hadn't noticed that Bernard was abusing Gigi then some responsibility rested on his own shoulders.

What had he been thinking? His fury at himself made his face a fearsome visage. It took all his strength not to drag this miscreant excuse for a man to the curb and thrash him within an inch of his life.

Laurent's face told more than his words would have because Bernard began to move more quickly in the direction of the main road, tossing ever weaker insults and threats over his shoulder as he went.

Laurent watched him disappear around the curve in the drive, then studied the lock on the front door. Bernard wouldn't be able to get through the door and the windows in the back and sides were too high off the ground to afford easy access.

He looked over at the people from the houses. He'd need to talk with them later—perhaps when he came back to start work on the house. Always before they had been friendly and responded amiably to any questions he had.

Clearly I hadn't been asking the right questions.

Still angry with himself but determined to at least have learned from his mistake, he made his way back to the car.

He should have dealt with this sooner. And then he would have been calmer. In the end it wouldn't have mattered. He'd still have tossed him out. But Bernard might have had time to prepare better.

As if these types prepared for anything.

No, he'd been distracted and allowed other matters to take precedence. He'd known it was building and in the back of his mind he was also aware that he needed this house—a house that now would need too much work to be useable this season.

He was disgusted—with Bernard. And with himself.

"Why do you think you can just do that?" Luc said under his breath when Laurent got into the driver's seat of the car.

Laurent turned to look at him. "What did you say?"

He watched the boy—fueled by anger—reach deep inside for his courage. He lifted his face to Laurent.

"You think you own people and can just do what you want with them."

Laurent had noticed that Luc had danced dangerously close to insubordination for weeks now. But this was the first time he'd actually crossed the line.

"It is my house to do with as I want," Laurent said mildly.

"That's what every rich man ever said as his excuse for cheating the poor!"

"Put your seatbelt on and stop spouting idiocy," Laurent said, turning away.

Later he'd remember that probably hadn't been his finest moment either.

"Screw you!" Luc shouted, throwing open his car door.

Laurent slammed on the brakes just as Luc tumbled out of the car, then scrambled to his feet and ran toward the woods.

24

W hen Maggie got home that evening, a pool of golden light shimmered on the polished foyer floor of Domaine St-Buvard from the small lattice window in the front door. The irresistible scent of rosemary, garlic and sautéed onions came from the kitchen.

"Helloooo!" she called as she dropped her heavy hand bag in the foyer. "Where is everybody?"

"In the kitchen!" Jemmy called.

Why am I not surprised?

Maggie came into the kitchen to see Laurent standing in front of his prized La Cornue stove, a dishtowel slung over his shoulder. Jemmy was beside him holding a bowl of pitted, dried plums. He looked at Maggie and grinned.

"We're making rabbit with plums," Jemmy said.

"Smells amazing," she said, noticing that Laurent had yet to turn around and greet her. "Everything okay? Where's Nicole?"

Maggie had run the tapes in her head for the whole ride back from Marseille of how she would present her news to Nicole about the impending arrest for the Leon Boucher murder. In Maggie's imagination, a teary-eyed Nicole flung her arms around Maggie's neck before gushing about how glad she was because she was already falling in love with Provence and now she felt she could really love it.

That sounded a little unlikely even to Maggie.

Not to mention the fact that, in spite of all the obvious benefits of telling Nicole that it was over, for some reason Maggie could not get over the fact that Gaston as the killer just felt wrong.

What happens if Jean-Baptiste brings him in, gets all tangled up in the interview and realizes Gaston couldn't have done it after all?

Maggie would have to go back to Nicole and tell her "never mind, the killer is still out there."

Or worse? What if Jean-Baptiste dug in his heels and tried to make the indictment against Gaston stick when with every passing minute Maggie felt more and more strongly that Jean-Baptiste was barking up the wrong *arbre*?

"You are late," Laurent said, finally glancing over his shoulder at her.

"Oh? I didn't think I'd given an estimated time of arrival," Maggie said coolly. She didn't know what the problem was with Laurent lately but he was clearly pissed off about something. And if she knew her husband at all, she knew that if he didn't feel like sharing why he was unhappy, he wouldn't.

She'd been down this road before.

She took down a wine glass for herself.

"What are we drinking tonight?" she asked cheerfully.

Laurent grunted and nodded in the direction of the open wine bottle on the counter.

He must really be annoyed.

Normally he poured her evening wine.

"Where's Mila?" she asked as she poured the wine into her glass. She knew perfectly well that Mila was staying the night at *Dormir*. She'd had a quick text exchange with Grace saying

Mila and Zouzou were baking a particularly challenging *tarte aux pommes* and needed the extra time.

"She is at *Dormir*," Laurent said gruffly.

"And Luc?" Maggie walked to the French doors and looked out. "Do you have him planting cotton out back?"

She meant it in a jovial way but at the sound of Laurent's metal spoon being tossed into the stockpot, it was clear he was in no mood to be teased.

He turned to look at her and she got the full brunt of his thundercloud expression.

"Laurent, what has happened?"

"Nothing!"

"Then where's Luc?"

"He ran off. He got mad at Dad and jumped out of the car!" Jemmy said.

Maggie's mouth fell open in astonishment.

"You don't know where he is?" she asked Laurent.

"He'll come back," Laurent said.

"He saw Uncle Laurent throwing some guy out of his little house," Nicole said as she came into the kitchen from the living room where she'd obviously been listening to the conversation. "I think Luc was thinking how that could have been *him*."

Laurent turned back to his stove. "We sit down in ten minutes. Jem, get the potatoes out of the oven."

"Which makes sense," Nicole said with a shrug. "I mean it's not like he's really family."

Maggie felt a trail of ice inch down her spine and she forced herself not to look at Laurent.

"Yes, he is!" Jem said. "Isn't he, Dad?"

"Set the table, Jemmy," Laurent said.

"Of course he's family," Maggie said. "Laurent, you need to go find him."

"I will after dinner."

"Why is he even here, anyway?" Nicole said. "And now you

want *me* to move in too? Are you trying to be the Angelina Jolie of Provence or something?"

"I see that you have not brought the salad to the table as I asked," Laurent said to Nicole.

Maggie wondered if anybody else noticed the sudden temperature drop in the room. Jem's hands were full of cutlery he was taking to the table and his eyes were wide and worried. Maggie pulled him from the kitchen.

"Come on, sweetie," she said. "Your papa and Nicole need a minute."

Jemmy dropped the cutlery on the dining table and Maggie ushered him out of the house and onto the back terrace. Both dogs were there and instantly began jumping around at their knees.

None of this made sense, Maggie thought unhappily.

Luc had seemed to love living at Domaine St-Buvard! What had happened that might make him jump out of a moving car and run off? What did Laurent know that he wasn't telling her?

"What's going on with Luc?" she asked Jemmy.

He shrugged. "I don't know."

"But he's unhappy?"

"How would I know?"

"Because you're not six and you can tell when someone's unhappy."

"I don't know. Luc is quiet."

"Why did he jump out of the car today?"

"I don't know, Mom. Ask Dad."

Maggie realized that Jemmy had reverted to the American name for both her and Laurent pretty much as soon as Nicole walked through the door at Domaine St-Buvard.

"Has Nicole talked at all about what she saw at the airport?" she asked.

"You mean the dead body in the trunk?"

Maggie swallowed. Was she trying to minimize what Nicole had experienced?

"Yes."

"Not to me." He turned and looked through the French doors where Laurent and Nicole were facing each other. Laurent stood with his hands on his hips. Nicole was looking down at her feet.

Maggie found herself glad she couldn't hear what they were saying.

"Is Nikki in trouble?" Jemmy asked.

"No, not really, she just...look, why do you call her that?" Maggie asked in annoyance.

"Uh, because she asked me to," Jemmy said with a shrug so reminiscent of his father that Maggie wanted to scream.

25

In the end, Laurent left his own amazingly delicious plate of *lapin aux pruneaux* to go track down Luc, leaving it to Maggie to put the rest of dinner on the table. Nicole and Jemmy ate quietly and after a few futile attempts to make conversation, Maggie also went silent. She glanced around the dining room and tried to see it from Nicole's point of view. In Atlanta, things were flashier, brighter, faster.

Here at Domaine St-Buvard, life was walks in the vineyard, throwing a ball to the dogs, picking blackberries, and taking a half a day to shop and cook a basic meal.

She knew that life in France wasn't looking very desirable to Nicole—between being scolded by Laurent as only Laurent can do—and seeing people jump out of moving cars...

Not to mention dead people being stuffed in your trunk.

Should she be surprised that Nicole—a typical American teenager—didn't want any of it?

Except she's not a typical American teenager, Maggie told herself. *She's special. She's in a category of her own. And this—this land, this way of life, this food—is her birthright.*

She'd been wrong to keep Nicole away from France for so

long. It had just been easier to let her live there in Atlanta—especially with her mother so determined to have Nicole in her life.

And I'm paying for that now.

"Do you think Dad will find Luc?" Jemmy asked.

"I'm sure he will," Maggie said. She looked over at Nicole. "Do you know why Luc got so upset?"

"I told you. Laurent threw this poor guy out of his house for doing something..."

"He was drunk, I think," Jemmy said.

"And Luc just flipped out," Nicole said. "I don't know all he said. You do remember I don't speak French, right?" Nicole looked at Jemmy. "What was he saying to your dad?"

"I wasn't really listening," Jemmy said as he focused on his plate.

Like father like son, Maggie thought as she watched him. Obviously Jemmy didn't want to tell her what had happened with Luc this afternoon. Whether he was protecting Luc—or Laurent—she didn't know.

"There's flan in the fridge," Maggie said to him. "You can bring it to the living room if you want."

Jemmy looked up. "Can I bring it to my bedroom?"

"Fine. Just be sure and bring your dish down when you're finished."

Jemmy jumped up. "Excuse me from the table, please," he said, snatching up his plate to take to the kitchen.

Maggie looked at Nicole who had eaten very little and was now engrossed in her cell phone.

"Nicole?" Maggie said, wishing she'd mentioned when Nicole first came that they had a zero-tolerance cell phone at the table policy.

Who was she kidding?

Without Laurent here to enforce it, Maggie would never be able to make it stick.

"No dessert for me," Nicole said, moving away from the table and leaving her plate behind.

Maggie washed the dishes, wrapped two plates for Luc and Laurent and put them in the oven to keep warm. Nicole had followed Jemmy upstairs.

While Maggie cleaned the kitchen she kept glancing through the kitchen window for a glimpse of Laurent's headlights in the driveway. She wondered for the hundredth time why she was hesitating to tell Nicole that the Leon Boucher case had been solved.

She topped up her glass of wine and settled down in her office to watch the rally video of Mohammed Olivier that she hadn't had time to watch before now. It was only about fifteen minutes long and Maggie was able to fast forward through it to confirm that Olivier had indeed talked for the full time.

She squinted at the description of the speech on YouTube but it was only listed as *Campaign Rally*. While there was a date for when the video was uploaded, there was no proof that it had been shot when Olivier said it was.

So not really an alibi, Maggie thought. *At least not until a time determination can be confirmed.*

Something else bothered her about the video and she went back through it more carefully to confirm what she thought she'd seen.

Or more specifically, what she *hadn't* seen.

Nowhere in the video could she find any sign of Cayenne Olivier.

Suddenly Maggie heard her phone vibrating on her desktop. A photograph of her mother appeared on the screen, and her stomach constricted as she picked up the phone.

"Hey, Mom," she said, forcing a lighthearted tone into her voice.

"Hello, darling. I'm just calling to see if you're going to let Nikki come home yet. I'm really worried about what she suffered seeing that horrible body."

"I know, Mom," Maggie said, moving to the living room with her wine glass. "Which is why I think cutting bait and running is not the best thing to do at this time."

"I know you want Nikki to like France, darling. And I know you want her to spend more time with you and Laurent—"

"Mom, I want her to *live* with us. I know I made that clear. I think she should move to France."

"Well, she absolutely doesn't want to do that, darling, so I think you need to revise your expectations."

"She might want to do that if you and Ben weren't constantly drilling into her head what an unsafe place France is!"

"Now you know that is not at all what we're doing, Maggie, but she has yet to discover a dead body in her trunk here in the US so I really believe you need to listen to what *she* wants."

"Is that what you did with me, Mom?" Maggie said heatedly. "When I wanted to eat candy for dinner or wear my Cinderella costume to school or any number of things that weren't the best thing for me?"

"This is not the same thing."

"Look, Mom. It's late here and I'm tired. I don't think we're going to agree so can we just table this for now?"

"Of course. But I need you to be open to hearing what Nikki has to say about what she wants."

"Yes, fine. Okay. Will do."

"All right, darling. I can tell when you get snippy like this that there's no point speaking to you. Give the babies my love and Laurent too."

"I will. Goodnight, Mom." Maggie disconnected and tossed her phone onto the couch.

"So you're never coming back to the US?" Nicole asked from where she stood in the shadows by the main staircase.

"Oh!" Maggie said, spilling her wine when she jumped. "I didn't know you were there."

"So you're never coming back home?" Nicole repeated.

Maggie sighed and went to the kitchen to get a towel to dry off her hands.

"I can't imagine why I would."

Nicole followed her. "Uh, because you were born there?"

"That doesn't mean anything. I came here and looked around and assessed the situation and decided I'd found something better than where I was born."

"I thought you were here because Uncle Laurent had a vineyard here so you had to stay if you wanted to be with him."

Maggie flushed because of course those were the facts, bald and unadorned.

When Laurent first suggested they "try out" living in France she had to be convinced. At the time France's superiority as a country to live in and raise children hadn't been so obvious.

As if she could read her mind, Nicole said, "Uncle Ben told me you used to hate it here and you were constantly trying to get Laurent to move back to Atlanta. Isn't that true?"

"I admit it took me a while to get comfortable here and until then I'm sure I acted immaturely."

"Is that what you think I'm doing? Acting immaturely?"

Maggie wanted to say *only because you are immature.* But she was pretty sure, true or not, that wouldn't be received well.

"It just means that I of all people understand why you might not be in love with this country at first sight. Which is why I'm hoping you'll give it a chance."

"But I don't have a husband or a vineyard here. I don't have any reason to be here."

"You're French."

"*Half* French. That's not a good enough reason."

Fully French, Maggie found herself thinking, but of course couldn't say.

As Nicole signaled she'd come to the end of her willingness to talk by turning away to the staircase, Maggie's phone chimed from where it lay on the sofa. Turning it over to see the screen, she was surprised to find it was a text message from Jean-Baptiste.

Maggie stared at the brief text and felt twin surges of relief and annoyance war inside her.

<Had to let Gaston go. Will explain later>

26

Laurent knew things could go one of two ways.

Either the drive down the winding village road to find Luc would jack up his anger at him or it would force him to take a breath and calm down.

Neither option was ideal as far as he was concerned.

It was like Luc had literally lost his mind. Somewhere between Christmas and Easter he had turned into a raging, snarling miscreant while giving absolutely no hint as to why.

Do all teenage boys go through this?

Laurent had no idea. All he knew was that he was missing his dinner and driving up and down the local *chemin de Rapine* in search of a surly brat who wasn't grateful for all he'd been given.

Why did Luc even care about Bernard? What the hell did Bernard—a drunken vandal who'd had every opportunity and tossed it all back into Laurent's face time and time again—have to do with Luc?

His phone rang and he saw the number of the monastery was showing on the screen. He hesitated and then answered.

"*Allo?*"

"*Bonsoir* Monsieur Dernier. This is Frère Dominic. We are needing to replace the eastern plot of the monastery garden tomorrow and I need help. I'm asking all the farmers in the area."

What is this monk up to?

"What kind of help?"

"Just a strong back or two and willing hands," Dominic said pleasantly. "Some of the boys here have been asking to see Luc. It has been a while since he visited, no?"

Laurent didn't know what the monk was up to but he did know he'd never find out if he didn't play his game.

"I will bring both boys," Laurent said and disconnected before Dominic could respond.

What was that about? Surely Dominic had more helpers than he had hectares to plant. What was he up to?

As Laurent turned the final corner, he spotted a lone figure at the crest of the hill. It wasn't totally dark yet but it was gloomy and Laurent had to squint to confirm that it was Luc.

Laurent drove to within ten meters and then slowed to a stop. He flashed his headlights at him—still walking in the opposite direction—until Luc turned and saw him.

Laurent wasn't surprised to see Luc hesitate. But he'd had time to cool down and consider his options. Straight ahead was hunger, foot blisters and a future with no more choices—if he could even see that far ahead.

Luc walked toward the car. Without looking at Laurent, he opened the car door and slipped into the front seat.

"What do you have to say for yourself?" Laurent said.

"Nothing," Luc mumbled.

"I will have to teach you what to say in that case," Laurent said, slamming the car into gear and executing a tight arc as he turned around to head back home. He caught his breath as he drove.

The light from the car interior had briefly illuminated Luc's scowling face as he'd climbed in. When Laurent saw him, he saw—as clearly as he had every day of his life growing up—the bitter, unhappy face of Laurent's younger brother Gerard.

The nose, the full lips, the hunted deep-set eyes. It was Gerard come to life again.

Sixteen angry years old all over again.

"There are consequences for lack of self-discipline," Laurent said, still stunned by what he had seen.

"Madame Alexandre said I've suffered enough."

"Don't listen to old women unless you want to sound like one. You'll work repairing the wire fence in the upper vineyard tomorrow."

"I'm not your slave!"

"You are if I say you are."

"You wouldn't tell Jemmy to do that!"

"What an idiotic thing to say."

Luc crossed his arms angrily and turned his head away, refusing to say another word.

Which suited Laurent just fine.

It was after nine o'clock by the time Maggie saw Laurent's car pull into the driveway.

Jemmy and Nicole had gone to their rooms an hour earlier. Had it taken Laurent this long to find Luc or had the two of them gone some place to talk?

She turned on the kitchen light to let them know someone was still up and went to let the dogs out one last time for the night. By the time she came back inside, Laurent was in the kitchen and Luc had disappeared upstairs to his bedroom.

"Where was he?"

"Almost to *Dormir*." Laurent pulled out both plates from the oven and put one of them in the refrigerator.

"Have you eaten?"

"*Non.*"

Maggie knew Laurent didn't eat between meals but like most French he had no problem eating late. He sat at the kitchen counter with his dinner.

"Isn't Luc hungry?" she asked.

"I don't feel like sharing a meal with him. Or providing room service."

"Laurent, what happened? Why are you so angry at him?"

"I would prefer to enjoy my meal without conversation."

"Well, then this is not your lucky day. Tell me what's happening with him."

"He is reverting to who he was last fall."

Last fall was when Luc was picked up by the police for petty theft and vandalism. Last fall was before he'd come to live with Maggie and Laurent.

"Why?"

Laurent looked at her and frowned.

"You don't know why?" Maggie asked.

"I don't need to know why. It is enough that he's doing it. I don't need excuses."

"But you do need reasons," Maggie said as she poured him a glass of wine. "Luc has been a model child for ten months. So if he's blowing up on us, we need to know why."

"There is no reason why."

"Of course there is a reason. You just don't know it."

"*Oui,*" he said, eating his dinner. "I don't know it."

Unspoken: *and I don't want to know it.*

"Luc deserves better than that," Maggie said.

Laurent looked at her with eyes flecked with anger.

"Better than his own room, three meals, warmth in the winter, a good school, and new clothes to wear?" he asked incredulously.

"Yes, of course. That's the minimum of what he deserves. Luc is a good kid. You know that."

"I don't know that. He has been behaving the opposite of that."

"Which is why you need to find out what's going on. Stop reacting to him."

"I am finished talking about this."

Maggie nearly laughed out loud. Frankly she was surprised he'd talked with her about it this long.

"I'm going to bring his plate up to him," she said, going to the fridge. "He must be starving."

"Suit yourself."

27

The next morning, Laurent was up again before anyone else. He woke both boys and had them at the far end of the vineyard before Maggie even had her first cup of coffee. Last night she'd only got a murmured *merci* and a hooded look as Luc took his dinner from her in the hallway.

She hated that she couldn't talk to him about what was upsetting him—or Laurent—but it was clear he wasn't interested in discussing it with her.

While she sat in the kitchen nibbling an almond croissant which had been frozen after Laurent bought it at the village *boulangerie* last week and then revived in the oven this morning, she called Jean-Baptiste to get clarification on why he hadn't arrested Gaston after all. Her call went straight to voicemail.

She drummed her fingers on the kitchen counter and then impulsively picked up her phone again and dialed Grace.

"Hey, you," Grace said. "I thought you'd be working."

"I've got the use of Laurent's Citroën today. Why don't you see if Zouzou and Mila want to join me and Nicole for a shopping trip to Aix?"

"Seriously? They'd love it."

"I think we can all use a little retail therapy," Maggie said, feeling her mood start to lift. "Nicole and I will be by to collect them in an hour."

The drive to *Dormir* was a short but pleasant one. Unfortunately, Nicole stayed focused on her cell phone and effectively shut down all conversation attempts on Maggie's part. Maggie hadn't expected more. But she had high hopes that a day walking the Cours Mirabeau, shopping and stopping for gelato and *socca* would help her niece relax and finally open up.

Just before they reached *Dormir,* they hit a particularly bumpy part of the road which reminded Maggie that the broken latch on her Peugeot trunk would've been evident to anyone inside the parking garage when she hit any of several speed bumps there.

The lock wasn't just broken. The mechanism wouldn't shut all the way so anyone watching her drive into the parking lot at the airport—especially when she hit the first speed bump— would have seen the trunk lid bounce at least a little, indicating that it wasn't fully closed.

Maggie had to think this was important because it meant that there was no significance to the body being placed in her car.

"I think the killer choosing our car to hide the body was just a random thing," she said to Nicole. "There was nothing intentional about it at all."

As she was speaking it occurred to her that Nicole might be upset *because* it was so random.

"On the other hand, of course the murder itself wasn't random. Boucher's wallet was still in his pocket, so his death probably had to do with his politics. It was only the method of the body disposal that was random."

"Dear God," Nicole said. "Can you please stop talking about it?"

Every time Maggie thought she'd come up with something that might mitigate the terrible experience Nicole had endured, she was wrong. She knew Nicole didn't want to talk about it but she couldn't help but think that talking was the only way Nicole was going to help relieve the trauma.

Even so, she allowed silence to envelop them until they arrived at *Dormir* to pick up Mila and Zouzou.

Aix was one of Maggie's most favorite cities. A tad on the touristy side but the shopping was the best in all of Provence.

She drove straight to the underground parking facility at *Les Allées Provençale* next to the Aix-en-Provence tourist center. Parking in Aix—although something Laurent somehow managed to do with no problem—was notoriously difficult. Not just the narrow lanes and avenues but there were never enough parking spaces.

Maggie had planned on taking the girls to lunch at one of her favorite bistros. But because this trip was largely about pleasing Nicole and Nicole said she didn't want to go to "some fancy-schmancy French restaurant," Maggie agreed to pizza slices from the first kiosk they came to. The pizza was terrible and Zouzou complained about her stomach burning for the next hour.

Maggie had had a fantasy about walking down the wide pedestrian avenues with her girls, their hands full of shopping bags with one-of-a-kind treasures and the memory of an afternoon together that they'd take into adulthood with them.

But the morning quickly transformed into something else entirely.

First, Nicole was on her phone with a girlfriend from

Atlanta nearly the whole time. Mila didn't seem to mind since she had Zouzou but Maggie found herself getting irritated.

"Oh, God, Denise, you're not going to believe all the dog crap over here!" Nicole said on the phone. "It's like every step you take."

Mila and Zouzou tittered.

"And forget finding a fountain Coke. Everything is in a can. I know, right? We're doing what passes for shopping now. No Nordstrom's, no movie theaters—or if there are they're all in French! Don't even get me started on the nonexistent Wi-Fi over here!"

It was all Maggie could do not to snatch Nicole's phone and toss it in one of the Cours Mirabeau fountains.

How can anyone not be enchanted with Aix?

By the time they'd gotten the obligatory ice cream which Nicole took one taste of and threw in the garbage, Maggie couldn't wait for the outing to be over. As she strode down the beautiful Cours Mirabeau, she couldn't help but think that if Nicole wasn't stirred by the avenue's timeless elegance and majesty, then Maggie just needed to give up.

Nicole continued to give her running commentary to the apparently insatiable Denise about how dirty the famous boulevard appeared to her.

As they were walking toward the new Apple Store anchoring one corner of the square that held most of the chain clothing stores, they passed a small group of teenagers with skateboards. They were speaking French of course and because Nicole couldn't understand them, she began mocking how they sounded to her.

Worse, Mila and Zouzou joined in and laughed at the French teens. It was all Maggie could do not to scold them and tell them to be quiet if they couldn't behave, but she knew that would only make things worse.

Like Jemmy, Mila had barely spoken a word of French since Nicole arrived.

Feeling a sudden lack of mental and physical energy, Maggie couldn't get them in the car fast enough.

On the drive back to Domaine St-Buvard, Mila and Zouzou promptly fell asleep in the backseat while Nicole studied her cell phone as if nuclear codes were about to be sent to her and the planet's very survival depended on it.

Maggie hadn't said a word since they got in the car but she was pretty sure Nicole hadn't noticed. She was now completely sure that Nicole had gone through a personality change in the last year. The fact was, the girl was a total brat. Maggie had to fight the urge to just let her go back to the States and be someone else's problem.

And then she thought of her sister Elise. And she remembered that terrible, terrible day in Cannes when Maggie knew that Elise was never coming home again. And the promise she'd made.

And she took in a big breath and resolved to try again.

By the time they pulled into the long gravel drive of Domaine St-Buvard, Laurent was standing out front with both boys. He'd texted her that he needed the car to go to the monastery and would be bringing the boys with him.

Jemmy was happily tossing a ball in the air. Luc was staring down at his feet.

"Wake up, you two," Maggie said to Mila and Zouzou. "We need to hand the car over to the men."

As she, Nicole and the younger girls climbed out of the car, Maggie's phone rang from inside her purse. Ignoring it for now, she greeted Laurent with a kiss and handed over the car keys.

"The start of the potato *gratin* is in the fridge," Laurent said. "I will make the fish when I get back tonight."

Once in the house, Zouzou and Mila instantly went to the

kitchen to find a *gouter* of some kind since it had been sixty whole minutes since either of them had eaten.

A couple of years ago Zouzou had a weight problem but since then—and with Laurent's help—she'd been able to put her passion for baking into perspective with a healthy diet and her weight had returned to normal.

Nicole went upstairs to her bedroom. Maggie heard her say into her phone, "Uncle Ben? Did I wake you?"

Sighing, Maggie went to her office where she pulled out her phone to see who'd called, half guessing it might have been Ben.

She was surprised to see the numeric exchange was the same as Jean-Baptiste's when he called from the Marseille police station.

She quickly hit *Call back*.

"Madame Dernier?" an oily male voice answered.

"Yes," Maggie said, perplexed. "Who's this?"

"This is Denis Chevalier. We met a few days ago at the Marseille police station?"

It was the forensic tech who'd interrupted Jean-Baptiste's interview with her.

"Yes, Monsieur Chevalier. Of course I remember you. How can I help you?"

"I was told you were consulting on the Leon Boucher case. Is that not so?"

Maggie felt her heart rate speed up.

"Yes. That's exactly right," Maggie said. "Do you have some information for me?"

28

A fter her conversation with Chevalier, Maggie sat back in her office chair and pondered the call for a moment. The Marseille forensic tech had said he had something to show Maggie but the conversation had been too brief to determine whether or not it was with Jean-Baptiste's sanction.

Why would he tell me anything unless it was with Jean-Baptiste's approval?

Is it a new lead? Is Jean-Baptiste hoping to make Chevalier his new point person?

"*Bonjour!*" Danielle called out from the foyer, followed by happy greetings from Zouzou and Mila. Maggie got to her feet and went to join them.

Danielle held a bag of plump red plums which she gave to Mila and then turned to Maggie to greet her properly with a kiss.

"Do you have time for a coffee?" Maggie asked. "I think Laurent has *palmiers*."

"I would never say no to coffee and *palmiers*," Danielle said, her eyes crinkling in delight as she set down her purse on the bench in the foyer.

Zouzou and Mila disappeared upstairs to Mila's bedroom while Danielle settled in at the kitchen counter. Maggie put the electric kettle on.

"How are things at *Dormir*?" Maggie asked. "Last time I talked to Grace she was being rushed off her feet."

"Yes, it is our very busiest time. There is always something to do. Or something that has broken!"

"Grace said you had two sets of American families there at the moment?"

Maggie knew that the American guests were usually the ones who were the most demanding. She ground a half cup of coffee beans and spooned them into the French press.

"Yes, but they are delightful," Danielle said. "And they have a small child too. So Philippe has a little friend to play with."

Maggie poured the hot water over the beans and looked at Danielle. "You're pretty crazy about that boy."

Danielle laughed. "I truly am. And me! A woman with no children at all to have so many grandchildren! It is a blessing I could not have expected."

"Still, boys are a handful," Maggie said as she pulled the flaky *palmiers* from the bread box and arranged them on a plate.

"Philippe is active, to be sure. He is all boy."

Maggie set the plate of cookies between them. "Does Grace worry that Taylor will show up some day and take him back?"

"I think Grace believes that is extremely unlikely."

"For Philippe's sake, I hope so."

"It is impossible to believe that his mother could walk away from him."

"Well, Taylor didn't leave because Philippe wasn't adorable enough," Maggie pointed out. "She left because she's who she is. Speaking of people who are who they are, do you know what's going on with Luc and Laurent?"

Danielle bit into one of the *palmiers*. "Bechards?" she asked, referring to the famous *patisserie* in Aix.

"Yes."

"So light. So flaky."

"It's not like you to stall, Danielle. Has Laurent sworn you to secrecy?"

"We have not spoken of it at all."

"*What* have you not spoken of?"

"*Chérie*, I think Laurent and Luc must sort this out themselves."

"So there *is* something to sort out?"

"You yourself have noticed as much."

"Men! It makes it so much harder when they won't talk!"

"They are different from women. *Vive la différence.*"

"I assume you're being sardonic, Danielle."

"Laurent will find his way in this."

"I just hope Luc can survive the process."

"Have faith."

Maggie turned and poured the coffee into two cups.

"I had an opportunity to talk with Nikki on the picnic," Danielle said. "She is a delightful girl. And growing up to be a fine young woman."

"That's not her name."

"She seems to think it is."

"Did she tell you I'm keeping her here against her will?"

"She mentioned she is ready to return home."

"I hope you can see that would not be the best thing for her right now. You see that, right? I mean she's upset. She's had a shock. She needs to take a breath and think."

"I would venture to say that is good advice for you too. Nicole is old enough to decide what she wants to do."

"You mean like Taylor was old enough to decide to ditch school and run off with that biker guy? And get pregnant?"

"Nicole is not like Taylor."

"You don't know the whole story about Nicole," Maggie said, crumbling a *palmier* between her fingers, "and I'm not at liberty to tell you but if I did, you'd think differently."

"I'm not sure I would, *chérie*."

An hour later after Danielle and Zouzou had gone home, Mila was happily making a lemon mousse in the kitchen and Nicole had still not come downstairs. Feeling at odds and more apprehensive than ever after her conversation with Danielle, Maggie put a call in to Marie-France—Leon's widow—which was not answered. She knew that as soon as she finally did connect with her all holy hell would break loose on Team Jean-Baptiste, since the widow was the number one person Jean-Baptiste really did *not* want her talking to.

But if Maggie knew one thing it was that it would be worth whatever hell it caused if she could get some new information on the case.

Thinking of Jean-Baptiste made Maggie think of the strange phone call from the forensic tech, Denis Chevalier. Should she assume Chevalier contacted her with Jean-Baptiste's blessing? What other reason would he have for reaching out to her? And what was it he had to show her?

Maggie sat at her desk, drumming her fingers and thought back to what Jean-Baptiste told her about how he was sure the killer couldn't be a woman because the body had been moved and a woman couldn't have managed it.

It could have been a woman with an accomplice. And the fact that Leon was killed with a hypodermic needle meant the murder was premeditated.

Who walks around with a hypodermic needle fully loaded with poison?

Was the fact that a woman couldn't transport the body easily the only reason Jean-Baptiste wasn't looking at a woman for this?

Suddenly Maggie turned to her computer and went to the last browser window she'd opened on Leon Boucher's website. She scrolled through the photos of him at his most recent rally, realizing what she hadn't particularly noted the first time she'd visited the site.

Leon was short. Not just short, but slight too.

Maggie stared at the pictures of him and then closed out the browser window and hurried upstairs to her bedroom.

She went to her closet and pulled out the largest of her luggage pieces, a thirty-two-inch hardside Pullman on wheels. She stood next to it and tried to imagine what she was thinking.

Could someone transport a body across the top of this? Using it as a sort of dolly?

She sat down on her bed and stared at the luggage piece.

Was there DNA on the parking lot floor between her car and Leon's vehicle where he was killed? Would there need to be? He wasn't bleeding. As long as he wasn't being dragged, anyone could position a body on a roller bag and for at least a few yards, scoot him to the other car.

Maggie felt her pulse quicken.

Jean-Baptiste is wrong.

A woman could definitely have killed Leon and gotten him to the other car.

Which meant Leon's killer could be Leon's wife.

Or his mistress.

Or his campaign manager.

29

Not surprisingly, the ride to the monastery was quiet. Laurent spent only a very little time trying to figure out what Dominic might want with Luc. He'd quickly dismissed the possibility that the monk would try to turn Luc in to the authorities or spirit him off to the refugee camp he'd talked about.

Laurent was a good judge of people—he'd had to be in his prior line of work. From what he could tell, Dominic was a bully. And like all bullies, he was a coward at heart. That meant that whatever he was planning wouldn't be arrived at by the direct approach.

They pulled into the parking lot. Jemmy was in high spirits. He hadn't been to the monastery in over a year and the thought of working in the garden sounded like a lark to him. Luc was much less happy.

He lagged behind Jemmy as they walked from the parking lot to the front of the rectory where a group of young people were standing.

"Hey, it's Lucky Luc!" someone called out. A few people

turned their heads to look at Luc but none met him with anything resembling a greeting for a friend.

Laurent knew Luc had hung out with two other boys—both troublemakers and both gone now—but he didn't know if he'd had any other friends at the monastery. Unless he was misreading the unfriendly sneers and jeers on the faces of these young people, Luc hadn't.

Laurent walked purposefully through the crowd to the monastery garden. Leaning against the stone wall that enclosed the garden was a line of shovels and pickaxes. Dominic stood by the wall, watching them approach.

"Does Frère Jean know you're doing this?" Laurent said as he looked out over the garden.

He could feel Dominic bristle at the question.

"I do not need to report to Frère Jean," Dominic said.

"You appear to have many more workers than you need."

"We can always use more," Dominic said, glancing at Luc. "So this is the boy?" He clapped a heavy hand on Luc's shoulder. "Frère Jean says you are not afraid of a good day's work. Is that true?"

Luc glanced at Laurent and then looked away in disgust, crossing his arms stiffly.

Laurent was not aware he'd agreed to let Dominic have the boys for more than a few hours.

"Hey, Luc!" one of the boys from the group called out. "We've missed you!" The rest of the group laughed.

Laurent narrowed his eyes at the speaker and then turned back to Dominic.

"What exactly do you need them to do?"

"I really only need Luc," Dominic said. He smiled condescendingly at Jemmy. "This one is too small for the work I require. It is a big job as you can see." He waved his hand at the field. Half the rows were dug up. Piles of weeds and dead roots topped the rows in unattractive lumps.

"I will need Luc until dark. And then I believe some of the boys are planning a bonfire later. You will of course allow him to stay for that?"

Laurent frowned. He looked at Luc. "Do you want to stay for that?"

"Oh, so I get a vote now?" Luc said bitterly, and then glared at his own feet. "What difference does it make?"

"Then it's settled!" Dominic said.

Laurent saw what was happening but wasn't sure it was in Luc's best interest to stop it. He didn't know what Dominic was up to, but he didn't think it was something likely to hurt Luc.

And perhaps a night away would do everyone some good.

"Do you have room in the dormitory?" Laurent asked. "I thought you were short of beds."

"We have a bed for him."

Luc twisted on his heel and walked away as if he couldn't bear to stand near Laurent any longer than he had to.

"Fine. I'll collect him in the morning."

"Why not wait until I call?" Dominic said. "That way the boys will have all the time they need together."

Laurent hesitated, glancing at Luc but the boy would not return his look. Finally, Laurent turned and walked with Jemmy back to the car.

Dominic watched Dernier go, his heart pounding in his chest at how he'd been able to talk with him as if nothing were wrong. He wasn't surprised to see that Luc—who was probably being held against his will for the free labor—clearly hated Dernier. If it weren't for the fact that Dominic knew that hurting Luc was the most effective way to hurt Dernier, he would feel sorry for the boy.

He watched Dernier get in his car.

He was once a criminal and now he's Lord of the Land?

How did that happen? The bastard avoids prison, keeps the loot, gets a beautiful American wife, a vineyard, and a house anyone would kill for on land that is worth millions?

He felt a pulling sensation in his gut and his throat went instantly dry.

The malice seethed through him like heartburn.

And then to see everyone kowtowing to Dernier like he's a god?

As far as that went Frère Jean was the worst.

When Dominic wasn't praying for his brother monk to get well, deep in his heart he was praying he would die.

"*Mon frère?*" Luc said. "Where do you want me to start?"

Startled out of his reveries, Dominic tore his eyes away from the retreating tail lights on Dernier's car and turned to regard Luc.

Why this boy? Of all the ones who needed a home? Why had Dernier chosen him? There was nothing special about Luc Thayer.

"Pick up a spade," Dominic said and pointed to the garden plot. "You see those piles of dirt? Make more. That's all."

Luc selected a shovel from the wall. He turned to look over at the five boys standing a few yards away, watching him. He looked back at Dominic with a puzzled expression.

"You don't need to worry about anyone but yourself," Dominic said. "They have other work to do."

Luc turned and looked again at the destroyed garden plot. "I'm to do all this myself?" he said incredulously.

"Oh, all this and more," Dominic said, smiling.

Until you'll wish you'd never been born.

Until you'll wish you'd never pretended to belong where you don't.

M aggie was surprised at how quiet the evening was without Luc.

There seemed to be a large hole at the dinner table with his absence. Jemmy and Mila must have felt it too because they were both quieter than usual.

Nicole had pled a headache and eaten a sandwich in her room.

While Maggie had intended to have a serious conversation with Laurent about Luc, her evening had quickly become dominated with calls from vendors and artisans she'd promised to feature in her next newsletter. She knew she'd been spending so much time thinking about the Leon Boucher case that she'd dropped the ball on her own work.

She decided her talk with Laurent could wait a day but if she didn't put out a few fires on the next newsletter, she would be out of business.

The next morning Laurent was again up early, this time with Mila and Jemmy as there was a one-day summer camp in Aix that they'd both been looking forward to. Laurent would drop them off, then visit the monastery before returning before dinner time to collect them.

Nicole was still sleeping when they left. Maggie had forgotten last night to mention to Laurent that she had to go to Arles. In truth she was going to Marseille to meet with Denis Chevalier. She wrote a note telling Nicole that she'd have the day to herself and that her lunch was in the refrigerator.

Maggie walked out to the car where Laurent and the two children were preparing to leave.

"Are you sure you are okay without a car?" Laurent said with frown.

"No problem. I'm the Queen of Uber these days."

Laurent snaked an arm around her waist and drew her to him—unusual behavior for him when he was set on his day's agenda.

"This is a nice surprise," Maggie said, draping her arms around his neck.

"What are you really up to today?"

"I'm just going out for a couple of hours," she said, standing on tip-toe and kissing him. "No biggie."

"This has nothing to do with the Marseille murder?"

"Dad! We'll be late!" Jemmy called from inside the car.

"Yeah. Go on, Dad," Maggie said with a grin. "Please stop at Bechards while you're in Aix and pick up more of those *palmiers*. Danielle and I finished off the others."

He kissed her without another word and climbed into the car. By the time he reached the end of the driveway, Maggie had already pushed the Uber button on her cell phone.

Ends justify the means.

I just need to convince Nicole that she belongs here. And how I do that is by erasing this terrible event that happened the moment she landed in France.

Confident that her plan was a good one, Maggie stepped outside to wait for her ride.

Luc stood knee deep in the horse manure, his arms trembling as he strained to hold the laden shovel from falling into the muck as the stench filled his nose. The horses were standing in the nearby paddock while he attempted to clear their stalls with a broken wooden pitch fork.

He'd started the job with a stainless steel one he'd found in the tack room. But Frère Dominic had taken it from him, telling him it didn't belong to the monastery and he needed to use the tools they owned.

Luc wiped the sweat and filth from his brow and felt in his pocket for his cell phone. He hadn't been at the monastery thirty minutes yesterday before he remembered to turn it off so no one would discover he had it.

He'd lived here before. He knew what happened to people who had nice things.

Last night he'd worked until dark and could barely find his way back to the rectory. Hungrier than he ever remembered being, he went first to the monastery dining hall only to discover he was too late. Everything had been washed and put away.

An old woman found a half a baked potato for him and he'd eaten it in the shadows, ever watchful for the gang of boys he knew were on the lookout for him.

Again, he'd lived here before. He knew the drill.

He wasn't a part of their tribe anymore. They'd be waiting for him.

His arms and back ached so much that just holding his head up hurt. This wasn't the kind of work he was used to doing at *Dormir* or Domaine St-Buvard. This was relentless, endless toil with no rest at the end but only hunger and a gang of boys waiting to show him he was no better than they were.

Had Laurent left him here knowing this would happen? Was this the "consequence" the bastard had talked about?

Frère Dominic was Laurent's ally. That—if nothing else— was clear.

He probably set all this up with the monk. He pretended like he didn't know what was going on but Laurent is smart. Wily smart. Nobody takes him by surprise.

So last night he'd finished his potato and limped to the stable where he knew he'd find a pallet of straw—hopefully not too badly pissed on—to sleep on. His other option was to find a bed in the dormitory.

And he was fairly positive that wouldn't turn out well.

Not for him anyway.

Suddenly Dominic's shadow filled the doorway of the stall. Luc put down the wooden pitch fork.

"I am wanted at home," he said to the monk. "I have chores to do there."

"Monsieur Dernier called to say you were not needed there today. You are to stay here for the weekend. He was glad to know you could be of some use to me since I regret to say he said you were not at all useful at his *mas*."

Luc felt his stomach drop. As hard as he worked at Domaine St-Buvard? Heat flushed through his body and he clenched his fists by his side.

Why was he surprised? Nothing he did was ever good enough for Laurent.

"When you finish here," Dominic said, "you may begin digging a ditch over by the rectory before it gets dark."

"I...I haven't eaten anything," Luc said.

"Then that will teach you to pay attention to meal times. This is not a cruise ship. We do not have twenty-four hour all-you-can-eat buffets for half-breed refugees who refuse to work!"

Luc felt his gut tighten when he realized the man didn't intend to feed him.

Dominic began to turn away and then stopped.

"By the way," Dominic said, "where did you sleep last night?" he asked. "Some of the boys were wondering."

31

N icole lay in bed half awake listening to the cooing of the mourning doves outside her window. She knew they liked to hop on the outdoor dining table to peck at the crumbs that were always there from last night's dinner or this morning's breakfast.

She tried to remember if she had seen many birds at her grandmother's house in Atlanta. She had to admit the bird songs and the sight of the sun as it rose over the vineyards were a somewhat pleasant feature of living here.

Suddenly an uncomfortable consciousness sliced into her and she sat bolt upright, her adrenalin spiking, her heart pounding.

The house was too quiet.

Ripping back the duvet cover, she leapt out of bed and ran to the bedroom door, flinging it open.

She stood for a moment in the hall. And she just knew.

There was nobody in the house.

"Aunt Maggie?" she called as she took a few tentative steps toward the staircase.

Silence.

Perspiration popped out on her forehead and she reached for the bannister of the stairs.

"Jemmy?"

Her voice echoed back at her in the empty house, seeming to mock her. Her mind flashed back to the night before and she tried to remember if they'd told her their plans for today. Something crept into her memory about Jemmy andMila going to Aix but she couldn't remember who was to take them.

Surely Maggie and Laurent wouldn't both go?

Panic began to inch its way up her throat, closing her breath off. She edged her way down the staircase, feeling the cold marble beneath her bare feet. Chills trembled up and down her arms.

Not even the dogs were here.

Why would they do this? Why would they leave me alone here?

When she reached the bottom of the stairs, she stood for a moment and held her breath. She could hear the big hand-painted Victoria Station clock in the dining room as it clicked off the seconds. The refrigerator hummed in the kitchen.

Standing at the foot of the stairs she could see through the sidelights of the front door that the car in the front drive was gone.

Suddenly she was aware of a sound behind her. A low insistent whine. Whirling, she turned with dread and creeping fear to face the French doors onto the terrace.

Outside, the two family dogs stood watching her, waiting expectantly.

With a shiver of relief, Nicole sighed. Normalcy. At least the dogs were still here.

She hurried to the French doors and pulled them both open. Instantly the dogs bounded inside, jumping on her and pushing past her to the kitchen.

Her heart was still pounding and she stood there for a moment, looking out onto the garden. And for a moment she got a flash of memory of the time when she was little and had come here with her grandparents for Thanksgiving.

She had found something terrible in the vineyard. Something that had given her nightmares for weeks afterward.

She licked her lips and found herself mesmerized by the view of vineyard—green and undulating and stretching far to the horizon.

That was the time someone got murdered in the basement of this house.

A cold sweat broke out across her top lip and she hurriedly shut the French doors against the sunlight and the scent of rosemary and lavender in the garden. For some reason the mingled fragrance prompted a nausea deep in her gut. She turned away from the garden view to go back toward the stairs. She needed to get dressed, to be ready…

…And then she saw it.

The front door was ajar.

Had it been closed a second ago? Why hadn't she noticed it was open when she came down?

Because it hadn't been open then.

Spots formed in her vision and she felt suddenly weak.

She needed to get to her phone! But it was upstairs in her bedroom. She turned and raced up the stairs. She hit the top landing, aware that one of the dogs had followed her. She ran to her bedroom where she snatched up her phone.

Her hands trembled as she looked at the screen. Her mind went blank.

Is it 9-1-1? Or Operator?

Her mind whirled as she tried to remember what the emergency number was in France. Her panic escalated at the thought that whoever had opened the front door *was now in the house*. At this very moment he might be creeping up the stairs toward her.

Her skin was crawling. Desperate and filled with terror, her mind was blinded by her panic.

She had to get out. *Get away.*

She stumbled toward the stairs still in her nightgown.

The dog stayed by her side as she ran down the stairs. The door was open wider now, no longer simply ajar. But she couldn't stop. She had to get out!

She reached the door and pushed it open wider as she stepped outside on shaking legs.

Immediately she froze, a scream stuck mute in her throat.

32

L aurent sat in his car in front of Domaine St-Buvard and picked up his phone. He frowned. There was no message from Dominic about when to pick up Luc. He debated whether he should just go get him.

On the other hand, perhaps Luc would be more ready to come back to Domaine St-Buvard after spending a little more time with the other boys.

Or perhaps he would prefer to stay at the monastery with them.

Whatever Laurent had been thinking of last fall when he opened his house to Luc, it was possible that some things had changed. If not for Laurent, then for Luc. Perhaps the search for Luc's papers or thoughts of making forgeries were premature.

A phone call from his contact in Nice on the drive back from Aix had suggested another way around the problem of Luc's legal status but if the boy genuinely did not prefer to stay at Domaine St-Buvard then that was a moot point.

He drummed his fingers on the steering wheel.

Did Luc understand that his options did not include going back to the monastery but to a refugee camp?

Even if the boy preferred it, could Laurent really allow his nephew to go to one?

Before he could sort out his thoughts in any greater depth, a motion out of the corner of his eye made him open the car door to get a better look. It was Izzy, one of the dogs.

Laurent frowned and got out of the car. He called the dog and it bounded over to him.

"What are you doing out front, eh?" Laurent said tousling the dog's ears.

He looked up at the sound of the front door swinging open and banging loudly against the house. Nicole flew out of the door, barefoot and in her nightgown.

He turned toward her and she ran to him and fell into his arms. He held her and felt her limbs trembling in his arms.

"What is it, *chérie*? What has happened?" He pulled back to look into her face. "What has scared you, *chérie*?"

She gripped his arms tightly and looking over his shoulder toward the road. Laurent frowned. Perhaps Maggie was right after all and the girl needed more guidance than the typical teenager?

"I woke up and everyone was gone!"

He walked with her to the house. "Aunt Maggie did not leave you a note?"

"If she did I didn't see it. I...I just..."

"Never mind, *chérie*," Laurent said, patting her shoulder. "I am here, yes? Why don't I make you something to eat?"

A few moments later, Nicole returned to the kitchen dressed and looking much more herself. Laurent slid a glass of orange juice across the counter to her with a baguette he'd spread with mashed strawberries and sprinkled with sugar.

"Eat," he said.

"Maggie says food is your answer to everything," Nicole said, smiling weakly.

Laurent tried to imagine what could have upset the girl so much. She was too old to be afraid to be home alone. Again he found himself wondering if Maggie wasn't right after all. Nicole had been traumatized by the event at the airport. And clearly the last thing she needed was time to herself.

Nicole drank the juice and picked up the piece of baguette.

"Uncle Laurent?"

"Hmmm?" Laurent turned back to the kitchen to begin the process of planning tonight's dinner.

"Can you please talk to Maggie about me going home? She'll do what you tell her."

"I do not find that to typically be the case. I think your aunt wants to make sure you give this a chance."

"No offense, Uncle Laurent. I just want to be in my own country. You can see that, right?"

"Bien sûr."

"I guess that means yes?"

"You really remember no French at all?"

"Why would I? I just want to be with my own kind, you know?"

"Other Americans?"

"Well, Maggie is an American too. We're not so bad."

"You no longer call her Aunt Maggie?"

Nicole blushed. "I meant to say Aunt Maggie."

Laurent patted her hand. *"Ce n'est pas grave, chérie.* And you are right. Some of my most favorite people in the world are Americans."

❧

Maggie glanced at her watch. Amazingly, her Uber had shown up at Domaine St-Buvard within thirty minutes of her call—a definite record. She now stood once more in the upscale neighborhood of La Corniche with its dramatic Haussmann-style apartment façades, wide avenues and green sculpted landscaping.

Since she had ninety minutes before she was to meet with Chevalier she had the driver drop her at Gaston and Marie-France's neighborhood.

This time, waiting on a park bench would do no good. Maggie straightened her light cotton blazer and marched up to the elegant and glossy black front door.

There was a buzzer and an intercom and Maggie pressed it and cleared her throat. The intercom didn't appear to be for the whole building but only the Boucher apartment.

"*Oui*?" a voice came through the speaker. Whoever it was spoke French but not like a native.

Does the anti-immigrant candidate employ aliens?

"I am here to see Madame Boucher," Maggie said firmly. "She is expecting me."

"Madame Boucher no taking visitors." The intercom shut off.

Maggie hesitated and then pushed the intercom button again.

"I am here to see Gaston Boucher," she said.

"He no here."

The intercom went silent again. Maggie stood for a moment, debating whether she should buzz again but it seemed pretty clear that beyond finding an open window for breaking and entering, only a frustrating and ultimately futile conversation over the intercom was the likely outcome.

She turned away from the front door. As she glanced down the street, it occurred to her that she could walk to Angeline Sauvage's apartment from here. She shouldered her handbag and started out. Because of how she'd left it with Angeline the last time there was every reason to believe that the woman wouldn't be quite so open to talking with her this time.

Rather than get the door slammed in her face before she got a sentence out, Maggie decided since there was no real urgency she would wait the remaining hour she had at the café on the corner by Angeline's apartment. If Angeline was like most people she would be in and out of her apartment several times a day—going to the market, running errands, picking up lunch.

It was worth a wasted hour sitting in a café on a pleasant weekday.

Maggie walked to the first café on the street nearest Angeline's apartment building. On any given day she imagined this café would be full of mothers with strollers, lovers canoodling and office workers grabbing a quick bite. Today was no different.

Maggie grabbed a table on the sidewalk with a clear view of the front of Angeline's apartment building door. And waited.

After two Coca-colas and a dish of peanuts, she was about to grab a taxi to take her to the police station for her meeting with Chevalier when she saw her.

Angeline stepped out of her apartment building, blinked against the bright sun as though she hadn't been outdoors in a while, and then turned toward the café. Maggie watched her stop at a small green grocers, examine the produce in the bin out front without buying anything, and move on.

Maggie quickly dumped change on her table and walked to intercept Angeline as she strode down the sidewalk.

Angeline slowed her pace when Maggie blocked her path and seemed about to walk around her when she suddenly recognized her. Maggie was close enough to see Angeline held a cigarette in one hand.

Hardly the sort of thing an expectant woman would do. Even in France.

"You!" Angeline said, her lip curled in a snarl. "I could have you arrested for forcing your way into my apartment."

"You invited me in. Why didn't you tell me you threatened to kill Leon the week before he died? Do the police know about this?"

Angeline blinked rapidly in either fear or fury, Maggie wasn't sure which.

"You've been talking to that bitch Joelle, I see. She would say anything to blacken my name."

"She says there were several people who heard you say it."

Immediately Maggie saw revealed on Angeline's face that what Joelle had said was true. Angeline *had* threatened Leon's life.

Which didn't of course mean she'd killed him.

But it wasn't good.

"Who are you anyway?" Angeline flexed her hands. "Why are you harassing me?"

"I'm someone who's trying to find out the truth about what happened to Leon—something I'd assume you'd want too—that is, unless you...." Maggie let her words hang indictingly in the air.

"I did not kill him! I have an alibi for the day. I was having dinner with a friend."

"He was killed mid-afternoon."

"Then lunch! I was having lunch."

"Except I heard from Joelle that the person you were having lunch with changed his mind about the time. So you *don't* have an alibi."

Maggie was flying blind on this one because up to this minute she didn't know that Angeline had even given the police an alibi, let alone with whom. But because of the kind of person Angeline was, Maggie assumed she probably didn't have too many girlfriends so the alibi she'd given must have been with a man.

Maggie realized she'd nailed it when Angeline's face went bone white at her words.

"That...bastard," Angeline sputtered, throwing her cigarette down and grinding it out with the toe of her black Ferragamos. "After all I've done for him!"

Maggie didn't want to imagine what that might be. She made a mental note to tell Jean-Baptiste to push harder on whoever provided Angeline's alibi. Clearly he'd been asked to lie for her.

Angeline now had motive *and* opportunity. So the only thing that kept her from being a Class-A suspect in Leon Boucher's murder was the fact that supposedly she hadn't had the means.

There were no CCTV cameras in that section of the Marseille airport but just because Angeline wasn't spotted in the area didn't mean she was home free.

"I don't know what you think you're doing but this is harassment! I am a French citizen!"

"Congratulations. But what I'm doing isn't against the law. In fact, I think the police will thank me for the information."

"Danon put you up to this, didn't he? The *putain!*"

Unable to stop herself, Maggie retorted, "Gee, Danon has nothing but nice things to say about *you.*"

"That deviant! Nobody will believe anything he says! Leon was no more gay than I am!"

"That's not what Danon says."

"Is *Danon* carrying Leon's baby? Is *Danon* the one Leon was going to marry?"

"No, but from what I can see neither are you—on either count."

Angeline's hand flew to her stomach and then she glanced at her ground-out cigarette on the sidewalk and she flushed as she realized she'd given herself away.

Without warning, she pushed Maggie, knocking her into a nearby café table.

Taken by surprise, Maggie flailed her arms to stay upright, grabbing at the table and knocking over Perrier bottles and ceramic ashtrays before crashing to the sidewalk.

33

Late that afternoon Laurent arranged for Danielle, who was in Aix on an errand, to pick up Jemmy and Mila from school and drop Jemmy off at Domaine St-Buvard. Mila had begged to be allowed to spend the night with Zouzou so Danielle would take her back to *Dormir*.

Jemmy jumped out of Danielle's car when she pulled into the driveway and Laurent met him there.

"I'm starving!" Jemmy said. "How come Luc gets to work overnight at the monastery but not me?"

"You are too young. Perhaps next year," Laurent said, motioning him into the house. "There is a hazelnut *crêpe* on the counter."

Laurent had planned on swinging by to pick Luc up from the monastery as soon as Maggie got home. Clearly Nicole was not comfortable being home on her own. He'd called the monk twice but the monastery only had a landline phone with no voicemail capability so the calls just rang and rang.

"Why don't you stay for coffee?" he asked Danielle, still in her car.

"No, thank you. I have things to do at *Dormir*. We have yet more guests coming tomorrow and their cottage is not ready."

"If you need help I can send Nicole back with you."

"I think Nicole would do better spending more time with Maggie."

When Laurent didn't respond, Danielle said, "Is everything all right with Nicole? Maggie asked me to come and keep her company yesterday. I was sorry I could not."

"She did?" Laurent was not aware that Maggie had been gone so long yesterday that she'd thought it necessary.

"I fear all our young people are stretching their wings lately," Danielle said.

"I have an asparagus quiche for you to take with you," Laurent said, tapping the backseat passenger window. "Mila? Can you come in and get it? It is on the counter."

"Yes, Papa," Mila said, jumping out of the car and running into the house.

"I have been meaning to say something to you about Luc," Danielle said.

"What has he done now?"

"He has done nothing. My thoughts have to do with what *you* are doing."

"You speak in riddles, Danielle."

"No, I speak words you don't want to hear, Laurent. There is a difference between not understanding and not wanting to understand."

Laurent snorted and turned away to watch the front door. "Mila must be having trouble finding the quiche."

"You think you can prevent Luc from turning out like Gerard. But you cannot. Ask yourself, was Gerard anything like Luc? Did he remember always to open the door with a smile for your grandmother? Did he play with the babies and never complain when asked to sweep the beetles from the back terrace? Did he always try so hard to please his father?"

Laurent didn't answer.

"Luc is not Gerard," Danielle said firmly.

Mila came out of the front door, her hands holding a large pie dish.

"Good girl," Laurent called to her before turning back to Danielle. "Be sure to warm it up first."

"Who are you telling, *mon chou*?" Danielle said with exasperation as she waited for Mila to get in the car. "Think about what I said, Laurent."

"*Bien sûr*," Laurent said, leaning over to kiss Mila through the open window. "Behave yourself, eh?" he said to her, brushing his fingers lightly down her cheek.

"Love you, Papa!" Mila said cheerfully as Danielle began to back the car up, giving Laurent one last admonishing look as she did.

As Danielle drove away, it occurred to Laurent that Danielle was so delighted to finally have grandchildren that she could no longer objectively evaluate anyone.

But one thing Danielle was not wrong about was the fact that—for all Maggie's talk about how much she wanted Nicole to be here—she had been gone a lot lately.

He'd clearly been too focused on his problems with Frère Dominic. He would need to have a word with Maggie. As he walked back into the house he passed Jemmy who was coming out with a remote-control helicopter in his hands.

"Do not get that on the roof again," Laurent said as he felt his phone beginning to vibrate.

"I won't, Papa."

He stepped into the house and answered the phone.

"*Allo?*"

"It's me," Maggie said. "I had a few minutes and thought I'd see what you were up to."

"Where are you?" He could tell by the noises in the background that she was calling from some kind of office.

"I have a meeting. I told you about it."

"You are leaving Nicole on her own too much. Come home."

"I can't. I have...business that must be dealt with."

But Laurent was in no mood to be put off. As he made his way to the kitchen, he could hear the sound of the television upstairs.

Few things set him off more than the thought that one of the children was watching daytime television—even if that child had lived most of her life in the US.

"Nicole has come here to visit this family," he said, "and you have taken every opportunity to be gone."

"That's not true! We all went shopping in Aix just yesterday."

"You have been gone every day since she arrived."

"I'm doing it for her! You saw her, Laurent. She was so upset about what happened."

Laurent turned to look out the kitchen window. Jemmy had set his toy helicopter in the gravel drive to avoid the trees and bushes. Laurent watched his son walk over to the side of the driveway where some of Laurent's hired workmen from the village had been repairing a broken placard by the front gate.

"You cannot undo what happened," he said.

"I'm not trying to do that!"

"Yes. You are. Besides, Detective Moreau does not need your help. But your family does."

"That's just it! He *does* need my help. I can't tell you how wrong he's getting this whole investigation."

"Enough, Maggie. That is his job. Your job is here with your family. If Nicole is feeling vulnerable then you need to be with her, not leaving her alone."

"I make sure she's not alone."

"You mean by asking Danielle to come be with her so *you* can go to Arles?"

"I... that was different."

"Or *today* when I came home this morning and she looked like she would burst into tears at the sight of me?"

"Did she really?"

Laurent could tell Maggie was losing steam. She must know he was right. It was not an easy process and after his conversation with Danielle, he could personally attest to that. But all in all, the truth must be faced. No matter how painful.

"And you know why you are doing it, too, *chérie*," Laurent said, more gently now. "It is because Nicole is not really Elise's daughter that you feel you need to fix what happened."

A crash behind him sent a sickening shock up his spine. He turned, knowing with sinking certainty what he would see.

Nicole was standing in the kitchen doorway with her mouth open and her eyes wide and unbelieving.

Laurent saw the cell phone on the floor where Nicole had dropped it. He heard the kitchen clock ticking and Maggie still talking on the phone he held in his hand. He didn't need to ask how much the girl had heard.

It was written on her face.

Nicole stood perfectly still, her eyes darting around the room as if looking for escape or another way to interpret what she'd just heard.

"I'm not....I'm *not* Elise Newberry's daughter?"

"Nicole, Nikki, *ma petite*..." Laurent said, tossing his phone onto the counter and taking a step toward her just as Jemmy burst into the kitchen.

Jemmy's face was bloodless as he held his arm out in front of him. A long rusty nail jutted out from his palm.

"Dad...Papa," he said tremulously and then his eyes rolled

back in his head and he sagged to the floor. Laurent caught him before his head hit the tile.

At the same time, Nicole stepped over her dropped cell phone and bolted out the open front door.

34

"Hello? Laurent?"

Maggie pulled her phone from her ear to see that her call had disconnected. It wasn't Laurent's style to hang up on her so the call must have been dropped. It happened more often than not at Domaine St-Buvard. There wasn't a nearby cell tower and reception was often spotty.

She sighed and settled back in her seat in the waiting room at the Marseille police station and replayed their conversation in her head.

Did Nicole really freak out from being left alone today?

A police officer walked by and stopped in front of her.

"You need to turn that off while you're in here," he said sternly, nodding at her cell phone.

Maggie smiled and made a show of turning off her phone. The officer moved on.

Maggie knew Laurent was right about her being gone too much. It was just that she'd been so sure that solving the murder would do more to help Nicole get over what happened than shopping trips to Aix or lavender tours. At least this way she was doing something!

She glanced at the clock on the wall. Chevalier was fifteen minutes late.

She'd been half hoping to see Jean-Baptiste while she was in the departmen—but only half. There were still too many people who could have called him by now to complain about her interference and she wasn't sure she had the emotional energy to go head-to-head with him all over again.

Why does he make everything so hard?

She gingerly touched the knee that had taken the brunt of her fall after Angeline had knocked her down on the sidewalk in front of the café.

Talk about someone who can't control her impulses!

If it weren't for the fact that carrying a loaded hypodermic needle into that parking garage was so clearly premeditated, Angeline's impulsiveness might count against her. As it was, she *still* ticked both boxes for motive and opportunity.

Now I just need to find if there is a way she could have gotten her hands on the drugs that killed Leon.

And then I'll have the complete trifecta for her—motive, opportunity and means.

Laurent glanced at Jemmy in the passenger's seat as they raced toward Aix and the emergency room there. He'd wrapped the hand tightly with gauze to stop the bleeding. Jemmy was alert and doing his best to be brave. There was no point in asking him if it hurt. It was whatever it was.

Twice Laurent had tried to call Maggie to have her meet him at the emergency room in Aix and twice the call had gone to voicemail.

He felt his stomach tighten in mounting frustration.

Since when does she turn her phone off?

As he maneuvered the narrow, winding country road, lined

on both sides by towering plane trees, he tried to imagine where Nicole would go. She was upset and running blind. She didn't know the area. There was nothing but vineyards and farms for miles. Would she try to go to the village?

He thought back to the moment when he saw Nicole's face. The disbelief written there tore at his insides.

How could he have been so careless?

Jemmy groaned softly and Laurent turned to look at him. He looked pale and was biting his lip.

Laurent put a call into Grace and then Danielle but both calls went to voicemail.

Cursing silently, he accelerated on the narrow village road and prayed he wouldn't run into a slow-moving produce truck or tractor before he hit the A7.

Wherever Nicole had gone, Laurent would just have to believe no harm could come to her.

There was no way he could be in two places at the same time.

Not even him.

The killer slammed the car into a lower gear to handle the small hill in order to better navigate at the slowest speed the car could manage without stalling.

It was still unbelievable that she was really out here on her own!

That was unbelievable, after a morning spent walking around the *mas*—way too hesitantly—and then giving up and just being grateful to have escaped undetected when Dernier's car came unexpectedly down the main road.

Looking on the side of the road, the killer could tell that this was where the girl had left the road. And glancing ahead there was a spot to hide the car. The rest of this would need to be done on foot. The killer patted the pocket that held the needle.

A smile that could not be contained slithered across the killer's face.

But as heady as it felt right now, nothing could match that moment of sitting in the rental car wondering what the next move should be and then seeing the American girl come running down the road in front of the Dernier *mas*.

All alone.

Running like she didn't care if anyone saw her.

Warmth radiated from fingers to toes as the killer got out of the car.

It is about time I came into a little bit of luck.

35

"Madame Dernier?"

Maggie looked up to see Denis Chevalier standing in the hall before her. He was wearing a white lab coat over checked wool gabardine trousers and clasped his hands in front of him.

Maggie tugged down the hem of her cotton dress where she'd been inspecting the abrasion on her knee and stood up quickly, sticking out her hand—hopefully forestalling any other more creative ideas he might have had for greeting her—and smiling broadly.

"*Merci*, Monsieur Chevalier, for meeting with me,"

"*Absolument*," he said, his Adam's apple working hard around the words as he waved a hand in the direction down the hall. "First double doors at the end, please."

Maggie walked in front of him and felt his hand on her back.

Low on her back.

She fought the impulse to knock his hand away. He hadn't ventured into dangerous territory yet and there was the whole cultural thing to think of. What was out of bounds in America was not necessarily so here.

Plus, there was information she needed out of him that an admonishment or abrupt education of #metoo politics would likely torpedo pretty quickly.

Maggie stiffened her shoulders and her resolve.

Suck it up and get what you came for.

Long countertops stretched the length of the police forensics lab alongside bins of safety goggles and protective clothing, an eye wash station, scales and a raft of locked cabinets.

Maggie looked around. It was lunch time. Nobody else was in the lab.

Chevalier led Maggie to a small office off the main lab and closed the door behind them. Inside a small table with a goose-neck lamp was shoved up against the wall with two chairs in front of it. Once settled across from him, she noted again that he seemed to be having a hard time keeping his eyes on her face. They strayed first to her knees...*why had she worn a dress today?*...and then to her breasts.

"So, Monsieur Chevalier," Maggie said, perching her purse on her lap and hugging it to her chest. "What have you got for me?"

"Well," Chevalier said, rubbing his fingers along the sides of his mouth and then inspecting them as if to see if any residue had come off, "I think you will be very interested to hear what I have discovered. And I think I should mention that I have not yet shared this information with Detective Moreau."

That last part did not hearten Maggie. There was no good reason for Chevalier to withhold information from Jean-Baptiste.

Maggie bit her tongue in order to overcome the urge to ask him why he hadn't told Jean-Baptiste.

She had a sinking suspicion she knew why.

Chevalier turned in his chair to pick up a folder off the desk and held it out as if he was going to give it to her, but then he pulled it back at the last moment.

"I know Detective Moreau's theories are based on his belief that the assailant could not have been a woman," he said, licking his lips in slow lizard-like movements that made Maggie's stomach roil. "But it is possible—just possible—that I have information to dispute that. You know, the forensics division of any homicide department is often treated as, how am I putting this? second class citizens. Forensics inevitably comes up with the facts to close a case. But it is the detective who gets the accolades."

Maggie was seconds from snatching the file folder out of his hand and it took all her willpower not to do it. If this baboon had proof that the killer could have been a woman, it opened up the suspect pool. And since Maggie now thought Angeline Sauvage might well have killed Leon Boucher, she needed that supporting groundwork.

"I couldn't agree more, Monsieur Chevalier."

"Denis, please," he said, his eyes dropping to where her breasts were hidden behind her purse.

"Denis." Maggie held out her hand and he slowly gave the file over.

Inside, she saw a copy of a cranial x-ray. The words *Leon Boucher* and the date he was killed were tagged in the corner of the copy.

"What am I looking at?"

Chevalier scooted over to Maggie on his chair which had caster wheels. As he leaned into her and pointed at the x-ray, her stomach lurched at the combined smell of onions and a strongly floral aftershave.

"You see this?" He pointed to a squiggly line across the back of the skull. "This happened postmortem." He then pointed to another line. "And here too."

Maggie frowned. So Leon was whacked over the head *after* he was killed? What sense does that make?

Chevalier laughed at her confusion and dropped a hand to her thigh.

"You don't understand, do you?" he said, his face inches away from hers.

Oh, I think I understand pretty well.

Maggie kept her eyes glued to the photocopied x-ray. Her thigh was literally burning under his fingers although she knew his hand was actually quite cold. She wasn't sure how much longer she could sit still.

She cleared her throat. "Can you explain?"

Chevalier leaned in even closer on the pretext of pointing out again the same lines on the skull. His lips were now nearly on Maggie's ear.

"The body was dropped on its head. Twice."

The revelation hit Maggie immediately. Dropping the body once might be a man in a hurry. Dropping it twice opened up the possibility that it was a woman having trouble carrying it.

Even Jean-Baptiste would have to see that.

Maggie nodded and made a show of closing the folder and leaning over to put it on the desk—which moved her body away from him.

"That's very helpful. It means the killer could have been a woman."

"There's more."

Maggie forced herself not to look at him. Instead she rummaged in her bag for a tissue to blot at nonexistent perspiration on her top lip.

"Warm in here," she said. "You said there's more?"

Chevalier stood up next to Maggie so that his pelvis was eye level with her. He turned on the light box hanging over the desk. When he did, she saw a negative of a photograph of the injection site on Leon Boucher's body. Her stomach gurgled unpleasantly but she steeled herself.

"You see this?" Chevalier, said, shoving his hips close to Maggie's face and pointing at the picture.

There was a tiny red dot on the left side of Leon's neck, obviously the point of entry for the needle.

"The puncture wound is not clean. It indicates a user awkwardness, as though injected by someone not used to doing it."

Maggie felt her pulse quicken.

"So possibly someone *not* in the medical profession?"

"Exactly. Or it could be in the struggle it just went in badly. Let's just say it wasn't a clean injection."

"So it *could* be someone with medical experience."

"Or it might not."

"Hardly helps narrow the field. Excuse me, Monsieur Chevalier, you are too close. Please step away."

Chevalier sat back in his chair and grabbed the arms of Maggie's chair which up to then she did not know also had caster wheels on it.

"I do not think that is what you want me to do," he said as he jerked her chair toward his, his mouth launching into her face as he did.

"Blecch! Stop it!" Maggie yelped, turning her head in time to avoid the kiss and giving the man a mouthful of her thick hair instead.

"You know you want this, *mignon*," Chevalier said, breathing heavily before he pushed himself on top of her. She felt his hands grab for her purse and toss it aside.

"I think we both like a little fight in our lovemaking, *n'est-ce pas?*"

Unable to get out of the chair and horrified to feel her dress beginning to creep up her thighs, Maggie grabbed Chevalier's forearms. As he positioned himself over she brought her knee up as hard as she could between his legs.

He let out an agonized groan and collapsed on the floor.

"Gosh, Denis. Too much?" she said, squirming out of her chair. "I never can get the amount of fight just right."

She snatched up her purse before smoothing down her dress. As she stepped over his still writhing body, he grabbed for her ankle.

"You will pay for this," he gasped before she kicked free of his grip.

36

Nicole felt the burning in her legs as she ran.

She welcomed the pain.

She welcomed the agony as the hard uneven stones of the road jarred her joints and cramped her feet. She wanted to hurt, wanted to let the physical discomfort blot out everything racing through her mind.

The relentless replaying of Laurent's voice came to her again.

"It is because Nicole is not really Elise's daughter."

And the look on his face when he saw that she'd heard him!

Not the expression of someone confused or unsure of why I might be upset but the horrible dreadful certainty that I'd got it right.

Because I'm not Elise's daughter.

She pressed her hands to her head as if to squeeze the words out of her brain. But they pounded into her skull and repeated themselves over and over again...

Because Nicole is not really Elise's daughter

Because Nicole is not really Elise's daughter

Because Nicole is not really Elise's daughter

She screamed to obliterate the sound of the refrain in her

head and then turned and bolted into the field next to the road. Instantly, she felt the uneven terrain as it punished her knees and hips.

She didn't see the ditch until the last minute and jumped it awkwardly. One foot made it, the other dragged down the side into the mud, destroying her sandals.

Screw the sandals! she thought as hot tears streaked down her cheeks and she scrambled up the other side of the ditch. *Screw everything!*

She didn't know where she was going. She didn't care.

The flatness of the village road was gone now and she was glad of it. She refused to slow down. She needed to wipe out her mind.

Her foot turned in a hidden pothole and she went down hard, slamming into the ground. She felt her lip burst as her chin hit and she tasted the salty blood in her mouth.

Good! More!

She scrambled to her feet, scraping her knees, and limped on.

I belong to nobody! They all lied! I'm no one's!

Her sobs gathered in her throat and she threw back her head and wailed, not looking where she was going, not caring if she fell again, not caring if anybody heard her. Just wanting to push the words, the punishing, horrible words from her head.

Nicole is not really Elise's daughter.

"No!" she screamed again. "I hate you all! I'll hate you 'til I die!"

She stumbled on through the sparse thicket of grapevines that were set in haphazard rows as if they'd been planted centuries before and then forgotten. She ran through them, not caring when the branches and limbs snatched at her sundress and scoured her bare legs.

She ran until her lungs felt they would burst and still she ran, hoping they *would* burst, hoping she would die and all the lies and the horrible truth and the voice in her head would be silenced forever.

She ran until the vineyard gave way and there was only rock and gravel. A shelf of stone that seemed to suspend in space appeared out of nowhere. She ran to the edge, stopping just in time, her sides heaving. The only sounds she heard were her own harsh gasps of breath trying to force air into her lungs.

At the bottom of the cliff were more vineyards. And rocks. It was just a little promontory, an aberration in a field of ancient grapes. The reason why nobody planted here anymore.

Just rocks and a drop to your death with one wrong step.

Nicole stood at the edge and stared over the rim, her mind whirling. A sob caught in her throat and suddenly the weariness of her run and her family's betrayal welled up inside her and she felt her legs give way. She fell hard to the ground on bloodied knees and bent slowly forward at the waist until her head touched the ground. She let all the sobs inside her out.

She grabbed handfuls of grass on either side of her and let the torrent of misery take her, let it deplete her until it was done. Then with one last whimper, she opened her eyes and focused again on the bottom of the cliff.

Such a long way down.

And then she heard the sound of a twig snapping. Behind her.

Instantly the fear was back, replacing her sadness and her anger, cascading over her in a tsunami of terror. She turned in the direction of the sound, her eyes looking everywhere at once.

"Who...who's there?" She flinched at the sound of her own voice, so full of fear.

A flutter of breeze touched her hair and with it came the scent she'd smelled once before.

His scent.

He had found her.

37

Adrenaline shot through his entire body. His muscles felt tight and coiled inside him as he ran across the unfamiliar terrain.

He stumbled at one point. He was going too fast. His lungs burned. He was laboring for every breath. But he couldn't let her get too far ahead of him.

He caught a glimpse of a flash of color. Her blouse.

She was moving fast.

Where is she going?

Something told him he couldn't just run her down. Something told him to hold back, to watch. He slowed and dropped to one knee, the bushes camouflaging him. He watched her turn and stand with her back to the cliff.

"Who are you?" she screamed.

He could see her fear, even taste it from where he crouched, half hidden in the bushes.

He cupped his hands around his mouth. "Nicole!"

She snapped her head in his direction, her eyes searching, imploring.

"Where...where are you?" she screamed. "Show yourself!"

Slowly, he stood up, his hands out as if he were walking toward a frightened animal.

Would she run? Would she jump into the ravine?

"*Je suis ici,*" he called to her, willing his voice to sound calm and friendly.

She stared at him, frozen. Then her shoulders sagged and she fell to her knees, her head bowed.

He reached her in a dozen strides. This time he knew he wouldn't hesitate.

He put his hands on her shoulders, small and vulnerable, and felt her collapse into them, her sobs choking the air.

"Nicole," he said, helplessly, wishing he knew enough English to make her understand.

"I thought...thought you were..." she murmured as she wept. "Oh, Luc, I was so frightened!"

Luc pulled her into his arms and patted her back, not completely sure of her words but sure enough.

"*C'est moi,*" he said more firmly as he held her close. "*Je suis ici.*"

Wispy streaks of clouds drifted across the stark blue sky.

Luc kept his arm around her and they sat with their backs to the stone cliff and watched the clouds. He could feel the heat of the day's sun still in the rock face, warming them both. They sat like that for what seemed like hours. He had never held a girl before. He'd never come to anyone's aid before. He'd never been a source of comfort to anyone before.

When Laurent called and ordered him to drop everything and go find Nicole, at first Luc hadn't believed him. While it was true Laurent was not typically given to testing him for no reason, it had been unbelievable that he would be calling *him*, entrusting *him* with such an important task.

But even as his mind had rebelled against the logic of what Laurent was asking of him, he could hear the paging system at the hospital on Laurent's end and quickly realized that it was real.

Laurent couldn't go after Nicole. So he had called Luc to go in his stead.

Luc leaned his head against Nicole's. He still couldn't believe it.

"I still can't believe it's you," Nicole said softly.

It was like she could read his mind.

Luc's grasp of English wasn't great but after ten months living with Maggie and Laurent where they both largely spoke English, he was astonished at how much he'd picked up.

"I was so scared, Luc."

"Je sais." I know.

She pulled out from under his arm to look at him, her beautiful face serious, the tracks of her tears still visible against her cheeks.

"He was here. Following me. I heard him."

"It was me you heard, I think."

She shook her head. "No. When you called my name your voice came from over there." She pointed in the direction Luc had come from. "But at the same time I heard the bushes rustling there." She pointed directly in front of her. "And I smelled him."

An animal, Luc thought. *A vole or a mouse.*

"But you didn't see him?"

When she didn't answer, he said, "You think France is full of...*des violeurs*, yes?"

"Does that mean rapists? Because then yes, I do," she said, nodding. "And murderers."

"Is not true. No more than your country. Less, even, I think."

She seemed to think about that for a moment and then turned and settled herself again in his arms.

"I heard something today I wasn't supposed to hear. Something terrible."

Luc wasn't sure exactly what she was saying. But he could tell she was relaxing. He was helping just by being here, holding her, and listening. Even if he didn't understand all of her words.

"I heard that I'm not really related to Maggie and Laurent."

When Luc didn't react, she turned to look at him. "I basically found out I'm adopted. Do you know that word?"

Luc nodded slowly.

"The person I thought was my mother, isn't. The people I thought were my grandparents, aren't. Nothing is what I thought it was."

"Are they...throwing you out?" Luc asked.

Now it was Nicole's turn to frown. "Throwing me out? No."

He shrugged. "What has changed is inside your..." He tapped her head. "Not here." He tapped his chest over his heart.

"Okay, maybe, but why did they have to lie to me? Why didn't they just tell me the truth?"

Luc shrugged helplessly. "I do not know this."

"I can't believe I'm not related to them. None of them. Instead, somewhere in this godforsaken country are my real people." She waved a hand to encompass the land around them.

"I think Maggie and Laurent are your real people still, " Luc said, struggling with the words and the building revelation that was forming in his own brain. "I think they feel the same."

"Your English is better than I thought."

Luc grinned.

She leaned against him again. "Do you think I'm over-reacting?"

He frowned at the word and Nicole rephrased.

"Do you think I shouldn't be so unhappy about what I found out?"

"I don't know who your people *en* France are being," he said. "They are wonderful or maybe they are not. But I know Laurent and Maggie. I am choosing them for you."

A fluttery feeling formed in his belly as the words came out of his mouth.

Words he had no idea he was about to say. Or felt.

Nicole narrowed her eyes at him. "I thought you did not like them."

Luc blushed. He'd been a fool. A baby. An idiot.

"They choose you too," she said. "When you were gone... last night... they said you were family."

Luc looked at her. "Laurent says that?"

Nicole shook her head. "I don't remember who said it."

As he took in her words Luc could see it was so. He saw it in the way Laurent watched him closely to make sure he learned a task correctly and in the way Maggie always made sure he got the largest tart slice because he was the oldest. He saw it in a hundred different ways that he'd not had his eyes open to see. Before today.

"I think I am now believing that blood is not so important," he said. "Maybe is not important at all."

"You mean because the people who love you and me aren't blood-related to us?"

Again, he didn't understand all of her words but he was pretty sure he got the gist of it.

"I think you and I are a lot alike, Luc," Nicole said, bringing her face close to his. "And I really hope *we* are not related."

For a moment he forgot to breathe as he was aware that his world had changed in the last few seconds. And was about to change again.

"*Moi, aussi,*" he said, and then leaned over and kissed her.

38

M aggie took in a long breath and took stock of her situation.

The detention area of the Marseille police department was a combination of old and new facilities, including wooden benches that hugged the perimeter of a large room and an exposed broken toilet in the corner which Maggie didn't imagine had actually been used for decades.

It seemed that when a somewhat respected forensic tech of the Marseille police department goes screeching down the hall insisting that a civilian had stolen an important piece of lab equipment—even though none was found on her person—that person might expect to be forcibly detained as Maggie had learned much to her discomfort.

When Chevalier decided to retaliate by accusing her of theft instead of assault which would have left Maggie with no choice but to tell the truth, she had to decide if she wanted to play it cool or plead self-defense against sexual assault—which she knew would effectively end her association with Jean-Baptiste and the Boucher investigation.

In truth she knew that although annoying and repulsive

there had never really been a moment when she felt Chevalier would succeed in forcing himself on her.

They were in a public police department for crying out loud!

Whatever his intentions Maggie believed it was likely just overzealousness. And since she'd effectively taken care of the problem on her own she wouldn't turn it into a fight she'd be sorry she started.

Plus, there was an argument to be made that if anybody had assaulted anyone, *she* had assaulted Chevalier.

This was France! An attempt at a stolen kiss had ended in a man writing in agony on the floor? Every person in the police station—women included—would think Maggie had grossly overreacted to a little good-natured flirtation.

In the end, she'd opted not to make it worse. There had been no real harm done.

Except possibly to Chevalier's chances of fathering children someday.

Of the twenty or so women sitting with her in the detention room, five women—clearly belonging in the lady of the night category—glared at her as if Maggie were the reason they were there instead of someone actually sharing their same fate. Maggie had made a special point not to speak to any of them. Not that she thought being friendly would be a bad thing.

But being recognized as American might be.

Turning away from her audience of glowering fellow inmates, she turned on her phone, which hadn't been taken away, further underscoring to her that her detention was largely for show. When the phone powered back up, she saw that Laurent had called and also Gaston Boucher.

She called Gaston back.

"Oh, thank God," he said. "I didn't know who else to turn to. I need your help. I'm being followed."

"Whoa, slow down, Gaston. How do you know?"

"How does anybody know? I see them on the street! Hiding behind newspapers! Slinking around corners! I'm being followed!"

Why would anyone follow him?

"Have you told the police?"

"I can't call them! They think I killed my father!"

"That's the opposite of what they think, Gaston. The lead detective told me you're in the clear."

Should I be telling him this? Is this the reason Jean-Baptiste doesn't tell me anything important?

"Really?"

"Yes. So you need to call the cops if you're worried."

Could the killer be trying to intimidate Gaston? Or is Gaston setting this up as a ruse to throw suspicion off himself?

"I don't believe you. The cops are just looking for an excuse to lock me up."

"They're not. I swear they've eliminated you as a suspect."

"Really? Oh, thank God!"

Maggie heard the tears in his voice.

"What about your mother?" she said. "Have you told her about the people following you? She could arrange a security detail for you."

"She's impossible. All she does is drink champagne."

"Have the police talked to her?" Maggie couldn't imagine that they hadn't but you never knew.

"Yes, but what could she tell them? Papa was away on business. We knew he would be late getting home—"

"Wait. How? Did he call and say he'd be late?"

"No, I think Joelle called. Is it important?"

"I'm not sure."

"Anyway, instead of him arriving home as expected a pair of

police detectives showed up on our front doorstep to tell us he was dead. It was pretty shocking."

"I can imagine. I still haven't been able to get a hold of your mother. I've called and even knocked on the door."

"I told you. She stays drunk all the time."

"I really need to talk to her, Gaston."

"I have to go now but I'll text you a time to meet with her. I don't guarantee she'll be sober though."

Maggie disconnected and bit her nail trying to figure out what she'd learned.

On the one hand Gaston had the necessary medical experience, no alibi and plenty of motive. But she was convinced he didn't have the stomach to do it. Angeline had motive and opportunity. Joelle too.

And then there was Danon. Was his desire to be publicly acknowledged as Leon's lover so important to him that he'd murder for it?

What about Olivier? Sure he hated Leon, but enough to murder him? And would he really do it himself? Wouldn't he hire it out?

The sound of the mechanized main door opening was accompanied by the sound of a loud buzzer that made all the women in the room stand and crowd around the door. Maggie remained seated.

"Madame Dernier!" a police officer shouted as he stepped into the room and waved the line of women back to their benches.

Maggie slid her phone into her pocket and got to her feet.

"*Ici*," she said, moving to the door.

"*Suivez-moi*," the stern-faced man said. *Follow me*.

Maggie felt a chill as she stepped into the hallway and

immediately saw Jean-Baptiste leaning against the wall, waiting for her.

"So," he said, straightening up. "Have you learned your lesson?"

"Using your position to toss people in jail without due process is illegal," Maggie said with all the indignation she could muster.

He held out her purse to her.

"I told you what I'd do if you didn't stop interfering," he said and then led the way down the hall.

"How is having a date with Denis Chevalier interfering?"

Jean-Baptiste stopped suddenly and turned slowly to look at her.

"You were meeting with Chevalier romantically?"

"And since when is that a crime?"

"Well, it isn't, of course, Madame. But your husband may think differently."

"Why does he need to know?"

Jean-Baptiste narrowed his eyes. "Were you really rendezvousing with Chevalier? The man is a pig."

"I'm appalled at your shallowness, Detective Inspector. He's beautiful on the inside."

"Now I know you're lying."

"Are you releasing me?"

"I'm still thinking."

"I've found a lead you need to follow up on."

"You need to stop telling me what to do."

They continued walking down the long hallway toward what Maggie now saw was the main entrance to the building.

"Angeline Sauvage told me that she asked a friend to lie and say he was with her during the time of the murder," Maggie said. Jean-Baptiste looked confused.

For a moment Maggie felt lightheaded. "Don't tell me," she

said. "You didn't confirm her alibi? Were you just going to take her word for it? Or did you even talk to her at all?"

"You, Madame, are extremely offensive, even for an American. I am astonished you have any friends in France at all."

"And I'm astonished you ever made it to detective. Tell me why you no longer suspect Gaston for the murder."

"You are relentless."

Maggie began ticking off the points on her fingers. "He had access to the drugs, he hated his father, and I assume he can't account for his whereabouts on the day."

"How in the world do you know all this?"

"This is Detective Work 101! *Why* is Gaston Boucher not your prime suspect? What made you go cold on him?"

"Why should I tell you anything? You are already too...rude and invasive."

"Tell me and I'll stop talking to people about the case. I promise."

"Your promises are meaningless! Already you have talked to the son, the head of Leon's campaign office, the head of his opponent's campaign office..."

"Just tell me why you released Gaston without charging him!"

"He's under suspension at the hospital."

"What does that mean?"

"He is having trouble performing his duties."

"Do I really have to pull this out of you? *Why* is he having trouble?"

"It appears he's developed an aversion to needles."

"You have got to be kidding me."

"It was established three months ago. A psychiatrist confirmed it. It can't be him."

Even though she had herself ruled Gaston out, it was still a surprise. She looked at Jean-Baptiste.

"He says he's being followed," she said.

"Who does?"

"Gaston."

"How in the world do you know this?"

"Does it matter? He's afraid to call you but he thinks he's being followed."

"Or perhaps he's just afraid. He appeared very timid when we interviewed him."

"So you're not going to do anything?"

"I'll do something if he calls. Meanwhile, I have called someone to take you home."

Maggie felt her mouth go dry.

"That wasn't necessary, Jean-Baptiste. I'm perfectly capable of getting myself home."

Jean-Baptiste smiled wickedly. "Of course you are, Maggie, but when I told him where you were, I'm afraid your husband insisted."

39

"You were *flirting* with the coroner?" Laurent said angrily as they reached his car outside the police station. Maggie was having trouble keeping up with his long strides.

"I don't think he's the coroner."

"Do you really think that is my question?" Laurent boomed out, nearly rattling the car windows as he jerked the car door open.

Maggie was trying to think if she'd ever seen him so mad. *With her.* There had been plenty of other times she'd seen him seriously unhinged but until now, *she* hadn't been the source.

She slipped into the passenger seat of the car and turned to him once he was in.

"Laurent, I'm sorry. I admit I led him on a very tiny bit so he would tell me what he knew."

"Did it not occur to you that it might be dangerous?"

"No. He's a little weasel of a guy. And we were surrounded by his colleagues. *In a police station.*"

"I wish I could communicate to you how furious I am."

"You're doing a better job than you know."

He glanced at her. "Mocking me? *Vraiment*?"

"No, no! It's just I need you to understand why I need to do this."

"I have no trouble understanding why you *think* you need to do this. You want to erase the event for Nikki by solving the murder *rapidement*."

"Correct. So why don't you see—"

"Because currently we have a problem that I need your entire focus on."

"Laurent, I am interested in whatever's going on at the monastery but surely you can see that this—"

"Nikki has run off."

"What?" Maggie froze as she stared at him.

"She overheard our phone conversation earlier."

Maggie felt a lead weight form in her stomach. "What exactly did she—?"

"She heard me say she is not the real Nicole."

"Oh, Laurent. No. Oh, no." Maggie gripped the armrest of the car door and shook her head as if she could somehow deny it had happened.

"And then she ran off."

"Oh my God. I can't believe this."

Maggie held her head in her hands. Of all the times she imagined having this conversation with Nicole when she finally told her the truth she always envisioned Nicole receiving the news with understanding and a wistful acceptance. She tried to imagine what Nicole must have heard.

"We should have told her sooner," Laurent said matter-of-factly.

"You *think*?" Maggie said shrilly. "Laurent, we have to find her! Why didn't you—?"

"I could not search for her because Jem had a little accident and I needed to take him to Aix."

"Oh, Laurent!" Maggie stared at him in horror.

"He is fine, *chérie*. But I could not go after Nikki myself."

"Where is he now?"

"Danielle came to Aix and picked him up from the emergency room."

"What happened?"

Laurent shrugged. "He got a nail in his hand when he was playing in the front drive."

"A nail? I *told* you to get Jemmy or Luc to clean up that mess!"

Laurent gave her a sidewise glance as he started to back the car up and Maggie swallowed her words.

"Never mind that now," she said. "We have to find Nicole!"

His phone dinged indicating a text had come in and he pulled it out and glanced at it.

"Nikki is with Luc."

"Thank God. Thank God!" Tears welled up in Maggie's eyes.

"I agree it is a relief, *chérie*, but it is not over. Not with Nikki and certainly not between you and me."

"Do you have to call her that?"

"It is what she wants to be called! Why do you resist her every effort to be who she is? She does not want to be French!"

"But she is French!"

"*Non, chérie*. She is not. Not any more. This is what everyone sees but you."

"But she...but Nicole..."

"Maggie, stop. You are driving everyone crazy. You are driving *me* crazy. She is not an abandoned waif or a kidnapped French national. She is no longer either of those things. Why can you not see this?"

A tear streaked down Maggie's cheek.

"You cannot change the past," Laurent said, more gently now. "She is an American teenager with no more interest in France than your brother Ben."

"Ben is probably the root of her antipathy toward France."

"And if he is? It changes nothing."

"We should have brought her back to France years ago."

Laurent threw up his hands in frustration. "And told your parents what?"

"We could have come up with something."

"Why is how things turned out so unsatisfactory? Is it because you'd planned something different? Take a breath and adjust to it."

"I can't."

"You can. And you must."

As they pulled onto the road, Maggie's eyes were stinging with tears of shame and frustration, the silence deepened between them. She glanced at Laurent and could see he was still angry with her.

"I'm sorry," she said. "I've had blinders on."

"I do not know what that is but I am sure it is probably true."

"There's been a problem with Luc lately, hasn't there?"

"I am handling it."

"We parent the kids *together*, Laurent. I know I haven't been a team player lately and I'm sorry about that. What's going on with him?"

"He is reacting to something."

"But you don't know what?"

"Not yet. It helps Nikki being here."

"Do you have to call her that?"

"*Chérie*, I will stop this car if I hear you say that one more time."

Those were the same words she and Laurent used when the children were acting up in the car. A laugh bubbled up in Maggie in spite of herself. She put a hand on his thigh.

"Sorry. I guess I'll get used to it."

He smiled back at her and covered her hand with his.

"I know it is hard, *chérie*. But you must let her be who she wants to be. Not who *you* want her to be."

"It sounds terrible when you put it like that," Maggie said, wincing. "So Ben wins, I guess?"

He looked at her with surprise. "Was this a competition between you and your brother?"

"No. Well, maybe a little. I just hate that he was right."

"If it's any consolation, *chérie*, on this subject *everyone* was right."

"Except me."

Laurent squeezed her hand. "I am glad we have resolved this."

Her phone vibrated and while Laurent was navigating the on ramp to the motorway, she glanced down and saw a text had come in from Gaston.

<My mother will see you at thirteen hundred hours tomorrow. But I need to see you first. I have something I should have told you before. Something BIG>

40

L uc forced himself to stand tall.

Unfortunately, he couldn't do anything about the sweat dripping off his chin or his trembling hands.

After delivering Nicole home he'd stayed until Danielle, Jemmy and Mila had showed up, but he knew he had to get back to *l'Abbaye de Sainte-Trinité* if for no other reason than to return the bicycle he'd borrowed when Laurent called him.

The moment he rode back through the gates of the monastery, the group of teen boys grabbed him.

He fought them but there were too many. They dragged him and the bike to the forecourt by the rectory where Frère Dominic was waiting.

"So you have returned?" Dominic said. "And with the bike you stole."

Luc shrugged off the boys' hands. He looked at Dominic. "I had a family emergency."

"And you knew of this so-called emergency, how?"

"He has a mobile phone, *mon frère!*" one of the boys shouted. "I saw him with it."

Dominic turned to Luc and held out his hand.

"It is my property," Luc said.

"You have no personal property here," Dominic said. "None of us do."

"I am not your prisoner," Luc said, not touching his phone but feeling it burn inside his pocket. "I only came back to return the bike."

"Give me the phone," Dominic said, his eyes hooded and cold.

Perhaps he only wants to check that I really got a phone call from Laurent.

Luc dug out his phone and handed it over.

"Laurent called me at—"

"Be quiet," Dominic said, holding the phone in his hand but not looking at it. He turned to the crowd of boys. "Where is the bicycle?"

A younger boy around fifteen—who Luc remembered had been friendly last summer when Luc lived at the monastery— emerged from the crowd and walked the bicycle to the center of the circle.

Dominic nodded. "And where is Aimee? The owner of this bike?"

"*Ici, mon frère,*" a girl said, stepping forward. She looked at Luc with revulsion and triumph. Luc did not know her. He figured she must be one of the new summer refugees. It was clear by the way she looked at him that she had been listening to the boys at the monastery.

"This girl has been wronged by this boy!" Dominic said loudly to everyone.

The group of teens agreed loudly with shouts of "*Oui!*" and "*C'est vrai!*"

Dominic walked over to Luc. He held Luc's cell phone with one hand and gripped the handlebars of the bike with the other.

"Theft in this community will not be tolerated! Do you

admit to stealing this bicycle?"

"We saw him, *mon frère!*" one boy shouted.

Luc looked at the group of young people. Some he knew, some he didn't. All of them were dressed, if not in rags, then in ripped and mended clothing, many of their faces looked already old before their time.

"I didn't steal it," Luc said carefully, his eyes on Dominic's face. "I had an emergency. I borrowed it."

Dominic scowled at Luc as if he were looking at the devil himself. "Thieves always use language to absolve themselves. Does anybody here think Luc *borrowed* Aimee's bicycle?"

Everyone shook their heads or shouted "*Non!*"

"The punishment for theft in this community is severe," Dominic said. "It is ostracization."

Luc bit his tongue. He didn't say that ostracization couldn't come soon enough for him.

"Normally I would let the authorities handle this. But because Luc is a special case—he was once one of you—I feel more severe measures must be observed."

"Beat his ass!" a boy called from the group. "He thinks he's better'n us!"

"In cases such as this, I feel it is important to let the community have a voice. Your crime is against *l'Abbaye de Sainte-Trinité*. You have wronged every single one of us standing here today, Luc. And for that you must pay and pay dearly."

Luc felt his scalp prickle uncomfortably at the monk's words.

"Grab his arms."

41

As soon as Maggie arrived home she intended to go straight to Nicole but the girl had heard the car in the drive and had fled upstairs to her bedroom.

Danielle and Jemmy were sitting at the dining room table. Just seeing Jemmy's bandaged hand made Maggie want to cry.

"It's fine, Mom," he said when Maggie sat down and tried to gingerly pick up his hand. "They gave me a tetanus shot. That was worse than the nail."

"How did you get the nail in your hand?"

"Just messing around in the front yard."

Laurent had gone to the kitchen. Maggie could hear him moving pots and pans around. When he came out he greeted Danielle, then opened the French doors and whistled for the dogs. It was late afternoon and the grapevines were easily visible in the dull light.

In five weeks there would be a four-day burst of activity in the fields that would dominate all their lives as they rushed to get the grapes picked in time.

"Where is Luc?" Laurent asked.

"I do not know," Danielle said.

"Luc brought Nikki home on somebody's bike," Jemmy said. "But he said the monk had more work for him to do."

Laurent stared at Jemmy for a moment as though trying to process what his son was saying.

Maggie turned to Laurent. "What in the world are they having him do over there?"

Suddenly Nicole appeared at the foot of the staircase.

"If you want any more evidence about what a backwards country this is," she said, flushing with anger, "Luc slept *in a stable* last night. With only a half baked potato for dinner. I'm telling you this is the Middle Ages over here. And you want *me* to move here? Un-believable."

Maggie turned to glare at Laurent. "They had Luc sleeping *in a stable*? What the hell is going on?"

But Laurent was already on his way out the door.

By the time Danielle headed back to *Dormir*, the sun was sinking low behind the house, its golden light making dappled patterns through the leafy canopy of chestnuts and plane trees by the front drive.

Maggie was in the kitchen trying to concentrate on making *Hachis Parmentier* for supper.

She'd looked at her cell phone no fewer than a dozen times but there had been no message from Laurent.

What was going on with Luc? What did Laurent know that he was refusing to share?

Maggie moved restlessly around the kitchen before settling down to chop shallots and carrots.

Jemmy and Nicole were watching television in the living room. The way Nicole kept looking up at the slightest sound made Maggie think that if Nicole hadn't been so determined to avoid her she would be in the kitchen helping to make the meal.

While it was true that Nicole was no more interested in cooking or baking than the average American teenager, she had still spent many a happy hour in the kitchen with Laurent over the years—as had all the children.

Maggie placed two pounds of russet potatoes peeled and cut into a large saucepan and added water to cover them. Then she took out a heavy-bottomed skillet and placed it on the gas stovetop.

As she looked at Nicole and Jemmy in the living room watching television, she was immediately struck by how relaxed Jemmy looked—even with his wounded hand.

His world is at peace. Everything is as it should be.

Nicole on the other hand was leaning forward rigidly, her shoulders stiff and resistant.

Things were not right with her world. Not by a long shot.

Maggie knew that if the crisis with Luc hadn't come to a head this evening, Laurent would have taken Nicole to task for running off in spite of the reason.

Laurent had never been on the back foot for as long as Maggie had known him. Being in the wrong wasn't something he had trouble admitting.

It was just something he often had trouble feeling bad about.

After she got the skillet hot, she poured a glug of olive oil into it and waited for it to shimmer before adding the chopped vegetables.

There was no doubt in her mind that fussing at Nicole for leaving would effectively breech the wall of silence on the dreaded subject. Painful or not, Maggie felt that would be a good thing.

She watched the teen as she sat on the couch. Nicole's eyes if not her mind were rivetted on the television program.

"Nicole," Maggie called. "Can you give me a hand in here, please?"

Maggie turned to focus on the hot skillet and not Nicole's slow and begrudging manner as she entered the kitchen.

"What do you need?"

Maggie pointed to a bunch of freshly rinsed parsley. "Can you roughly chop those for me?"

With a sigh, Nicole reached for the parsley.

"Look, Nicole. About what you overheard today—"

"Did you just lure me in here on a pretense?"

"Nicole, listen to me—"

"*No,*" Nicole said firmly in a low voice so as not to be overheard by Jemmy in the other room. "I don't want to listen."

"Look, I understand how upset you must be," Maggie said in a strained voice. "It's a terrible thing what you overheard."

"Is that the reason you wanted me to live here so bad? Because you stole me away from my real family and you're trying to make it right? I can't believe you let me believe your sister—a grubby drug addict—was my mother! How could you do that?"

Maggie was speechless. Should she tell Nicole that she'd come from an abusive family? With a mother every bit as bad if not worse than Elise?

No. The day had already held too many harsh revelations. Nicole needed time to digest the fact that she wasn't Elise's child.

Wasn't really a Newberry.

"I'm just so sorry, darling. I don't know what else to say."

"Well, that's a switch," Nicole said as she tossed down the parsley and turned on her heel to leave the kitchen.

Maggie let the kitchen resonate gently with the sound of

Nicole's words and then turned back to the stove and moderated the heat, her vision blurred with tears.

How did she ever think solving the riddle of who put Leon's body in her trunk would help anything?

42

Laurent saw the outdoor lights in the forecourt from the parking lot. Two monks stood at the open monastery gates. When they saw him, they turned and hurried up the steps of the chapel.

That was when Laurent heard the cheering. He quickened his pace. When he entered the forecourt, the first thing he saw was Luc hanging by his arms, held by two boys twice his size. In front of Luc stood Frère Dominic.

"What is the meaning of this?" Laurent bellowed as he pushed into the scrum of boys.

Luc did not look up. But Laurent could see blood dripping from his mouth.

"Tell me you didn't hit him," Laurent said loudly as he walked up to Dominic.

"It was necessary to—"

Without warning Laurent's fist smashed into the center of the monk's face, dropping him to the ground like a sack of cement. A few girls in the group screamed.

Laurent put his boot against the monk's neck. And pressed.

Dominic flailed with his arms and Laurent pressed harder.

A voice of warning bubbled up from within Laurent. The rage that burned inside him was enough to kill the monk. Easily. He *wanted* to kill him. His hands twitched in his effort to hold himself back.

He heard Maggie's voice in his head. A soothing sound, a peace-making sound. A sane sound.

He removed his foot and Dominic began coughing and slapping the ground in an attempt to get air back into his lungs.

Laurent turned to Luc. The boys holding him quickly released him and melted into the crowd.

When the boys dropped their hold on him Luc staggered to stay on his feet. He tried to shake the fog from his head. It seemed that Laurent had suddenly materialized and was standing over Frère Dominic who lay on his back gasping on the cobblestones of the courtyard.

Laurent's face was a thundercloud of fury as he looked around the crowd of young people.

"Do you think you can treat this boy like this because he belongs to no one?" he roared. The boys at the front of the group cowered away from him.

"He belongs to *me*. He is *mine* and if someone, if *anyone* hurts what is mine, they will pay."

"The boy was being disciplined," Dominic said, wiping blood from his nose.

"He is not yours to discipline," Laurent snarled.

"He's not yours either! You have no legal adoption papers for him."

"I don't need adoption papers. He is my heir. That is a matter of law. Recorded at the Municipal Council in Aix."

A hush swept the crowd. Everyone knew that the Dernier's were one of the wealthiest families in this part of Provence. To say that Luc was Laurent's heir was incomprehensible to them.

Luc shook his head as if to make his jumbled thoughts make sense. Laurent must be bluffing.

But he said the Municipal Council. Does he not think Dominic will check?

A tremor of disbelief raced through Luc.

Can it be true?

"Well, that has nothing to do with *l'Abbaye de Sainte-Trinité*," Dominic blustered, his hand to his face where it was still bleeding. "He still stole a bicycle. I will contact the authorities."

Luc watched Laurent's face contort in disgust.

"You will contact nobody. You are gone. Tonight. You will leave on your own two feet or in an ambulance. I will tell you my preference."

His face ashen, Dominic looked at the crowd and then back at Laurent.

"But the boy stole! We have rules for stealing in our community! Even you should understand that."

"He does not belong to your community. Your rules are not for him."

Laurent turned to look at the bike and then scanned the crowd. "Whose bicycle is this?"

Aimee raised her hand meekly.

"I told Luc to do what he must do to rescue a girl in trouble," Laurent said.

When Aimee just stared at him, Laurent raised his voice.

"Is it *you* accusing my son of stealing your bicycle?"

Aimee shook her head. "No, no. It's fine. I didn't know he needed it. Sorry, Luc."

Laurent turned back to the monk still wiping the blood from his face.

"Is that Luc's phone?" he asked.

Dominic hesitated and looked at the cell phone still in his

hand as if he wasn't completely sure how it got there. Luc could almost see his mind straining to figure out what to say. Wisely, the monk opted to just hand the phone over.

"A misunderstanding," he muttered.

"I'm trying to imagine what would have happened to my niece today if I hadn't been able to reach Luc," Laurent said, taking the phone from him. "I'm trying to envision a different outcome to this day with a not so happy ending."

"I misjudged the situation," Dominic said. "I apologize."

"I do not feel your apology is enough. You must leave. *Now*."

"You can't...you can't throw me out!"

Dominic looked around the group as if hoping someone would step forward and stop this humiliation. A monk emerged from the back of the crowd. He pulled Laurent aside and spoke to him in a low voice.

If Dominic thought this might result in a reprieve for him, he was wrong. When he finished talking to Laurent, the monk looked at Dominic.

"We have packed your bag, *mon frère*," he said.

Then the monk went to Luc. "You are not badly hurt?"

Luc shook his head. He didn't blame this monk, or any of them, for not trying stop Dominic. He didn't need Laurent to tell him that many men who took orders did so because they were too weak to manage life outside the friary.

"Luc, *allons-y*," Laurent said gruffly over his shoulder.

Laurent stopped on his way to the parking lot to address Dominic.

"If I see you back here again," he said in a voice so low that Luc was sure only he and Dominic could hear it, "I will put you in a wheelchair."

Dominic whitened.

"And Dominic," Laurent said, holding the monk's gaze. "I do remember you."

Dominic's shoulders sagged in what amazingly looked like relief to Luc.

"Luc!" Laurent barked again and turned to leave.

Luc's head was buzzing loudly as he hurried to catch up with Laurent. In fact he wasn't sure he was ever going to hear properly again.

Not because of the blow that Dominic had dealt him—he'd had worse in his life. But because of the words Laurent had spoken for the whole community to hear.

Words that continued to reverberate in Luc's head that blocked out all other sound.

"My son."

43

The headlight beams from Laurent's Citroën flashed through the kitchen window.

"Dad's home!" Jemmy called from the living room.

Maggie wiped her hands and pulled off her apron.

Jemmy and Nicole were already in the foyer by the time she walked to the front door. Jemmy jerked open the door with his good hand.

Maggie had a sudden fear of overwhelming Luc. He'd been acting so strangely lately that a confrontation with the whole family seemed like something he might find uncomfortable.

Luc was the first one out of the car. They watched as he walked up the front steps, his head down, his expression unreadable. Maggie really wanted to give him a big, long hug. But she was fairly sure that was the last thing Luc—a Frenchman to his core—could comfortably handle.

"Hey, Luc!" Jem said.

"*Salut*, Jem," Luc said. He touched fists with Jemmy as he stepped inside. "What happened to you?"

"Knife fight," Jemmy said with a grin. "You should see the other guy."

Luc smiled and then his eyes sought out Nicole. Maggie was surprised to see him blush. When she turned to look at Nicole, her niece was having much the same reaction to Luc.

"Did you put the potatoes in the baking dish without packing them down?" Laurent asked as he stepped into the foyer, a look of concern on his face.

Ignoring him and her own better judgment, Maggie stepped up to Luc and pulled him into her arms. To her astonishment, he hugged her back.

That night at dinner, Luc was more talkative than he had ever been since arriving at Domaine St-Buvard. His lip was cut and there was a bruise forming on his jaw, but he was smiling through his injuries. Nicole had moved her place at the dinner table next to his and from time to time he reached over and held her hand.

Whatever had happened when he'd found her and brought her back home had clearly helped Nicole process her shock. And helped Luc as well.

Maggie caught Laurent's eye over the *Hachis Parmentier* but he only shrugged. Something had happened at the monastery but she would hear about it tonight in bed. Until then, she would try to relax and enjoy the refreshing lack of tension around the dinner table.

"We are doing Sunday lunch at *Dormir* tomorrow," Laurent said to Nicole. "A day of rest for all except possibly Luc and Jem. They are required in the garden."

"Aunt Grace wants a stone wall around her *potager*," Jemmy said to Luc. "Have you ever built a stone wall before?"

Luc grinned. "How hard can it be?"

Laurent turned to Maggie. "Detective Moreau mentioned to me today that your car is ready to be picked up."

"Grace and I will run by there tomorrow and get it," Maggie said, wondering why Jean-Baptiste hadn't mentioned to *her* that the car was ready. It galled her when the good ol' boy network was still so obvious in so many human interactions in France.

Laurent cleared his throat. Nicole and Luc, who had their heads together in silent conference, both looked up at the same time.

"When you're ready to book your flight home," Laurent said to Nicole, "get the credit card from either me or Aunt Maggie."

"Thank you, Uncle Laurent," Nicole said with a small frown.

Maggie wasn't surprised to see that Nicole appeared at least mildly conflicted. She looked at Luc who was now staring at his plate.

"May Luc and I be excused?" Nicole said, standing up. Luc also stood and grabbed both of their plates.

"Let the dogs out while you're up," Laurent said, as he spooned up another serving of the potato-topped pie.

Nicole and Luc left the house through the French doors that led to the garden.

"Are you sure your hand doesn't hurt, Jem?" Maggie asked.

"Nope. Is there dessert?"

"There is *chocolat* mousse," Laurent said. "You may eat it in the salon."

Jemmy jumped up, plate in hand, to disappear into the kitchen.

"Luc seems much better."

Laurent grunted.

"We need to talk to Nicole," Maggie said, "about what happened today. This is the sort of thing that can erode trust and ruin families."

"You are so American."

"Laurent, this is a very big deal! Nicole now knows she was adopted. No! It's worse than that because we never even bothered to legally do that."

"I am fairly sure she is too old for it now."

"None of this bothers you at all? The fact that we lied to her? To everyone? For years?"

"It bothers me that Nicole is upset. But other than that what has really changed?"

Maggie sagged in her chair and looked through the French doors where she could no longer see Luc and Nicole.

"Only everything," she said.

44

L aurent put the leftovers away as Maggie retired to her study. He knew the situation with Nicole was very upsetting for Maggie. He cursed himself that he'd been so sloppy as to have been the one to reveal the secret.

But in the end, it was still the truth and a truth he and Maggie had always intended to give to Nikki when the time came. He patted his shirt pocket for his cigarettes and glanced through the French doors where he could see Nicole and Luc walking back to the house in the dusk.

It had been fortuitous after all, sending Luc to find Nicole today. He had helped settle the girl. Laurent could see that it had helped settle Luc too.

Orphan to orphan, Laurent thought as he watched them.

Laurent still didn't know what to make of Luc's behavior. Hot one minute, cold and angry the next. Perhaps it was only being a teenager—something Laurent had no parental experience of dealing with.

He watched Luc reach for Nicole's hand and they walked hand in hand. Laurent tried to imagine Gerard doing something so simple and sweet.

He stood up when they came in, both dogs bounding ahead of them.

"Start on the dishes," he said to Luc. "Nicole, you can help him."

He didn't wait for her response but went to the door and stepped outside, closing the French doors behind him.

He gazed out toward his vineyard which was cut into four quadrants by two narrow dirt tracks. In the fall when the weather was pleasant, he and Maggie would often take the dogs for an after dinner walk down one of the tracks.

He walked to the edge of the terrace and lit a cigarette, allowing his thoughts to quiet.

Laurent often imagined his Uncle Nicolas, the man who'd left him Domaine St-Buvard, standing on this back terrace and surveying his vineyard. He sometimes wondered what the man must have thought as he gazed out at his land.

Without a wife or family, it was hard to imagine what the vineyard had meant to Uncle Nicolas beyond its ability to support him.

Still, the fact that he'd left it to Laurent—his only living relative but also someone he'd only met a few times—in Laurent's mind spoke of Nicolas's desire to keep the land in the family.

To sustain his legacy.

Laurent heard the snick as the French doors opened but didn't turn around. Maggie's footstep was as familiar to him as any sound he knew in his life.

This tread was not hers.

"I remember the first time I came here," Nicole said from behind him. "Remember?"

"Of course."

"It was Thanksgiving and I found that horrible pumpkin in the vineyard. The one that had been left for us by that awful man. Later when I was older Grandad told me it had been a warning."

Nicole was leaning against the waist-high dry stone wall that enclosed the kitchen *potager*. At this time of year, the tomatoes and beans were ripe. The cabbages and lettuces were visible from where he stood.

"Don't think I'm not still super mad at you because I am," she said.

Even in the gloom of the dusk, he could see her scowl.

"*Je comprends*," he said.

"And I'm not ready to talk about it yet."

Laurent allowed the silence to grow between them.

"I can't tell you how betrayed I feel," she said.

"I know."

"On top of that I feel guilty because a part of me was glad Jemmy got hurt when he did because it meant you couldn't come after me."

She shivered and took a long breath.

"After Luc found me in the vineyard we talked—you know his English isn't that bad. He's just shy about it."

Nicole moved closer to Laurent and stared out at the vineyard.

"He told me that lately he'd been thinking along the same lines as me." She looked at him. "I'm not going to tell you the details because that's for Luc."

"I understand."

"But him being an orphan and then suddenly being rescued by you guys last fall was a little bit like what happened to me today except I never knew I was an orphan."

Nicole sniffed noisily. Laurent wanted to hold her but she wasn't ready. She had more to say.

Nicole wiped the tears from her face. "All I could think of was, well, now I'm totally alone," she said in a small voice. "I mean, even after all those years of birthday parties and my own pony and being loved by Grandma and Grandad and you and Aunt Maggie and Uncle Ben and everyone, all I could think of was that none of it was real."

She took in a long breath.

"Luc said he recently figured out that family is not really about who gave birth to whom."

Her words slammed into Laurent and he tossed away his cigarette, watching it make a fiery arc in the night air. He cleared his throat. "He said that?"

"Yeah. He said he hoped it wouldn't take me as long to figure that out as it did him because in the meantime it feels so bad...the feeling like you don't belong."

"Especially when you do."

At his words, she turned to him and Laurent caught her in his arms and held her. In a moment, she relaxed.

He kept one arm around her shoulders and looked back at his vineyard—the vineyard he knew he would someday hand down toMila, Jemmy and Luc.

And as he stood there, the sound of cicadas buzzing loudly in the air perfumed by the hedge of lavender that grew beside the terrace, he also knew without a doubt that Luc must never know the truth of his paternity.

45

Sunday lunch at *Dormir* was a weekly ritual of rich food, exotic *salade composées* and complicated desserts for the benefit of whichever guests were staying there, but also for family and friends.

Maggie knew it had taken Laurent time to adjust to the idea of having strangers at the big weekly meal, but she and Grace helped him see that just as the bedrooms of *Dormir* were outfitted in high-thread count sheets with fat lavender scented pillows and vivid prints of Cézanne and Matisse on its walls, providing an authentic French Sunday lunch was yet another feature on offer at the bed and breakfast that helped complete the whole experience.

Besides, they had all winter to enjoy their Sundays without paying guests.

Maggie was hoping that today would provide a better opportunity to talk with Nicole. Friends and family milling around a beautiful garden in a relaxed atmosphere might afford the perfect moment for Nicole to hear Maggie's apologies—as well as her reasons why she did what she did all those years ago.

Laurent had packed a hamper with the basics for the day's meal—his homemade tapenade and gazpacho as well as the lamb chops and salad ingredients. Normally they would take two cars, but since they were down a car, they all piled into Laurent's Citroën with Maggie and Laurent in the front seat, the three children in the back and the trunk and floor boards groaning with their provisions.

The meal would take the full afternoon to prepare and consume. Over the years Maggie had gotten used to the practice and come to enjoy these weekly lunches as a time to relax, to indulge and to reflect on the week.

Today, Laurent was planning on starting with Coquille St-Jacques scallops, a cold vegetable soup, grilled lamb chops and a salad, and end with a cheese course. Mila and Zouzou had made a *gâteau au citron* for dessert.

As they drove into the gravel drive in front of *Dormir* Grace met their car. She carried young Philippe on one hip. The child was dark-skinned with thick hair that Grace kept cut short. He always had a ready smile but particularly when he spotted Laurent.

"We've been watching for you," Grace said as Maggie and Laurent got out of the car.

"Papa!" Philippe squealed at the sight of Laurent. He reached both chubby arms out to him and Laurent paused long enough in unloading the car to take the boy from Grace. He kissed his cheek and gathered up the bags and baskets of the produce needed for today's meal.

Jem, Nicole and Luc were already heading for the house, their arms full of bags and baskets of food.

"Are we going to be able to eat outside do you think?" Grace asked as Maggie scooped up a bag of baguettes they'd bought on the way. She turned to walk with Grace into the main house.

"I thought it looked like rain?" Grace said.

"Laurent has forbidden it," Maggie said with a laugh. "Where are your guests?"

Grace made a face. "You'll meet them later but I think they're going to pass on lunch. Idiots."

Maggie entered the foyer of *Dormir*. Laurent was already in the kitchen with Luc, Nicole, Mila and Zouzou. Danielle stood by the stove conferring with him.

"*Bonjour*, Danielle!" Maggie called and made kissing noises in the air.

Danielle waved to her but continued talking to Laurent in very fast French.

The main kitchen at *Dormir* had been renovated when Laurent bought the place three years earlier. Since then Grace and Danielle had added their touches so that the room featured open cabinetry against the stonework and exposed wooden beams. Sunshine poured in from the front window.

"Do you want coffee, darling?" Grace asked.

"I've had too much as it is," Maggie said. "Can we get going? I promised Laurent I'd be back in time to help with lunch."

"Absolutely," Grace said, turning to pick up her car keys from an antique painted hall table. "I feel like we haven't talked in ages."

As soon as Grace settled into the driver's seat and maneuvered her SUV around the two rental cars parked in her driveway belonging to her American guests, and the further she drove away from *Dormir*, the more Maggie watched her relax.

"Crazy last couple of days?" Maggie asked.

"Why? Has Danielle said something?"

"What? No, not at all. You just seem a little tense."

"Well, honestly I could use a vacation from all the people on vacation if you want to know."

"I probably shouldn't let Mila spend so much time at *Dormir*," Maggie said.

"Don't be silly. She is a great help. And she's so good with the baby."

"He really is a little doll and so good-natured."

"He has his moments, trust me. But yes, when I'm not falling down exhausted at the end of the day I can actually appreciate how darling he is."

"You know, before everything at my house went ass-over-apple-carts I had this idea that Nicole might help you at *Dormir*. I'm sure she'd be a big help with Philippe."

Grace gave Maggie a sideways look. "Nicole has no interest in a summer job at *Dormir*."

"She might if she gave it a chance."

Laurent had told Maggie about his conversation with Nicole the night before and while it encouraged Maggie to believe that someday Nicole would forgive them for what they'd done, she knew that the important thing hadn't changed.

Nicole was still completely resistant to living in France.

"I see that Luc and Nicole have become very chummy," Grace said. "I already mentioned to Laurent that you need to be careful about that. Better to nip it in the bud now. They are after all brother and sister."

"Except they're not," Maggie said with a sigh.

Grace frowned and took her eyes off the road to look at her. "Does Laurent now believe that Luc is *not* Gerard's son?"

"No, that's unassailable. Short of having him take a DNA test we know he's Gerard's son."

Grace's mouth fell open. "Are you saying Nicole *isn't* your sister's daughter?"

"Pretty much."

Grace let out a small gasp. "How long have you known?"

"I didn't know when I brought her to Atlanta thirteen years ago. I found out later."

"How much later?"

"Pretty soon afterwards," Maggie admitted.

"Who else knows?"

"Well, everybody now except my mom and brother. But up until yesterday, only me and Laurent. And Roger Bentley and Gerard before they died. Gerard knew because the real Nicole died on his watch."

Grace clucked her tongue sadly. "How?"

"He was supposed to be taking care of her. They were living on a boat in the Cannes harbor. She fell overboard and drowned. Gerard didn't even notice until the next morning."

"May he roast in hell. And your sister never knew?"

"No. Elise was in Lyons in rehab at the time. She thought the child I brought back with me to the US was Nicole." Maggie sighed. "Obviously, as soon as Elise got back to Atlanta and saw the child she would have realized it wasn't her daughter."

"But that never happened."

"No, because Elise was murdered first."

"And Nicole didn't know any of this?"

"Not until yesterday when she accidentally found out."

"Poor girl."

"She's furious with us. Well, mostly me."

"You can't blame her. It's a terrible thing to wrap your mind around."

"I know. I just wish she'd let me help her but she's still too angry."

"I'm so sorry, sweetie. I'm especially sorry if Nicole can't see how much she's loved. But she will, once the shock wears off."

"Laurent said that she told him that Luc made her feel a little better about it when he told her *he* wasn't blood-related to us either but he knew we still loved him. She said it helped."

Grace frowned. "Except..."

Maggie sighed. "Right. Except Luc *is* related to us and now Laurent doesn't think he can ever tell him."

"Because then Luc will think you only took him in because he was Laurent's nephew."

"Exactly."

"What a mess."

Maggie watched the flat green scenery of the treeless landscaping fly by as they approached the city limits of Marseille.

"I was so convinced that if I found out who killed Leon Boucher," Maggie said, "it would fix things with Nicole. But none of that can fix this."

"How's the investigation going?"

"I talked to a bunch of people who knew the victim and they either loved him or hated him or they loved him *and* hated him."

"I Googled him after I talked with you," Grace said as she exited onto Canebière towards the city's famed harbor. "Leon Boucher really did seem like a very unpleasant man."

"He was a racist and a homophobe—except he had a boyfriend—and he was a serial adulterer."

"Gee. I wonder why someone wanted to kill him?"

"I know, right? Everyone I talked to had a reason to kill him."

"But who had the best reason?"

Maggie frowned at Grace's question.

"Who stood to benefit financially?" Grace asked. "His wife?"

"Possibly. She was divorcing him so she might not have come out of the marriage with much."

"So that's certainly a motive, wouldn't you say? And what about Boucher's political opponent? He wins the election now, hands down, right? That's a pretty big benefit."

"Mohammed Olivier. I talked to him but I have to say my gut told me he was just a nice guy trying to do right by Marseille."

"So because you like his politics, you think he's not capable of murder? I'm surprised at you, darling. Did you know that in the old days in Marseille the politicians would openly attempt to assassinate each other?"

"Times were more brutal back then."

"I'm talking 1965."

"Well, it doesn't matter. I promised Laurent and everyone else that I'd leave it alone."

"Oh, well then. If you promised."

"Don't be flip, Grace. The only reason I did as much as I did was because I thought it would help Nicole get closure on seeing Leon's dead body."

"You mean you thought it would change her mind about staying in France."

"That too."

"And now you don't think you need to do that?"

Maggie gnawed on a nail. "Well, frankly I don't see how it could hurt for me to wrap this up. And now that you mention it, Mohammad Olivier *was* a little evasive when I talked to him. For one thing he never mentioned that his wife worked with him."

"Is that important?"

"I don't know. It's not really a lie, I guess," she said and then sighed "See? He's just squeaky clean."

"*Nobody* in politics is squeaky clean. How much were you able to find out about his background?"

Maggie pulled out her cell phone and opened up the browser windows she'd bookmarked.

"He has a really impressive background of working for the community," Maggie said. "He's done hundreds of hours of community service and he even led the gay pride parade one year."

"He's gay?"

"No. He's just supportive."

As Maggie scanned the website page, she noticed a group

picture of Olivier's campaign office. She pointed to the small blonde in the back row. "That's his wife, Cayenne."

Grace frowned at the picture. "She's pretty," she conceded, handing the phone back.

Maggie scanned the rest of the crowd and then froze.

"Crap," she said.

"What is it?"

Maggie looked at Grace and then back at the picture. "I can't believe I missed this." She held the phone up to Grace and pointed to a tall man in the picture. "That's Danon Chastain. Leon's boyfriend."

Why didn't Danon mention he worked for his boyfriend's sworn enemy?

"Huh," Grace said with a shrug. "Hardly a surprise, is it? I mean a gay man can hardly work for a neo-Nazi party."

"I guess not," Maggie said. But it bothered her that Danon hadn't mentioned it to her.

They were silent for a moment.

"You know you need to let Nicole go back home to the States," Grace said.

"She's already booked her ticket."

"Sweetie, France works for you. For us. In spades. It's literally saved my life and I wouldn't trade it for any place on Earth. But at this point, Nicole is a dyed in the wool, card-carrying American teenager. Making her stay here will not change the past."

"That's what Laurent said."

"Well, he's right. You need to snap out of it. Otherwise people might think you're more interested in easing your own guilt about what you did thirteen years ago than about what's best for Nicole right now."

Maggie turned to her, her face stricken. "I've been horrible."

"Not horrible. Just not open to anyone else's view of things."

"It's because I was so sure I could fix this."

"I don't think there was anything that needed fixing, darling. Except maybe in your own head."

"And now look where I am. How am I ever going to get her to forgive me?"

"She will. In time. Things happen in families. Eventually we all find our way back home."

46

After picking up her car from the police impound lot, Maggie took her time driving back to *Dormir*, stopping to pick up yet more baguettes—Laurent preferred the *traditionales*—at a village *boulangerie* along the way.

Her talk with Grace had been helpful. If nothing else, she saw now that she'd been content to cross Olivier off her list based on just one visit and her gut instinct.

Fine detective you are.

Grace was right, she thought with fresh determination. Olivier had more to gain than anyone from Leon's murder. He definitely warranted another interview.

She arrived back at *Dormir* fifteen minutes after Grace but just moments before it was time to sit down. Grace's *gîte* guests —an American couple with a young child—had changed their minds about going off for the day and were now seated at the long wooden outdoor dining table that Laurent and Luc had dragged into the garden.

Because Laurent had designed the garden at *Dormir*, including its *potager*, it resembled the garden at Domaine St-

Buvard. A platoon of ancient olive and fig trees lined a pebbled path from the terrace leading to the grape fields beyond. Strong scents of rosemary, woodsmoke and lavender filled the air.

The luncheon table set up in the garden had been spread with Grace's good linen tablecloth. Zouzou and Mila had lined the center of the table with sunflowers and daisies in faience jars along with tapers in case the lunch extended into the evening as it often did.

Jemmy was busy positioning chairs around the table and showing off his emergency room bandage to any and all. Zouzou was minding Philippe although Mila was staying close too.

Nicole stood alone at the garden gate staring off into space, lost in thought.

Maggie handed the baguettes to Danielle. "Everything looks beautiful," she said.

"Thank your husband for that," Danielle said, taking the bread as she examined the table with a critical eye.

Whenever Maggie thought about it, it was always hard to believe that this house had once been the setting of Danielle's first marriage and of some of the most miserable and lonely years of Danielle's life.

But now Danielle lived here at the center of a bustling family. She was loved and admired, her days filled with activity and purpose, her words listened to and respected.

"Jemmy," Danielle called. "It's time to serve the *apéros*."

Jemmy hurried toward the kitchen where Maggie knew Laurent would have a tray of fluted glasses filled with *kir* and champagne.

Maggie walked over to Nicole. It was a typical summer day in Provence, but for a change not too hot. Maggie imagined they might even need cotton sweaters towards evening.

"Did I hear Luc trying to teach you some French this morning?" Maggie said as she approached. "You sounded good."

"It doesn't mean I ever want to come back to this horrible country. And I'm still really mad at you, Aunt Maggie."

Maggie didn't know whether to be glad or discouraged that Nicole had gone back to calling her "aunt."

"I know. And you have every right to be. I just want you to know that Laurent and I love you and that the only thing we ever intended to—"

Nicole held up her hand.

"Stop. Just stop. I hate good intentions. It allows all kinds of despicable behavior."

"Okay. But have you fully processed the fact that—in our defense—we thought you really were Elise's daughter at first? It's not like we intentionally kidnapped you."

"Uncle Laurent knew."

Crap. That's true. Laurent knew all along she wasn't the real Nicole.

Nicole made a face. "You act like you deserve a medal for not throwing me back once you found out I wasn't really your niece."

Maggie bit her tongue. No good would come from responding.

"The real crime wasn't in keeping it a secret from me," Nicole continued. "The real crime was kidnapping me to begin with!"

Maggie took a steadying breath.

"It's just that," Maggie said slowly, measuring her words, "I really believe that bringing you to the US did not negatively impact your life."

"How can you say that? I had a mother here! A *real* mother, not a ghost!"

Maggie knew that now was not the time to tell Nicole about her real mother. Nicole turned and walked away. She went straight to Luc and into his arms. Behind Luc, Maggie saw Laurent standing and watching them.

Thirteen years ago, after Roger Bentley had found the child he would later pass off as Nicole Newberry he'd told Laurent that she was an abused child.

As far as Maggie was concerned, the fact that Nicole today had no memory of her early life was nothing less than a blessing.

Lunch was its usual extravaganza. The scallops were poached in white wine, gratinéed and served in individual scallop shells. Danielle had pulled fresh green beans straight from the garden which were plated alongside the lamb chops which were grilled with lemon and rosemary sprigs.

Laurent allowed Luc and Jemmy to man the grill and the lamb was perfectly pink and aromatic. A simple vinaigrette salad and an expansive cheese course followed the lamb.

While Maggie noticed that Nicole spent much of the meal deliberately avoiding eye contact with her, she also knew they'd made strides in their brief conversation in the garden.

Little Philippe and the American couple's baby—an adorable toddler by the name of Hannah—both went down for naps after lunch before the cheese course and coffee, allowing their parents—or grandparent in Grace's case—a relaxing continuation of their Sunday lunch.

Laurent had outdone himself again. Maggie marveled at how many times she'd thought those very same words over the years.

When Zouzou and Mila brought out their *gâteau au citron* to gentle applause plus a few groans, Maggie slipped away to the house to freshen up.

All day she'd debated canceling out on the meeting Gaston had set up with his mother.

She was painfully aware that she had promised both Laurent and Jean-Baptiste that she would stop any semblance of an investigation. A raised eyebrow and a meaningful look from Laurent here and there throughout last night as well as today reminded her that he was still less than amused to have had to escort her from the Marseille jail yesterday.

While she didn't remember outright promising Laurent that she'd refrain from doing any more digging into Boucher's murder, she knew that *he* believed that that point had been agreed upon.

She went to the guest bathroom to wash her hands and run a comb through her hair.

Besides, she now knew that solving the murder wouldn't mean a thing to Nicole. It wouldn't help her view France differently.

As Maggie returned to the table she saw Grace and Danielle were making coffee in the kitchen. She paused and pulled out her phone to text Gaston and tell him she couldn't make it tomorrow after all.

Before she could find his number a text came in.

She blinked in surprise.

It was from Mohammad Olivier.

<theres something I should have told you. Meet me tonight?>

Maggie looked at her watch. Gaston had set the meeting with his mother for tomorrow at five o'clock. She felt a burst of excitement.

She could meet with Madame Boucher and then swing by and meet Olivier and be home by seven. Laurent had mentioned he had work to do at the monastery.

He would never even know she was gone.

"Coffee, darling?" Grace called to her.

Maggie gave her a thumbs up and quickly texted Olivier back.

<Tonight is no good. Tomorrow at fourteen hundred hours?>

She forced herself not to add any happy face emojis to indicate how truly delighted she was that she was going to get a second crack at him.

When he texted back <*OK*> she felt a flush of satisfaction. It wasn't like *she'd* approached *him*, she told herself. All she was doing was responding to a request as any polite, normal person would!

Meanwhile she'd need to outline a few crucial questions for him—starting with *why did you say your wife was with you at the rally the day Leon died when there's no trace of her on the video?*

While her adrenalin was pumping, Maggie scrolled through her message contacts until she found Danon's number and fired off a text to him.

<*why didn't you tell me you worked for Olivier's campaign?*>

Feeling in control once more with the direction of things, she made her way back to the luncheon table in the garden. Laurent was talking to the American wife and Maggie could already see that she was downright moony-eyed over him. She kept wetting her lips and laughing at everything he said. Her husband was a little less enthralled but Grace moved to sit on his other side and was doing her best to keep the peace.

Maggie noticed that now that Nicole had her ticket back home, she was much more relaxed. She and Luc continued to only have eyes for each other. They left the table to wander through the garden.

Laurent turned to Maggie and put an absent hand on her arm. Maggie thought she could see the American wife's eyes narrowing at the gesture and Maggie felt a burst of love for Laurent.

An eruption of laughter came from the garden where Jem, Mila and Zouzou were lighting lanterns. Maggie and the children would spend the night at *Dormir*.

Laurent would go home to Domaine St-Buvard to take care of the dogs. He had an early morning appointment with the new vineyard pickers but would swing by and pick up Luc and Jemmy before heading to the vineyard.

Maggie heard the melodic ping that signaled a text had come in on her phone. She looked and saw she'd gotten a response from Danon.

<Who'd you think Id campaign for? Goebbels? I loved the MAN. NOT his politics!>

Ignoring Laurent's annoyed frown when he saw her using her phone at the table, Maggie excused herself and walked away, punching Danon's phone number in as she went.

She didn't bother with a greeting when he picked up.

"That didn't upset Leon?" she asked. "Knowing you were working for the enemy?"

"He didn't love it naturally. In fact at first he tried to get me to spy for him. But only at first. He backed off after that. I'm sorry you never met him. He could be so charming he made you want to march to the beat of his tune. I mean, even *I* found the whole thing hard to believe—me, in love with a neo-Nazi?"

"So he really was a Nazi?"

"That's just it! No! He liked to put on that he was but it was mostly for show."

"Really?"

"Yes, really!" Danon laughed. "I mean, have I mentioned I'm also *Jewish*?"

47

That night Maggie surprised herself at how tired she was. Between treading a fine line with Nicole, helping to clean up after the Sunday lunch, the drive to Marseille and planning all her largely covert assignations for the following day, she fell into bed and was instantly asleep.

The next morning she was awakened by the insistent fragrance of just-brewed coffee. By the time she found her way to the kitchen, she was clearly the last one up. Laurent had brought *brioches*, croissants and *pains au chocolat*. He sat at the kitchen table in the kitchen with Philippe on his knee. Philippe was working on a brioche slice covered with jam.

The American guests had opted to skip breakfast in favor of an early lavender farm tour.

Maggie poured herself a cup of coffee and found the creamer on the counter.

"So is today the day you meet this year's pickers?" she asked Laurent.

"We have already met them," Luc said. "Now we are showing them the ropes."

"I'm going too," Nicole said from her seat beside Luc. "I want to see the process."

"If you stay a little longer," Laurent said, "you can see the harvest."

Nicole glanced at Luc. "Maybe next time."

"Zouzou and I are making a cherry *clafoutis* today," Mila said, looking from Laurent to Maggie.

"Is that okay with you?" Maggie asked Grace.

"Of course," Grace said. "Philippe and I welcome any and all attempts to make *clafoutis*."

"I will pick her up on my way home," Laurent said. "Everyone ready? Luc? Why don't you drive?"

Luc's eyes lit up as he took the keys from Laurent and hurried out the door with Jemmy and Nicole following.

"Looks like you have that all sorted out," Danielle remarked to Laurent.

He kissed her cheek and then leaned over and kissed Maggie. "Don't be late tonight," he said.

Maggie was astonished that he knew she was going out. She'd been all prepared to talk about the long hours of work she had to do on her newsletter. The truth was she *did* have several long hours of work to do on her newsletter.

Right after she got back from Marseille.

Within an hour of driving herself home and spending a frustrating morning trying to sort out which artist to showcase in her newsletter, Maggie was more than ready to shut her office door and set out for Marseille. She'd made a list of questions for both Madame Boucher and Mohammed Olivier.

She wanted to be able to ask them as unthreateningly as possible, so her sheet of questions also had tips about the way she should ask her questions.

She arrived in Marseille at just before one o'clock and parked on the residential street of the Boucher apartment. On the drive in she'd thought long and hard about exactly who

Leon Boucher was. In the end she decided he was a total conundrum. He was in love with a Jewish man and yet was campaigning on a platform of anti-Semitism, intolerance and racism.

Was Leon just so determined to be famous and powerful that he didn't care *what* the world thought he stood for? If you asked his son, Gaston would probably say yes.

Maggie also spent some time wondering what new information Gaston could possibly have for her.

And why he couldn't have just told her in a text or over the phone.

She walked to the front door, rang the bell and when the intercom crackled on once more asked for Gaston.

And once more she was told that Gaston was not in.

"No," Maggie said firmly to the disembodied voice. "Do not hang up on me! Gaston Boucher told me to come here today. I have an appointment to see him and his mother so do not tell me…"

"Madame Boucher is expecting you," the voice intoned as the buzzer released the lock on the outside door.

The dramatic entryway of the apartment showcased high ceilings, a marble foyer and a set of massive gold-framed mirrors that made the apartment look even bigger to Maggie.

She felt her sandals sink into the thick carpet as she followed the maid who led her into the main salon.

Maggie found it mildly annoying that Gaston had said he'd meet her here and then hadn't even texted her to tell her he couldn't. But at least she was finally getting to meet his mother.

"Madame Boucher," the maid announced in a voice laced with boredom.

Maggie wasn't sure whether the maid was addressing Marie-France Boucher or announcing her for Maggie's benefit.

At first she had trouble seeing anyone in the dim lighting. The room faced the street with floor to ceiling windows but they were clad with heavy drapes, possibly even black-out curtains.

"*Bonjour* Madame Boucher," Maggie said, probing the shadowy recesses of the room with her eyes to pick out the woman in it.

"Come closer so I may see you," a slurred voice said.

The unwelcome memory of a Grimm's fairytale came to Maggie's mind but she stepped toward the couch and the source of the voice. As she did, she saw the shape of a woman—nearly indistinguishable from the dark settee.

Maggie cleared her throat. Now that she was closer she could see the array of bottles on the coffee table. And not wine bottles either.

Gin. Vodka. Whiskey.

"My name is Maggie Dernier," Maggie said, opting to use her married French name in hopes it might feel less foreign and therefore less threatening to Madame Boucher. "I wanted to extend my condolences for your loss."

"Eh?" The woman sat up and a glimmer of light entering the room through the foyer revealed her face.

Madame Boucher blinked rapidly. "Are you Angeline?"

"What? No," Maggie said. "I hate to bother you at a time like this but I was hoping you could answer a few questions for me."

"You are not Angeline?"

Just how drunk is she?

Maggie moved closer to the couch and sat down on a nearby tub chair.

Did she dare ask Madame Boucher where she was during the time Leon was murdered? Had the police already gotten an alibi from her?

"If you're looking for Leon, you just missed him," Madame Boucher said with disgust.

Maggie pinched her lips together. "I'm not looking for Leon. I'm looking for the person who killed him. Do you have any idea who that might be?"

"What is your name again?"

"Maggie Dernier. I'm a reporter."

Maggie wasn't sure anything she said to this woman was going to make sense. But it was just possible Madame Boucher might say something useful.

"A reporter?"

When dealing with a crazy or drunk person—something Maggie had had considerable experience with over the years—she often found it helpful to be as provocative as possible. It usually tipped the drunk or crazy person over the edge into revealing things they might normally try to keep secret.

"We have a lead given to us that says that you, Madame Boucher, might know who killed your husband. Is that true?"

Marie-France Boucher stared at Maggie as if trying to make up her mind before slowly standing up. Maggie was surprised she was steady enough to do it.

"Very well," Marie-France said. "Since you asked, I'll tell you."

Does she really know who killed Leon?

Maggie tried to tamp down her excitement at the thought of at least getting a good lead.

"Do you know who killed your husband, Madame Boucher?" she asked.

"I guess I do," Madame Boucher said with a shrug. "Since it was me."

48

Maggie was sure she hadn't heard correctly.

"Come again?"

"I killed him," Madame Boucher said wearily, rubbing her stomach and looking around the room as if hunting for the thing that appeared to be making her nauseated. "I stabbed him with one of Gaston's needles. Here." She pointed to the front of her throat.

Maggie felt a wave of confusion.

Was she really confessing to killing her husband?

Maggie knew she should be thrilled to hear this but instead something bothered her about the confession. Something just didn't sound right.

Maggie pulled out her cell phone and turned on the recording function.

"Could I ask you to repeat that?"

"I killed my husband," Marie-France said loudly, wavering on her feet now. "Stabbed him in the throat." Then she snorted. "Do you really need to ask why?"

Yeah, probably not.

She would leave uncovering the motive—of which she had

no doubt there would be copious ones—to Jean-Baptiste's team.

"His whores. The way he treated our son. His verbal... verbal..." She looked dumbfounded for a moment.

"Abuse?" Maggie added helpfully and then cursed the fact that she'd done it on the recorder. She didn't want to appear to be leading the witness. Even one falling down drunk.

"Yes. Verbal abuse. All the time. Glad to kill him. Happy to kill him. Kill him all day long."

Could someone this screwed up have waited for Leon in a public parking lot, accosted him, killed him, stuffed him in the first available car trunk, and then disappeared without anyone seeing her?

It seemed highly unlikely.

But in Maggie's experience stranger things had happened. She had her confession. If Jean-Baptiste wouldn't accept her recording as admissible it shouldn't take too much official questioning to get Madame Boucher to repeat it in an interview room down at the Marseille police department.

Marie-France started to move but bumped her legs against the coffee table. She yelped and toppled backward onto the couch. Maggie stood up, unsure of how to help when the maid appeared.

The maid pulled Marie-France to her feet and with her arm around the older woman's waist began to walk her across the living room.

"Madame go to toilet," the maid said to Maggie. "You wait here."

Maggie waited until she heard the bathroom door close in the hall and then jumped to her feet and ran after them. The apartment was laid out with the salon in the center and a hall branching off to the bathroom and what looked like three bedrooms.

Maggie went to the first room she came to, glancing over

her shoulder at the hall bath although she couldn't imagine they would be finished any time soon. She opened the door and saw it was a bedroom.

An ornate Egyptian handmade window screen was perched over the top of a four-poster bed. The walls were decorated with a series of framed Impressionist oil paintings. Opposite the bed was a marble fireplace and mantle.

It was clearly Marie-France's room.

Maggie went to the dresser and pulled open the top drawer. Inside was a jumble of silk lingerie and lavender sachets. The second drawer contained nightgowns. The third, sweaters and pullovers.

Next she went to the bed and opened the drawer in the bedside table and was surprised to see there was nothing in it. Not a notepad or book or a pot of petroleum jelly or a tissue.

She turned and listened. She could still hear them in the middle bathroom but she knew she needed to hurry. She saw an ornately painted door across the room and hurried over to it. Inside she found two bars of hanging clothes, a rack of expensive Italian shoes and in the back, a matched set of lavender-colored luggage. A big brass G on the handle told her the luggage was Gucci.

Through the thin walls she could heard Marie-France coughing. She closed the closet door and turned to see another door beside it.

Praying she didn't open it and find Marie-France and the maid inside, Maggie eased open the door and saw it was a small half bath. She stepped inside and went straight to the medicine cabinet.

All she needed to find was a packet of needles. Needles, when Marie-France had no reason to have needles. Presumably the woman wasn't diabetic or a drug addict. Finding needles among her things would go a long way to supporting her confession—even a drunken one.

Hard evidence always trumped words.

Maggie sorted through the bottles of pills in the cabinet, the face creams and serums, and pots of unguent.

No needles. At least not here. She picked up a prescription bottle out of curiosity and stared at the label. *Loperamide.*

"What in the world is loperamide?" she said under her breath, starting to put the bottle back.

"It is medication for chronic diarrhea," a voice said from the bathroom door.

Maggie jumped, dropping the bottle in the process. The maid stood there watching her.

"You were to wait in the other room," the maid said.

"I...I had to use the toilet," Maggie said feebly.

The maid came into the bathroom and began to pick up the pills from the floor.

Had the maid just left Marie-France leaning against a wall somewhere? Surely she hadn't gotten her to the couch already?

The maid straightened up and put the pills back inside the medicine cabinet.

"I never heard of *loperamide*," Maggie said lamely, as if trying to explain what she was doing with the bottle in her hand.

"Madame has Crohn's Disease. Its symptoms are quite severe and immediate."

Oh snap! So that's why the maid hustled her to the bathroom. It wasn't to throw up.

"As a result of her affliction," the maid said ominously, "Madame can never be far from a toilet at any time."

49

W*ell, that settles that*, Maggie thought as she got in her car in front of the house. No matter what Marie-France said or how badly she wanted to confess, her affliction made it extremely unlikely she could have killed her husband.

Even waiting in the parking lot for Leon to show up would have been untenable for someone with Crohn's Disease. There were no public facilities in the parking lot and the killer couldn't have used the airport facilities—they were too far away —or he or she would have risked missing Leon.

Not only that but as she sat in her car it had finally occurred to her what had bothered her about Madame Boucher's confession. She'd pointed to the front of her throat to indicate where she'd injected her husband when she killed him.

But Denis Chevalier's photograph had clearly shown the injection site was at the side of his neck.

No, as nice and tidy as a confession would have been, Marie-France Boucher couldn't have done it.

Maggie drummed her fingers on the steering wheel. There was something else that bothered her about her visit that she couldn't quite put her finger on. It was either something Marie-France had said or something Maggie had seen that she now couldn't reassemble in her brain. But something had felt weirdly *familiar* to her.

She had to believe it would reveal itself in time.

She pulled her phone out and glanced at the address Olivier had sent her the night before. The address was close to the wharf. She wasn't familiar with that particular section of Marseille.

It definitely did not look like a nice area of town.

Maggie called up a Google Earth image of the address and as she suspected saw that the street was filled with warehouses and industrial storage facilities. It was not residential. Yes, the water was near. But the familiarity of that gave her no comfort. The whole area looked creepy.

On the other hand, she had to admit that most things she looked at on Google Earth looked vaguely creepy.

She had finished her visit with Marie-France exactly on time. Now if she could meet up with Olivier in the next thirty minutes, she could be on her way home with plenty of time to stop and pick up a *baguette* for dinner.

Tonight was Nicole's last night at Domaine St-Buvard before flying home in the morning and Laurent intended to make it an event.

As far as Maggie was concerned, tonight was just a manifestation of how badly she'd failed Nicole in every way. She'd failed to convince her to stay the full summer. She'd failed to mitigate her horror over what happened to her when she landed in Marseille. She'd failed to present the most sensitive and ultimately destructive information to her about her origins in a way that the girl could handle.

She'd failed miserably on every point.

As she followed the map on her phone to the address Olivier had given her she noticed that the street population had dwindled significantly until she pulled up outside a massive garage door.

The fact that Olivier wanted to meet her offsite told Maggie he had something to tell her that he didn't want his people to know—or perhaps, more specifically, his wife Cayenne. That was exciting to Maggie and the main reason she'd been happy to meet him here.

She checked to make sure the battery on her phone was good and then pulled out a notebook. Normally she would leave her purse in the car but the street didn't feel safe. She might not be overtly attacked—although that was always possible—but a car break-in was a definite possibility on a street like this.

In the end she decided not to lock the car so as not to come back to a broken window even though she was well aware that an unlocked car was how she'd gotten into this mess in the first place.

Let's just get this over with.

She left her car unlocked and walked up to the garage door. There was a small door beside it. Olivier's text said to punch in a code which he'd also sent and the smaller door would unlock.

Annoyed at all the cloak and dagger and telling herself that it had better be worth it, Maggie punched in the numbers from his text and slipped through the small door.

Inside she found herself in a narrow hall. She felt her irritation ratchet up with every step to match her nervousness.

This had better be worth it.

At the end of the hall was another door. She tried it and found it unlocked. But before going through the door she fished out her phone and sent Olivier a text.

<*Im here. Where R U?*>

Then she took in a breath and pushed through the door into a large darkened space. She fumbled on the wall for a light switch but found none. She turned on the flashlight feature of her phone and played its beam along the walls of the enclosure. Instantly she saw that she was in a large triple bay garage area. Empty wooden shelving lined the walls all the way to the twenty-foot ceiling.

"Monsieur Olivier?"

Furious and feeling her fear crawl up her throat, Maggie turned to go back through the door.

The handle wouldn't turn. The door had locked behind her.

Her heart began to beat fast. She forced herself to take a breath and then counted her heart beats to steady her breathing.

Olivier would be here soon. There was no reason to panic.

Mustering her courage, she stepped to the center of the space, playing her beam slowly down the nearest wall as her doubts began to crowd in on her.

This can't be right.

There was no way Olivier would have asked her to meet him here! There wasn't even any place to sit down! Had she gotten the directions wrong? Except the code outside had worked.

She turned her phone around to look at her texts again to see if he'd answered the one she'd just sent him. He hadn't.

None of this makes sense!

She felt a sudden hypersensitivity to sounds and knew her fear was about to get the better of her.

She breathed through her nose and tried to banish the mounting panic that was gnawing insistently at her nerves. She closed her eyes briefly to make her other senses work harder. When she did she thought she could smell the sea.

The harbor must be nearer than she realized. She also felt the humidity on her skin and she could smell mildew. As she took several steps, she heard the boggy scrape of wet grit underfoot.

When she opened her eyes again, she saw a pile of canvas wrappings on the floor.

Perhaps they would tell her what this place was being used for. She shined her beam of light on the bags on the floor and walked toward them.

She stopped when she was three feet away.

Because the bags were not bags.

It was a body.

On his back, his arms flung out to his side, his face open to the world.

Maggie took a step backward and dropped her phone.

It was Gaston.

50

The image of Gaston's dead sightless eyes seared into her brain.

She looked down in the darkness and saw a tiny rim of light where her phone had fallen screen-side down a dozen feet away.

With her heart pounding, she inched slowly toward the phone, one small step at a time, fighting a bucking stomach, trying to remember where the body was.

The last thing she wanted to do was touch it.

She stopped to try to get her breathing regulated, certain she was about to have a full blown panic attack.

In the dark.

In an abandoned warehouse.

With a dead body.

Kneeling down to reach her phone, she grabbed it with trembling fingers and held it out so that it illuminated the way back to the door where she'd come in. Then she stood up and ran.

She reached the door and paused just long enough to look at her phone to see if she could get reception.

Nothing.

She fought down the panic that threatened to engulf her.

You're trapped in a wharf warehouse with a dead body and nobody knows where you are.

Desperately Maggie ran her fingers down the flange where the door connected with the doorjamb. Then she grabbed the door handle and jerked it down hard and pulled at the same time with all her might.

It opened.

Her eyes filled with grateful tears as she fell into the hall, barely managing to stay on her feet, and ran to the exterior door. She repeated the gesture of jerking open the handle and pulling hard. The door opened onto the street.

It was only a little after three and after the warehouse's dark interior, the sunlight was bright in her face. She didn't bother looking down the street but raced to her car and jumped in, her heart throbbing in her ears.

"Thank you thank you thank you," she murmured, glancing in her rearview mirror as she slammed the car into gear and drove away from the warehouse.

She drove to Quai des Belges on the harbor which was already packed with a steady swarm of tourists. The sheer number of people helped to calm her. She slipped into the first parking spot she found. She sat for a moment in the car, her heart pounding. When she lifted her hands from the steering wheel, she saw they had finally stopped shaking.

There was no way she could call this in. No way she could call Jean-Baptiste. She knew that before she knew anything else. Before she was even fully out of the warehouse she knew she couldn't report it.

Nor could she tell Laurent. She had done a lot of things to him in their twelve-year marriage but tripping over a dead body twice in a single week was almost certainly going to test even his legendary patience.

She opened the glovebox in the car for the envelope of household cash she kept there and counted out a hundred euros. She locked the car and walked to the end of the block where she saw a corner café.

It wasn't terribly busy but it wasn't unpopular either. A man in his late fifties was leaning up against the exterior wall to the café and watching the pedestrian traffic. He was dressed cheaply with plastic shoes and a shirt worn and stained. If she had to guess, Maggie would have said he was a pickpocket except he wasn't near a street frequented by tourists.

She approached him. "Want to make a hundred euros?"

He looked at her in surprise and straightened up.

"I need you to make a call," Maggie said.

"That's all?"

She held out the money but pulled it back when he tried to take it. "I need you to call 999 and say somebody died at 48 avenue de la Corse."

He frowned. "Did they?"

"Does it matter?" Maggie flapped the money. "Yes or no?"

He pulled out his phone and punched in 999. "*Allo*, I want to report a death at 48 avenue de la Corse." He disconnected and Maggie handed him the money.

He grinned. "Anyone else you would like to report dead, Mademoiselle?"

"Nope," she said turning away. "That'll do for now."

She walked back to her car and tried to take stock.

She'd been lured to a warehouse where someone had killed Gaston. She'd been lured there in order to find him. Was she supposed to be implicated in his death? Was this a warning?

She pulled out her phone and looked at the text she'd sent Olivier. She looked at the number and frowned. Quickly, she went to her contacts list and found the phone number for Olivier that she'd gotten off his website.

They weren't the same.

She called the phone number that had sent her the texts. Nobody answered so she left a message.

"Call me back immediately or I'm going to the police with what I know," she said. She hung up and then sat in the car and chewed a nail. Why were the phone numbers different? Was that significant?

Her phone lit up and she saw it was the number she'd just called.

"This is harassment," Olivier said when Maggie picked up.

"So is luring me to an abandoned warehouse to show off the body of your latest victim."

"What are you talking about?"

"You know what I'm talking about! The text you sent me last night!"

"I sent you no texts!"

"I can prove it, you know! Erasing texts doesn't erase them for good!"

Maggie wasn't sure about that but she had to hope that Olivier was even less technologically savvy than she.

"I have no idea what you are blathering about but I've been assured by the police that your attempts to pass yourself off as a member of the press in order to interview me are illegal."

"Then why did you call me back?"

"To tell you once and for all to leave me and my wife alone."

Maggie had never said a word to his wife. Clearly Olivier was afraid she was going to.

Clearly that meant she needed to.

Olivier was breathing heavily. Something here didn't make sense. Why would Olivier lure her to the place of Gaston's execution and then deny doing it? He honestly sounded confused. Her mind whirled.

If Olivier didn't send the texts, who did?

"I need to meet with you. At your office."

"That is impossible. I'm giving a speech this evening. If you call me again, I'm notifying the police."

He disconnected and Maggie leaned her head on her arms on her steering wheel as if she could will her mind into order and away from the churning vortex of feelings and thoughts surging inside her.

Who would murder Gaston? Was it the same person who murdered his father? Was what Gaston had to tell her? Was the "BIG" thing he mentioned in his text the fact that he knew who killed his father?

Is that what got him killed?

Maggie tried to run through all the suspects she had—and anyone who might have wanted to hurt Gaston.

Even if Marie-France's disability hadn't effectively eliminated her as a suspect, the fact that she was Gaston's mother would.

That left Angeline, Joelle, Danon, and Olivier—the very one who had sent Maggie to the warehouse.

Did he do it so I'd discover the body? Or was someone waiting to kill me too?

That thought made her sit up straight. It was then that she realized that somewhere in the back of her mind the thought had been there all along. The fear that the killer was there in the warehouse with her, watching her, waiting for her.

She tried to remember if she'd heard any other noises before she bolted. Footsteps, breathing, movement of any kind.

A chime from her phone alerted her that a text had arrived. It was from Olivier and it was from the same number that had originally contacted her and sent her to the warehouse.

<I just got this text from you. There are no other texts to you on my phone. Please leave me alone>

His text showed up right under the text message Maggie had sent him saying she was at the warehouse.

So they are both his phone numbers.

But whether Olivier had sent the earlier text messages was another question. Anyone could have picked up his phone, sent the messages to her and then erased them from Olivier's phone.

It didn't clear Olivier but it didn't indict him either.

Maggie felt a wave of exhaustion pulse into her shoulders.

Should she have called the police herself? It was too late now. If she came forward now, she'd certainly be arrested for obstruction.

She looked again at her contact list of suspects on her phone. Somebody on this list, she thought, had access to Olivier's phone—that is if Olivier hadn't sent the messages himself —and someone on this list killed Gaston. Were they also the one who killed Leon?

Angeline, Joelle, Danon, and Olivier.

She looked at the names and then added Cayenne's name to the list. She would need to call each of them one by one and see how they reacted to the news of Gaston's death. Better, she would accuse each of them and see how they responded to *that.*

She called Joelle Mercier first.

"*Le Façade Nationale,*" Joelle answered mechanically.

"Gaston Boucher was just murdered," Maggie said bluntly. "But I think you already know that."

51

I t was only five o'clock but the campaign offices of the *Le Façade Nationale* were deserted.

Maggie wasn't surprised. There was no longer any candidate. Unless Joelle decided to run, *Le Façade Nationale* was presently the headquarters of precisely nothing.

When Maggie entered the campaign office she found Joelle sitting at the receptionist's desk. Maggie wondered briefly whether the unpleasant young woman who'd manned the desk three days ago was now unemployed.

Joelle's face was white and her eyes red-rimmed. Maggie reminded herself that just because Leon and Gaston hadn't gotten along, it was likely that Joelle had watched Gaston grow up.

Joelle stood as Maggie entered.

"There's nothing about it on the Internet," Joelle said. "If this is a ruse to get in to see me I will have you arrested."

"It's the truth," Maggie said. "I know someone on the force. Gaston was murdered today."

Joelle sat down hard. "How? When?"

Don't you mean why? Or do you know why?

Maggie leaned against the receptionist's desk. "I was hoping you might be able to tell me who benefits from his death."

"Me? What makes you think I would know?"

"Because you're close to the family. You know their secrets. You know things nobody else knows."

"You're wrong. I was out of touch with Gaston. When he turned against his father, I no longer saw him."

"Pity. He seemed like a sweet guy."

"He was," Joelle said sadly. "Poor Marie-France. This will finish her off."

Maggie wasn't sure Marie-France wasn't already so far gone that it would have much effect. On the other hand as far as Marie-France was concerned there were probably at least a few more levels of hell yet to be plumbed.

"I know about your brother," Maggie said. "There's no point in lying. I know he died because of Leon."

She watched Joelle's face pale at her words. And she saw the exact moment when Joelle decided not to bother lying about it.

"I admit that Leon hurt my family. Hurt Michel. But I believed in what Leon stood for. I was able to transcend all of the personal stuff for that."

"I don't believe you."

Joelle's eyes flashed. "So you think Mohammad Olivier is so wonderful?"

"I don't think he caused anybody to slash their wrists."

"Then I guess you don't know about the assault charge last year?"

Maggie frowned. "You mean like at a rally that got out of hand?"

"No. I mean as in domestic violence," Joelle said, enjoying the look of shock on Maggie's face. "He broke his wife's nose."

Maggie's eyes widened in surprise.

"Doesn't exactly jive with your image of Monsieur Olivier as a peaceful egalitarian, does it? Mohammad Olivier is a thug. Just ask the cops who came to his house that night."

Maggie told herself she would do exactly that the next time she had Jean-Baptiste in her crosshairs.

"Although in Cayenne's case, you can hardly blame him," Joelle said.

"I hope you're not defending spousal abuse, Joelle."

"Regardless of what she did?"

"Do you really think physical abuse is ever justified?"

"Even for adultery?"

"Of course not."

"How about adultery with your biggest opponent?"

Maggie's mouth fell open.

"Cayenne and Leon hooked up about three months ago," Joelle said.

"And Olivier found out?"

"Of course he found out! Do you know Leon at all?"

Then Joelle shook her head. "Of course you don't. Leon couldn't wait to tell Olivier. This wasn't your typical run-of-the-mill adultery. This was betrayal of the first order. And if Leon decided to make it public? You think it would be *his* ass in a sling? *Olivier* would be the one humiliated. You've lived in this country long enough to know the typical machismo French male. Of the two of them, Olivier would be the one who came out looking weak."

Maggie tried to process this information, reminding herself that Joelle would naturally try to throw suspicion on anyone other than herself.

"Can you imagine the fallout if *that* became known?" Joelle said.

"So you're saying Mohammad and Cayenne Olivier both had motives for killing Leon. But Mohammad has an alibi," Maggie said.

"All right. Fair enough. But what about Cayenne? Does *she* have an alibi?"

Maggie didn't know but she was tired of playing this game with Joelle. Whether or not Olivier or Cayenne were suspects in Leon's murder didn't alter the facts about Joelle's own motives.

"What about yourself? If you don't mind my asking," Maggie said. "Where were you that day?"

Joelle's eyes were cold and flinty. "I loved Leon. I would never hurt him."

So, no alibi.

"Even after what he did to your brother?"

"Michel did that to himself. I won't make excuses for Leon. He could be cruel. But it was Michel's decision to react that way."

"Wow. You really did love him."

Or you really want me to think you did.

"I will mourn Leon until the day I die."

"Most people hated him."

"That's not true."

"I've seen the YouTube videos, Joelle. Leon was a racist monster."

"You're welcome to your opinion. If we're finished here, I need to be somewhere else."

"Can you at least tell me how Cayenne and Leon met?"

Joelle stood up and then hesitated.

"It's probably not important but Leon met her when he broke his arm after a rally got out of hand last February."

"Met her how?"

"At the hospital."

Maggie realized with sudden clarity what Joelle was going to say before the words were out of her mouth.

"At Centre Hospitalier Avignon," Joelle said, smiling. "Where Cayenne worked as a nurse."

52

Cayenne Olivier was a nurse?

Maggie stared at Joelle, stunned.

If this is true then Cayenne knows how to get a hold of a deadly drug cocktail. And how to administer it.

Maggie felt a tremor of exhaustion creep into her shoulders. It felt surreal to her to realize she'd found a dead body just a few hours earlier. She very much hoped that the cops were already processing the murder scene. She had no expectation that Jean-Baptiste would give her any information about it and she didn't dare call and ask him in case it tipped her hand that she already knew about it.

She didn't know what else to ask Joelle and her sudden wave of weariness made her want to go home and hole up with a glass of wine in a hot bath.

"What about Gaston?" Maggie asked, her hand on the door handle as she was about to leave. "Can you think of any reason why someone might want to hurt him?"

"None at all. Unless he found out something."

"You mean about his father's murder?"

"Why else would someone want to hurt him?"

Maggie saw that Joelle's eyes were filling with tears. She heard police sirens in the distance and wondered if they'd discovered Gaston's body yet.

"Let yourself out, please," Joelle said and turned away to her computer screen.

Maggie walked to her car, oblivious of the scooters, electric bicycles and motorcycles shooting by her on the busy street. Something was nagging at her at the back of her brain. Something she knew was important.

Did Gaston know who killed his father? Did his killer know that?

She sighed. Even after everyone she'd talked to, she still didn't have any hard proof about anything. All she had were motives. For pretty much everyone.

But with the kind of man Leon was, that was hardly surprising.

When she got into her car, she opened up the YouTube channel live streaming Olivier's speech. It was set up like the one the day Leon was killed. It even looked like the same venue. Maggie watched as the camera scanned the crowd before coming back to focus on Mohammed Olivier.

Maggie wondered if Cayenne was there this time. When the camera left Olivier to pan the audience, she tried to see if she could find her on stage or in the audience but she couldn't tell.

On impulse, she called Olivier's Democratic Union campaign office. A woman answered the phone and when Maggie asked to speak with Cayenne Olivier, she was told to leave a message.

"I am happy to do that," Maggie said in a very thick Southern accent, "but I did want to say that I was referred to Madame Olivier by William Traiture and was told that I might be able to meet with her today. I'm only in Marseille this afternoon."

Through Maggie's research she'd run across the name William Traiture and knew him to be a wealthy sponsor for causes such as the Oliviers's.

Immediately, she was put on hold and when the woman came back on the line she said that Madame Olivier was in a meeting onsite and would be delighted to meet with Maggie within the hour.

Maggie thanked her and hung up.

She wasn't completely sure what she was going say to Cayenne Olivier beyond her usual tactic of blindsiding her with a startling fact to unsettle her—in this case it was a toss-up between the domestic violence charge and her affair with Leon—and then just sitting back and watching how she reacted.

The Democratic Union headquarters was only a few blocks away.

Maggie sat in the waiting room of the Democratic Union campaign headquarters. She kept her face averted. Although she didn't think Cayenne had gotten a good look at her when she was in the office before, she didn't want to get tossed out before she had a chance to talk to her.

A quick scan of the live-stream video on her cell phone showed Olivier was still at the rally fielding questions from his future constituents.

"Madame Olivier will see you now," a young dark-skinned woman said, approaching Maggie in the waiting room.

Maggie followed her to a large corner office.

Cayenne was seated at a desk but didn't look up when Maggie entered. The woman who'd led her in quietly left, closing the door behind her. Immediately Cayenne stood and walked around the desk, her hand outstretched to shake Maggie's hand. Then she froze and her mouth dropped open.

"*Bonjour*, Madame Olivier," Maggie said, stepping forward and shaking her outstretched hand. "We've not formally met."

Cayenne jabbed a finger toward the door. "Get out!"

"I was hoping you'd tell me if there was any truth to the rumor that you and Leon were sleeping together," Maggie said.

Cayenne jabbed at the intercom system on her desk. "Violet, please call security."

Maggie knew she needed to hurry if she didn't want to spend any more time in the Marseille police department holding cells.

"I also know that you and your husband are each other's alibis for Leon's murder but that your alibi appears to be unsubstantiated."

"Get out now or I will have you thrown out."

"I'm happy to go just as soon as you tell me where you were the day Leon Boucher was killed."

"I was here. No fewer than twenty campaign workers can attest to that."

"Okay, but your husband said he was giving a speech on rue du Soleil the day Leon Boucher was killed and that *you* were with him. I've seen the video and it only shows that *he* was there. So if what you say is true, your employees are your alibi but of course then you can't be your husband's alibi."

"I don't need to be," Cayenne snorted. "I think two hundred people watching a public rally at rue du Soleil would suffice."

"I agree. Except the video is not time stamped and second, why not just say that when the police asked where you both were? Why lie?"

Her face looked strained and a big bulky guy opened the door.

"Did you need help, *chérie*?"

Chérie?

Maggie turned to see a very good-looking man with dark brown hair and very blue eyes standing in the doorway. "Wait a minute," Maggie said. "So are *you* her alibi?"

Her brain was already recalibrating the situation with the new facts as the man blushed and looked helplessly at Cayenne.

53

Cayenne still threw her out.

As Maggie walked back to her car she tried to determine exactly what her visit with Cayenne had gained her. Just because Cayenne was having an affair didn't mean she *hadn't* killed Leon. It just meant she had an ironclad alibi for the time of the crime.

If she was willing to blow up her marriage in the process.

No wonder she was hoping her other two alibis—being in the campaign office or at her husband's rally—would hold up.

Maggie stood for a moment on the street outside the Democratic Union's offices. A group of tourists with their guide was wandering toward the Old Port. The guide's voice was just barely carrying on the sea air but his words were incomprehensible.

Maggie felt antsy and unsettled. When she glanced at her watch she saw that it was a little before six in the evening. She also saw a text from Nicole saying Laurent wanted her to pick up bread on her way home. Nicole had sent the message five minutes ago.

Maggie got in her car and pulled out of the parking spot.

For some reason all she could think of was the fact that the Marseille Airport was only ten minutes away.

And it was on the way to Domaine St-Buvard.

Sort of.

If Maggie pushed the speed limit a bit she could make it to the airport, check out something that had been bothering her for the last several hours and be back at Domaine St-Buvard before the steamed mussels were even cold.

As soon as she'd made up her mind to go to the airport, Maggie felt the tension in her shoulders relax. She was surprised she hadn't thought of doing this before—retrace her steps *as well as the possible steps of the killer*. Not that it would tell her anything she didn't already know.

But you never knew.

She kept her phone on the passenger seat and found herself continually glancing at it. She had no way of knowing if the police had found Gaston's body yet. She didn't expect it to be on the radio this soon.

Maggie felt a pulse of guilt in her stomach at the thought of how she had just turned and run when she found Gaston's body.

She reminded herself that it wouldn't have helped anyone for her to be held for hours downtown answering questions. She pushed down the rising tide of guilt every time she thought of Gaston, every time she recreated in her mind the image of his lifeless body on the cement floor of the warehouse.

She turned on her car radio hoping to distract herself from her thoughts.

Thoughts that were only going in circles and ending up back at the beginning.

She took the Marseille Airport exit and wound around to the parking garage entrance, bypassing the lane for departures and arrivals. She went to the short-term parking garage lane, collected her parking ticket from the automated dispenser and drove to the parking level where she'd parked last week when she'd come to pick up Nicole.

The combination of the darkness of the underground lot with its sudden dip in temperature, and the memory of what had happened the last time she was here sent shivers up and down Maggie's naked arms.

She parked in the same spot as before, brushing away the feelings of revulsion and *déja vu.*

The parking area was deserted. Perhaps that wasn't unusual for a Monday, Maggie thought. She sat for a moment and then got out of her car and walked to the spot where she knew Leon Boucher's car had been—and where he had likely been killed.

She stood and stared at the spot. She couldn't detect any stains on the cement or any physical evidence that something terrible had happened here.

She turned to look at her car to gauge the distance. It was close. Even now she could see the gap of her still broken trunk lid. Walking toe to toe, she marked off the steps to her car.

It was roughly twenty feet.

She turned and walked back to Leon's parking space. And this time she looked at the distance to her car as if measuring it for a trip taken with a lifeless body.

Just a few steps. Easily done if the body were resting on a rolling bag. She walked to her car and stood with her hands on the trunk. She could feel the heat of the summer day where it had baked into her car parked outside in Marseille most of the day.

Two people came from the direction of the escalators and walked past her.

Suddenly Maggie got a flash of memory of the couple she'd seen but last week had been too distracted to really see on the day of the murder.

Their rolling bag had been making the same loud clicking

sounds that she was hearing now. She closed her eyes, listening hard, and tried to remember their faces.

It was impossible. On the day of the murder, she hadn't really looked at them enough to be able to remember them now.

The sounds of the baggage wheels were louder as the couple passed her. It was an ugly discordant sound that seemed to drill deep into her brain, pulling the memory out of the recesses of her mind.

And then it came to her in a sudden flash. Last week she'd heard that same noise and she'd unconsciously glanced in the direction of the bag making it.

A purple hard side bag with flapping baggage ID tags.

Maggie felt a sudden need to sit down as the revelation hit her.

She'd seen that same bag recently.

Today.

In Marie-France Boucher's closet.

54

The lavender hardcase Gucci luggage!

The couple that walked past her in the car park last week had the same bag!

Maggie thought hard. Had the people even been together or had she just assumed it? Was it possible that *one* of the people was walking closely to the other to deliberately give that impression?

Had she seen the killer?

Maggie turned back to her trunk and leaned against it. She stared again at the spot where Leon's car had been.

But how would that work? The killer murdered Leon. Then he or she waited for someone to come along? Or waited for the coast to be clear. The killer saw Maggie drive up with her broken trunk lid, waited for her to leave and then stuffed Leon's body in her car trunk.

But why? Why not just leave the body in Leon's car? Had he been killed before he could unlock his car? But then the killer could just have used Leon's keys and unlocked it. Why the need to move the body to another car?

Maggie glanced in the direction that the couple with their rolling bag had come from.

And then what? Why would the killer be coming *out* of the airport with his bag? Why would he even have a bag? Plus, the timing was wrong.

She ran an agitated hand over her face and tried to reorganize the facts.

The murderer had to have been watching her get out of her car. That much fit. And when she left to go into the main airport terminal the killer put Leon's body in her car trunk. Also fine so far.

But why wouldn't the killer have just fled after that? Why would he or she then go into the main airport terminal? And if they had done that they would have had to do it *after* Maggie had gone in—in which case the person with the purple Gucci bag Maggie saw as she walked into the terminal couldn't have had anything to do with the murder.

She shook her head in confusion and frustration.

Besides, purple Gucci bag or not, it could hardly be Marie-France. Because of her affliction she was virtually housebound.

Maggie tried to think of how many luggage pieces she'd seen in Marie-France's closet. She hadn't paid close enough attention but it seemed that the smaller sizes were there but the bigger one—the one which was the size she'd glimpsed the day of the murder—was missing.

So who had access to Marie-France's closet?

Leon and Gaston, surely. Did Joelle?

Maggie turned and got back in her car.

What did any of this information mean? Was she a little closer? The puzzle piece of the Gucci luggage was tantalizing but Maggie couldn't make it fit to create a picture that made sense.

When she glanced at her phone she saw she'd received

another text from Nicole asking if she could have champagne tonight since it was her last night in France.

Maggie felt a throb of sadness.

She started the car and maneuvered it slowly out of the parking garage. Dejected and further away than ever from figuring out who stuffed Leon Boucher's dead body in her car trunk, Maggie focused on the thirty-minute drive back to Domaine St-Buvard and her waiting family.

And the goodbye party that everybody was looking forward to except her.

55

Maggie got home that evening with two *batons* of *pain traditionale* in her arms.

She heard the laughter before she was even fully in the house. Nicole and Luc were both in the kitchen making dinner. Laurent met her in the foyer, relieved her of the bread and gave her a kiss.

"I don't even want to know where you've been," he said. "Just tell me you didn't proposition the baker."

"What does *proposition* mean, Papa?" Mila said as she ran into the foyer and gave Maggie a quick hug.

"It means your father has a very French sense of humor," Maggie said to her daughter as he turned and went to the kitchen.

Dinner was grilled leg of lamb. Laurent loosely supervised the preparation but he clearly saw that the main focus of tonight was not a perfect meal but a congenial family evening. He plied Maggie with a glass of wine and she forced herself to relax in the living room while Jemmy and Mila set the table.

She still didn't know what her memory of the Gucci luggage
meant. But after what happened to Gaston and her conversation with Cayenne she'd already moved Olivier to the top of
her suspects list. If Olivier knew about the affair between
Cayenne and Leon, he had more motive than all the others put
together.

As far as his alibi for Leon's murder, there were only a thousand ways anybody with even a basic technological bent could
doctor a video date and time stamp. She made a mental note to
go back and look at the video again.

The airport crime scene was less than twenty minutes from
the rally site where Olivier supposedly had been. He could
absolutely have killed Leon and then shown up in time to strut
about on stage and pretend to have been there all afternoon
long.

And added to all that was Gaston's murder. Regardless of
what Olivier said, it was *his* phone messages that had led
Maggie to the murder scene.

From her chair in the living room she saw Laurent get down
a casserole pot from the highest cabinet in the kitchen. It wasn't
unusual for her to watch him when he didn't know she was
doing it.

When she first met Laurent she remembered being so in
love with him that she literally could not think straight when
she was around him. Normally she could push aside the
memory of the *circumstances* of how they'd met. Those circumstances were too painful and they weren't what she'd built a
life on.

They were just something that had happened.

But tonight, she couldn't keep the memory of those circumstances from crowding in on her attempts to be at peace.

She didn't need Laurent to tell her it was time to let it go.

She knew it was time.

Time to let Nicole go and time to let the killer of Leon

Boucher go. And time to let all her anxieties and self-determined beliefs about what was best for Nicole go too.

All of it, just let it all go.

"To the table!" Laurent called, clapping his hands, and making both dogs bark. Jemmy jumped up to set down the dogs' dinner bowls in the kitchen as Luc and Nicole began to bring platters of food to the table.

Maggie was dying to tell Laurent about Gaston and the warehouse but she knew when she did his level of annoyance with her—just now beginning to subside after the whole Marseille jail episode—would dramatically ramp up. Of course when he eventually found out about Gaston the fact that she *hadn't* told him would make things worse. Much worse.

"I need to have a word with you later," she said to him as she sat down at the dinner table.

He waggled his eyebrows at her.

"Not that kind of word," she said.

"Will this word make me unhappy?"

"It might."

He sighed and refreshed both their wine glasses.

Maggie heard the sound of a champagne bottle cork popping in the kitchen and Nicole squealed.

She looked at her cell phone. Why had she assumed Jean-Baptiste would call her? Surely he'd discovered Gaston's body *by now*. He had access to all the forensic data that would tell the tale of what had happened in the warehouse. Maybe he even had a suspect in Gaston's murder in custody?

"At the table, *chérie*?" Laurent said admonishingly. "On Nikki's last night with us?"

Maggie turned off her phone and gave him an apologetic look.

As Nicole, Jemmy and Mila came into the dining room and took their seats, Luc poured champagne into each of their glasses. Maggie looked at their faces, so exuberant and happy.

She pinched the area between her eyes and tried to make all the clues and the leads fade away so she could enjoy this evening, this last night with Nicole.

Between the mussels vinaigrette and the grilled lamb Laurent got up to stretch his legs, let the dogs out and have a smoke outside. He noticed that Maggie had been uncharacteristically quiet tonight but assumed she was just wistful about Nikki leaving.

If it was anything other than that he had no doubt he'd learn of it in due course.

He left her at the table, twirling the stem of her wine glass, lost in her own thoughts.

"Luc?" he said, as he opened the French doors. "Nicole can help Mila bring in the frozen vanilla custard." He indicated with a nod of his head that Luc should follow him outside.

The look on Luc's face was at first startled and he nearly knocked over a water goblet in his rush to join Laurent.

Laurent wasn't exactly sure what he was going to say to the boy but he knew that this was one of those times when he needed to say something. Luc had been mistreated and it had happened on Laurent's watch. Worse, he had put Luc in a predicament that arose for no other reason than Laurent had allowed the situation to evolve at Frère Dominic's pace. That was Laurent's fault.

He was well aware that Luc seemed to have done a miraculous about-face in attitude which could not be totally attributed to his present infatuation with Nikki.

Probably best for all concerned that Nikki go back to Atlanta.

Laurent walked to the end of the terrace while the dogs Buddy and Izzy sniffed the ground and bushes as they had an hour earlier.

"Everything okay?" Luc asked.

Laurent lit a cigarette and leaned against the stone wall surrounding the *potager*. He eyed Luc for a moment.

"I was proud of you, Luc," he said solemnly, "for doing what you needed to do to take care of Nikki on Saturday."

Even in the gloom of the evening light, Laurent could see Luc's eyes light up. The boy rubbed his hands on his jeans as though he didn't know what to do with them.

"And I'm sorry," Laurent said.

Luc's head snapped up. A stricken look across his face.

Laurent realized the boy thought he was apologizing for needing to withdraw his promise to include him in his legacy.

There was a reason everyone at the monastery had dropped their jaws when Laurent announced it. It was not believable.

Luc would have every reason to doubt that it was real.

"I'm sorry I gave you to Dominic for the night. I should have known he would take his problem with me out on you."

Luc stared at him and then he ducked his head and nodded. "I'm sorry, too," he mumbled.

"*Pourquoi*?"

Luc cleared his throat. "I've been a jerk." He stood up straight and looked Laurent in the eye. "So I'm sorry too."

Laurent smoked and gazed silently at him.

"I didn't say it for the effect alone," Laurent said finally. "I intend for you to inherit alongside Jem and Mila."

Luc leaned against the *potager* wall as though his legs were having trouble holding him up.

"Why?" he asked.

Laurent ground out his cigarette against the stone wall. He debated how much to tell him without revealing the truth. And of course the fact of Luc's paternity was only part of the truth. The larger part of it was that Laurent had felt a connection with Luc *before* he knew he was Gerard's son.

And before he'd been sidetracked by his own pessimism he'd also seen the boy's decency and goodness.

"I can't explain. Can you live with that?"

Luc nodded. "I don't understand it but I want to be a part of..."

Luc stared at the dark vineyards and then waved his hand to encompass the land, the house, and the glow from the lights that illuminated the people inside the house. "Part of everything."

"Good. Then that is all that is necessary. I think I see Jemmy in the kitchen trying to impale himself on the grill rotisserie. You'd better step in. I'll be there in a moment."

Luc turned and hurried back into the house. Laurent watched him go and then called the dogs.

❧

Dessert was a triumph for Mila, who basked in the accolades of her family—but as usual mostly Laurent's, Maggie noticed.

They all looked to Laurent for approval and praise. Even to a certain extent, she herself did.

It had been a lovely evening. Good food, much laughter and warmth, and a connectivity that Maggie realized was usually there but had been missing for the last week.

She knew Nikki was happy tonight because she was finally getting what she wanted—to go home. And Maggie knew that due to Nikki's newfound affection for Luc it wasn't as easy for her as it would have been.

So it was a bittersweet evening. Mila would miss Nikki but Mila would soon be happy to focus on her pastry making and eventually forget how it had felt to have a sister for a week.

Laurent had his hands full with the monastery, the refugees and the imminent harvest. He would be happy to talk with Nikki on the phone from time to time and see her at Christmas on visits to Atlanta. That would be enough for him. And like everything else that troubled Laurent but served no purpose in his life, he would put away his feelings of guilt—if indeed he even had any—and simply get on with things.

Maggie envied him that.

When the last bowl of ice cream had been eaten and Mila and Nikki had begun to clear the table, Laurent took a crystal decanter of Calvados and two glasses into the living room. While the boys began to clean up the kitchen, Maggie followed him to the sofa.

Ever since Nikki had come to France and made it clear she hated it here, Maggie had wrestled with the secret of what she and Laurent had done thirteen years ago. Up until then she'd had no trouble forgetting it had even happened.

But when the secret finally came out, well, it was all she could do on an hourly basis not to think about that time.

That time in Cannes when the world was blowing up around her—when she was falling in love with a man—a man who lied to her but made her feel alive—and when she was forced to illegally bring a French national into the US along with her murdered sister's ashes.

No, that time in Cannes was a watershed moment that had changed Maggie's life forever. It was one she would always look back on with equal parts longing and sorrow.

She remembered with painful clarity the day she and Laurent sat down and mapped out exactly how they would create and keep the secret of who Nicole really was—as if they would never be faced with the day when they would have to tell her the truth.

Laurent poured Maggie a brandy and handed it to her.

"She is going to be fine," he said.

"I know."

"And we will see her in Atlanta."

Maggie sipped her brandy and felt the burn go down her

throat as the essence of apples filled her nostrils. Tears welled up in her eyes.

"Don't be sad, *chérie*," Laurent said softly. "It will all work out for the best."

Maggie gazed into the golden core of her brandy glass and realized that there was someone standing behind the sofa. She and Laurent both turned to see Nikki standing there.

"I'm ready," Nikki said before walking around the sofa and sitting down on the chair across from them. She took in a long breath as if steeling herself.

"I'm ready to hear the truth."

56

A part of Maggie was secretly hoping they could just pretend nothing had happened. Nikki would go back to Atlanta and they would carry on as if this last week had never revealed what it had revealed.

Maggie cleared her throat but Laurent put a hand on her knee.

"I will start," he said to Nicole. "I need you to know that my work in those days is not something I am proud of today, *chérie*."

Nikki frowned and looked at Maggie. She was not expecting this.

"I thought Aunt Maggie said you were a chef at one of the big hotels in Cannes."

Laurent glanced at Maggie.

"So that was a lie?" Nikki said looking from one to the other.

This is not getting off to a very good start, Maggie thought.

"Were you a human trafficker or something?" Nikki said to Laurent, her bottom lip quivering.

"*Non*. Not like that. My work was different depending on the situation."

"So you were...a criminal?"

Laurent shrugged. "It's what I did in those days. *Je suis* désolé, *chérie*."

Maggie was amazed at how unembarrassed Laurent appeared.

"Is that an apology?" Nikki asked.

"*Oui*. I am sorry. A little."

"A little?"

"Okay, Laurent, no," Maggie said hurriedly, clearly seeing what he was leading up to saying and convinced Nikki wasn't ready to hear it. "She doesn't need to know that part."

Nikki turned to Maggie, her voice rising in volume.

"*What* part? More secrets? More lies? I want to know it all! Or I swear I'll never talk to either of you again."

Maggie squeezed Laurent's hand still on her knee.

"Let me tell it," she said.

She turned to Nikki. "Laurent was working with a man named Roger Bentley who was hired to find Elise Newberry's family in order to formally identify her body in the Cannes morgue."

Maggie swallowed hard. Just saying the words made her relive that nightmare all over again.

"Roger Bentley contacted your grandfather—"

"Except he's not my grandfather," Nikki said, her cheeks flushed with anger.

"Perhaps do not interrupt until your aunt has finished," Laurent said mildly.

"Bentley contacted my father who then sent me to Cannes to identify Elise's remains. But Bentley also told Dad that there was a child involved. And before that moment we had no idea Elise had a child."

Maggie took in a long breath to steady her nerves.

"So we made arrangements with Bentley to bring Elise's child back to Atlanta with me."

"How did you do that post-9/11?"

"Well, it was tricky. And it wasn't legal," Maggie said. "Because the child's father was still alive and we were essentially stealing you away from him, we had to pay for false papers, and a false American passport."

Nikki wiped the tears from her face as she listened.

"Anyway," Maggie continued, "we made all these arrangements with Bentley when, unbeknownst to us, there was in fact no child. Or there was but she—the real Nicole—had...died."

Maggie pushed past the lump forming in her throat.

"My dad had promised Roger a certain amount of money to help us bring the child to the States."

"So basically this Bentley dude had to come up with a kid," Nikki said flatly.

"Yes," Maggie said. "And that's why he found you. And the reason he was able to get you..." Maggie took in a breath to fortify herself, "...was because he knew nobody would miss you."

"How is that possible?"

Laurent leaned over and put his hand on Nikki's knee.

"I'm sure they noticed you were gone," he said gently. "Aunt Maggie means nobody would care."

Nikki's expression was stricken.

"You were living in an abusive family situation," Maggie said hurriedly. "Maybe a half a dozen people were living in the same hovel. Roger said your mother had disappeared. Probably dead of an overdose or maybe she just ran off."

"But not interested in me." Nikki's eyes filled with tears.

"People like the family you were taken from have very big problems," Laurent said. "They are surviving day to day. And sometimes not at all."

"What happened to the real Nicole? Elise's real daughter?"

"Her father—Gerard—was supposed to be watching her and she fell off a boat and drowned," Maggie said.

They were all silent for a moment before Nikki turned to Laurent. "The real Nicole was your niece. She was your brother's child."

He nodded, waiting for the question he knew was coming.

"Which meant you knew all along that the real Nicole was dead when Aunt Maggie came looking for her," Nikki said.

Laurent glanced at Maggie. She would have told this part of the story but she knew it was Laurent's to tell. And he was not going to come off looking well no matter how he did it.

"*Oui*," he said quietly. "I am not proud of taking advantage of Maggie's family in that way."

"For how much?"

"Thirty thousand euros."

Nikki turned to Maggie. "How could you ever forgive him? Or trust him after what he did?"

"Nicole, you *know* your Uncle Laurent. You know what a good, solid, kind man he is. He made a mistake."

"A pretty big one," Nikki muttered.

"And he was sorry for it. I thank God I was able to forgive him and put it behind us."

"And the money?" Nikki asked, looking at Laurent again. "Did you give it back?"

"He did," Maggie said firmly.

"How? If he never told Granddad who I really was? How did he give the money back?"

"It was put in a trust for you," Maggie said. "But you have to believe that your grandfather wouldn't have cared that you weren't really Elise's daughter."

"Except he wasn't really my grandfather."

Maggie sighed. "I hope someday you'll realize that the time you had with him—your whole childhood long—he was your grandfather in every way that mattered. And he'd have said so too."

"If that's true then why did you not tell him the truth?"

Maggie glanced at Laurent. "We did."

Nikki's eyes widened. "Granddad knew I wasn't the real Nicole?"

"We eventually told him," Maggie said.

"But not Nana?"

Maggie shrugged helplessly.

"You know your grandmother well enough to know it wouldn't matter two figs to her either. But your grandfather was being his usual protective self. He knew that for your grandmother the fact that you were Elise's daughter was like having a piece of Elise back. He didn't want to take that away from her."

"But Granddad knew." Nikki's eyes were misty. Maggie could tell she was remembering times with her grandfather, conversations with him, knowing now that her paternity had made no difference to him. Maggie watched the tension relax in Nikki's shoulders.

"You are loved, Nicole," Maggie said. "That's all that matters."

Nikki nodded. "Thank you for telling me." She stood up and walked into the kitchen. When Maggie heard her talking there with the others, she turned to Laurent and he was looking at her with an arched eyebrow.

"What difference does it make?" she whispered to him. "She'll never find out the truth and it helped put her mind at ease."

When Maggie saw the corner of Laurent's lips twitch into a half smile. A part of her wanted to slap him for being able to read her mind so well. But another part of her wanted to kiss him for the same reason.

57

The next morning began like so many mornings at Domaine St-Buvard. When Maggie came downstairs, Laurent was in the kitchen making pancakes surrounded by all the children seated at the counter.

Maggie noted it was the first time since she came to France that Nicole had joined in on the morning routine.

The day she leaves.

When Maggie came into the kitchen, Laurent leaned across the counter and gave her a kiss. "Coffee is hot," he said as he turned back to the stove. She poured herself a cup and turned to smile at the four young people eating pancakes at the counter.

"I could smell those from all the way upstairs," Maggie said.

"Dad had to put the dogs outside," Jemmy said around a mouthful of pancakes. "The smell was driving them crazy."

"You look pretty this morning, Aunt Maggie," Nicole said. "Is that just to drive me to the airport?"

Maggie sighed. "About that." She turned to Laurent. "I got a call last night from Cosette Villeneuve and I have to see them in

Arles this morning. I've already put her group off *twice*. Can you take Nicole?"

Laurent frowned but Nicole jumped in.

"You don't have to," she said. "I'll just Uber there. I do it all the time in Atlanta."

"No, I don't like that," Maggie said. She looked over at Laurent but he was already shaking his head.

"I am meeting with the wine co-op," he said. "And I'm taking Jem and Mila to their camp again in Aix, remember?"

Maggie looked at Luc. He didn't have his driver's license yet but he was a good driver. Before she could suggest it, Laurent interjected.

"*Non*. Luc has a dentist appointment in Aix."

"I could reschedule," Luc said hopefully but Maggie saw the hope die in his eyes when he saw Laurent's expression.

"I'm telling you it is *not* a big deal," Nicole said in exasperation. "Seriously. We'll all just say goodbye here." She leaned over and gave Mila's shoulders a squeeze.

"I wish I was going with you," Mila said wistfully.

"No, you don't," Nicole said. "You and Zouzou have that engagement cake you're making next week."

"Oh, yeah," Mila said, her eyes lighting up.

"I will take Mila and Jemmy into town first," Laurent said to Luc. "So you can at least stay with Nikki until her ride arrives."

Maggie saw the look of relief on Nicole's face and she felt a spasm of guilt. She prayed that being back in Atlanta would help Nicole feel safe again. She winced as it occurred to her that she never thought she'd ever hear herself say think *those* words.

"Everybody grab your bags," Laurent said, "and say goodbye to Nikki. We leave in five minutes." He pulled a dish towel from his shoulder and tossed it onto the counter.

Maggie turned to Nicole. "I hate saying goodbye like this."

"It's fine," Nicole said. She put her arms around Maggie. "I'm sorry for being such a pill."

Maggie eyes burned with tears. "You had every right to be," she whispered. "Give my love to your grandmother. And Ben. I assume he's picking you up at Hartsfield?"

"He is," Nicole said, before turning to hug Mila and Jemmy.

As Luc came downstairs with her bag, Nicole turned to Laurent and he lifted her off her feet in a big hug.

"Are you all coming to Atlanta for Christmas?" she asked him.

"We will if we cannot convince you to come to Domaine St-Buvard," he said.

"Luc too?"

"Of course."

As Laurent and Jemmy and Mila went to climb into the car, Maggie turned again to Nicole. Every molecule of her being said this was not the way she wanted them to say goodbye. Nothing about this visit had turned out the way she'd envisioned it.

As soon as they'd all waved off Laurent and Jemmy and Mila, Maggie looked at her watch. She'd have to speed if she was going to make her meeting in Arles on time, but she just couldn't leave Nicole yet.

"I'm hoping you'll think about college in the fall," Maggie said.

There were several community colleges in Atlanta and they all beat the tattoo webinar Nicole seemed to think she was going to make a living out of.

"I'll keep in touch," Nikki said evasively, smiling and giving Maggie another hug. "I love you, Aunt Maggie."

"I love you too, sweetie," Maggie said, her eyes stinging with tears as she finally let her go and turned to walk to her car."

"Ubers take forever to pick up from here," Maggie said. "So you probably should call one now."

"I already have," Nicole said.

Maggie nodded and got in her car. As she pulled out of the drive, she adjusted her rear view mirror and got a final glimpse of her beautiful niece standing with Luc in the driveway.

She blinked back tears and as she drove away she put a call in to Ben. He didn't pick up but it didn't matter. She left a long voicemail.

She wanted to remind him that if he ever needed anything at all for Nicole...anything at all...all he had to do was ask.

Nicole felt the sun on her shoulders as she stood in the drive of Domaine St-Buvard. She held Luc's hand. He was such a different sort of boyfriend—if she could even call him that. He didn't speak. Well, hardly ever. And when he did it was like he was hoarding his words.

Now that she thought of it, he was a lot like Uncle Laurent in that way.

She wondered if it was just a French guy thing.

She turned to him and smiled.

"You are nervous?" he asked, his brows knit together.

"Not nervous," she said. "Excited. But sad to leave you."

He smiled at that but his smile quickly faded.

"But not afraid?"

"You mean about going back to the airport?" She shook her head. "What are the odds I'll trip over *two* dead bodies there?" She tried to laugh but couldn't quite manage that.

She wasn't lying. She wasn't afraid. Not really.

I'm leaving.

All the stuff she had to be afraid of she was leaving here.

In fact, as much as she was going to miss Luc, she couldn't get on that plane fast enough.

Not that she'd tell him that.

She squeezed his hand. "I'll call you when I get home. And Uncle Laurent says you'll all come over at Christmas."

Luc nodded and looked at her in that way he did that made her want to melt.

Why couldn't Luc be in Atlanta with her? Why did he have to stay back here? Life was so unfair sometimes.

A car hesitated in the entrance of the drive and then turned to make its way toward the house.

"That was fast," Nicole said. "Aunt Maggie made it sound like Ubers had to come from Paris to pick up here."

Luc let go of her hand to talk to the driver. Nicole heard him say the word "*aeroport.*" She was grateful she didn't have to try to make herself understood. If she remembered correctly, almost everything at the airport was in French *and* English. So at least there was that.

She was already planning on going straight to the food court, grabbing a coffee and a roll, and positioning herself at the gate so she was the first one on.

She felt a subtle tingling in her limbs and she rubbed her damp palms against her sides.

Luc picked up her rolling bag and put it in the front seat of the car.

"Ready, *chérie?*" he asked, smiling sadly at her.

"I'll never forget how you helped me, Luc," Nicole said, suddenly not wanting to leave him. "I mean it."

"Me too," he said, taking her hand and pulling her gently to him.

The kiss was long and longing. Nicole wrapped her arms around his neck and sank into the comforting feeling of his arms around her.

"I'm really going to miss you," she whispered.

"*Moi aussi.*"

When she finally forced herself to pull away, she knew she had to go and go *now* or she wouldn't go at all. She gave his hand one last squeeze and then climbed into the back of the car.

The car slowly pulled away but Nicole turned to catch one last look of Luc. She blew him a kiss through the window and told herself she would always remember the sight of him standing in the drive of Domaine St-Buvard, the sun in his eyes and the breeze gently tossing his brown hair around his face.

She waved and then turned and sank into the seat, tears stinging her eyes.

She would study her French. She would surprise Luc so that when she saw him at Christmas...

Suddenly, her stomach lurched. Nicole gasped and immediately struggled to take a breath. Panic inched up her throat and she gripped the arm rests of the car.

She looked into the rear view mirror to see the driver watching her.

She recognized those eyes.

But it was the scent that told her before anything else.

Her hands began to shake uncontrollably.

It was him.

58

The walls of the Arles Municipal Council were decorated with pictures of the city's past leaders, as well as various logos, awards and plaques. As Maggie took her seat at the conference table, she noticed one of her newsletters had been printed out and framed on the wall too.

She winced when she saw it. A man had coincidentally lost his life rather gruesomely in the Arles Amphitheater during the time of that particular newsletter.

Cosette Villeneuve, the guild president, was already seated at the table with three other women when Maggie came in. She turned and smiled coolly at Maggie.

"*Bonjour*, Maggie."

"*Bonjour*, Cosette," Maggie said and then greeted the other women. "*Bonjour* Mimi, Michelle, Dede. I'm sorry we've been missing each other lately."

All four of the women were dressed impeccably in summer silks, high heels, and tightly coiffed hair styles, making Maggie feel shabby in her linens and espadrilles. One thing she'd learned a long time ago was not to try to compete with a French woman—or Grace for that matter—for style.

"We are all together now," Cosette said briskly. "Let us get to business, yes?"

Mimi Marchand turned and held up a remote control device that immediately opened a set of walnut cabinet doors behind Maggie that hid a small screen.

"I think first we need to be aware of the ways in which the gypsies will come into Arles," Cosette said. "Always by way of the Camargue, I think, yes?"

All the women nodded.

"First slide, please, Mimi," Cosette said.

The screen showed a map with multicolored arrows indicating pedestrian and vehicle flow around the Amphitheater.

"The gypsies will parade here and here," Cosette said, standing up and pointing to the colored avenues on the map.

Maggie knew it was no longer PC to say "gypsies" and she would take special pains to make sure the newsletter addressed the travelers in terms they preferred. Cosette on the other hand didn't care. Maggie happened to know that Laurent didn't care either. Honestly, most French people that Maggie knew didn't care.

The gypsies of course cared.

As she looked at the arrows and the colored arcs indicating traffic patterns as Mimi clicked from screen to screen, a sudden glimmering of awareness began to make itself known in her brain. She couldn't see what it was but something was playing at the edges of her mind. It was frustratingly like looking at an equation that she *knew* she should know but the numbers kept changing.

There was definitely something there. Something right below the surface that would not go away, that would not be ignored.

But Maggie could not see what it was.

"It would be wonderful if the person who is the whole

reason we are meeting here today could keep her mind focused on the topic at hand," Michelle said tartly.

Maggie turned to see all four women looking at her. But only Michelle's face was flushed with fury, her eyes glittering as they pinned Maggie.

"I'm so sorry," Maggie said. "I have some things going on at home."

"Is that meant to be an excuse?" Michelle said. "We all have busy lives. Perhaps you think your time is more valuable than ours?"

"No, not at all," Maggie said, feeling her face redden. "I do apologize."

"Bah! You are like all Americans. Arrogant! And I am sick of forgiving your constant inattention to detail."

Michelle stood up and tossed down the file folder she'd been holding. She snatched up her purse and stalked out of the room.

Maggie looked in horror at the other women, a thickness forming in the back of her throat. She didn't know where to begin to apologize for not being as conscientious as she knew she should have been. As the other women turned to regard her, Maggie couldn't help but remember every time in the last two weeks that she'd put them off or failed to answer an email.

Michelle Royer was normally very levelheaded and kind. Maggie had worked with her for the last five years on every imaginable project—from community flower and bake sales to park renovations. For her to exhibit this level of disgust at Maggie's less than diligent work habits was an unexpected but no doubt well-deserved rebuke.

Maggie swallowed hard. "I don't know what to say," she said to the remaining three women seated across the table from her. She knew her face was red with shame.

"Well, you must forgive her, of course," Mimi said matter-of-factly.

The other two women nodded. "Poor Michelle. She is not herself."

Maggie looked at each of their faces until Cosette Villeneuve leaned back in her chair and lit a cigarette.

"She did not tell you? Her husband has asked for a divorce. Such a pig."

"He does not deserve Michelle."

"Well, of course that is true," Mimi Marchand said, also reaching for her cigarettes.

Maggie's head began to spin. She stared at the door where Michelle had just stormed out of. Michelle Royer was the most even-tempered woman she knew. And she'd just come unstrung and stomped out of a meeting with friends.

She is not herself.

Maggie put a hand to her mouth in a sudden, terrible flash of understanding.

Nicole had always been a sweet deferential child. Even last fall when they were in Atlanta for Maggie's father's memorial service, she was as loving and even-tempered as ever.

But from the moment she'd stepped foot in France Nicole had been different.

Something happened.

Maggie began to gather up the folders on the table while her mind spun into a pinball pinging frenzy.

"Let's pick this up tomorrow," she heard herself saying. "We need Michelle's input to go forward."

Danon. Angeline. Joelle. Marie-France. Olivier. Cayenne.

Of the six suspects Maggie had compiled in her mind only Olivier's alibi was confirmable, although possibly Cayenne's too if her lover was to be believed.

That left four suspects.

Maggie said goodbye to each of the women in the room, her body moving as if on autopilot as she made her way out of the building and toward her car.

If I eliminate Marie-France because of her disability that leaves only three.

Joelle. Danon. Angeline.

The three people in love with Leon.

Which of them could have gotten their hands on Olivier's phone easily?

Only Cayenne or Danon.

And between those two only Cayenne was known to be comfortable with a needle. Maggie got in her car and pulled out of the parking spot.

She remembered what Chevalier had said about the awkward needle puncture.

The killer wasn't necessarily adept with handling needles.

As Maggie sped down the highway toward Marseille, she brought Nicole's face back to mind. She envisioned her as she'd been that day at the airport when she met her at baggage claim. It wasn't revulsion or pique she'd seen on Nicole's face then.

It was fear.

Something had happened at the airport.

At the baggage carousel.

Had Nicole seen Leon's killer? Had their paths somehow intersected? It would explain why she immediately ranted about how horrible all French people were.

No, Maggie reminded herself. How horrible all French *men* were.

If what Maggie now began to fear had happened and Nicole had somehow crossed paths with Leon's killer, that killer was a man.

And that only left Danon Chastain.

59

Danon Chastain.

Had anyone checked *his* alibi for that day? Had Maggie even asked him where he had been that day? Had the cops even bothered interviewing him? Did they even know he existed?

She hadn't asked Danon where he was that day because she was trying to be friendly and hoping he would spill what he knew about the other suspects. He'd never seriously registered on Maggie's radar for the murder itself.

All the facts began to tabulate and fall into place faster than Maggie could think.

If Danon was Leon's killer, it meant he knew when she interviewed him that it was her car he'd stuffed Leon's body in.

And because of what Maggie told him when they spoke, trying to make him comfortable, he also knew that Nicole had been with Maggie at the time.

Maggie groaned as the picture began to come together.

If Nicole had somehow seen or interacted with Danon that day at the airport—if she'd had some kind of run in with him —*she could identify him.*

Maggie's heart raced as she merged onto the A7 heading south toward Marseille. She called Nicole. The call went immediately to voicemail.

Why is her phone not on?

For a moment Maggie debated calling Jean-Baptiste but quickly dismissed the idea. There was no way he would be open to hearing a theory that Nicole had seen Leon's killer.

Danon Chastain.

But it made so much sense!

Danon killed Leon and then after he put the body in Maggie's car trunk, he went into the airport for some reason. There he had an altercation with Nicole—one big enough to upset her. Big enough to make her remember him.

Why had Maggie let Nicole go to the airport on her own today? To hell with the newsletter!

She would never be able to live with herself if something happened to Nicole today.

Why didn't I realize Nicole's temper was out of character for her? Why didn't I realize that something must have happened?

Maggie picked up her phone and scrolled through her contact list until she found Marie-France's number. She had no real hope that the woman would answer the phone. Especially not with her son recently murdered. But she had to at least try.

"*Allo?*"

"*Allo?* Is this Madame Boucher's maid?" Maggie cursed the fact that she'd never gotten the woman's name.

"Madame Boucher too sick to talk."

"Can I ask you then?" Maggie asked hurriedly. "Please? This is Maggie Dernier. I was there yesterday."

"I remember you. Snooping."

"That's right. Can I ask if you know the name of the drug that killed Monsieur Boucher?"

It was a long shot but Maggie had detected a certain pride in the maid when she'd told Maggie about the *loperamide*. It was just possible she knew. And if she did, she would want to let Maggie know she knew.

"Yes. It was Botox."

Maggie felt her heart sink. Why hadn't she asked this before? Anyone in France could get hold of prescription level Botox from their pharmacist. You didn't need to be a medical professional. It wouldn't have been surprising if every woman at the meeting with Maggie this morning had their own supply of Botox and their own needles.

It wasn't an exotic drug cocktail. It was something anyone could easily get their hands on.

Certainly someone like Danon.

"Thank you," Maggie said. "Please give my condolences to Madame Boucher."

"She no be good ever again now," the maid said sadly.

Maggie thought sadly that that was probably very true.

She glanced at her watch. It would take twenty minutes to get into Marseille proper. But only ten to the airport.

She called Nicole again. Again it went to voicemail.

Why isn't she answering? Her flight isn't for another hour! *What teenager isn't completely tied to her cell phone?*

As she drove, Maggie found the *Find My Friends* app on her phone. She had no doubt that Nicole—Nikki—would be furious if she ever found out what Maggie had done, not to mention the fact that Maggie was pretty sure it was illegal. She'd hated herself last week when she'd secretly installed the app on Nicole's phone. And then she'd felt terrible all over again this morning when she realized she'd forgotten to delete it before Nicole left.

And now she thanked God she hadn't.

She quickly clicked on Nikki's name and prayed the girl's phone was on. With one eye on the road for the exit that would lead to the airport, and the other on her phone screen, Maggie watched the app map come alive with a tiny circle with Nikki's photo in the middle of it.

Her stomach hardened as she saw where Nikki's icon was.

At the harbor of Marseille.

Nowhere near the airport.

Maggie felt sick. There was no way Nikki would be anywhere but on that airplane.

If she was physically able.

Maggie bypassed the exit to the airport and pressed down hard on the accelerator pedal, now dividing her attention between the road and the icon on the map.

She had to get to Nicole. She had to find her and...

Suddenly the photo disappeared.

Maggie stared at the map on the screen, her anxiety ratcheting up by the second, willing the photo of Nicole to reappear.

But it was gone.

60

Maggie's hands were clammy as she punched in Jean-Baptiste's private phone number. Unsubstantiated allegations against a possible murder suspect were one thing, but what she had to tell him now was unassailable.

Nicole was supposed to be at the Marseille airport about to board an airplane.

But her phone was sitting in a location off the Marseille harbor twenty kilometers away from the airport.

Jean-Baptiste's phone rang several times until it finally went to voicemail.

He's screening me. And I will never forgive him for this.

She ended the call, feeling the blood drain from her face. Next she put a call in to Laurent and it also went to voicemail.

In Laurent's case there was every reason to believe he hadn't even brought his phone with him when he took Luc to the dentist.

Luc! Maggie quickly called his number.

It too went to voicemail. Maggie groaned. Luc was probably

sitting in a dentist's chair, his phone somewhere vibrating uselessly, unheard and unseen.

Maggie kept checking and rechecking the map on her phone—now absent Nikki's icon photo—to try to remind herself of where she'd last seen it.

She thought about calling Grace but Grace would have no more luck reaching Laurent than Maggie had and what would Maggie ask her to do anyway?

I'm on my own.

She punched in the street intersection for the location where she'd last seen Nikki's GPS icon on her phone.

The only plan she had was to go to the place where Nikki's phone had last been detected. She would follow the onscreen prompts to take her there.

And just pray that the phone—and Nikki—was still there.

Had Danon found her? Did he grab her at the airport? Had he been watching Domaine St-Buvard?

Maggie looked at her phone and for a moment thought about calling him.

But if he answers then he'll know I know the truth.

And he might do something drastic.

If he hasn't done it already.

She drove down rue de la Douane and for a moment had a brief, eerie glimpse of the Chateau d'If perched on its rocky islet west of the Port Vieux. Although she'd never visited it, the place always gave her the chills since it was the prison immortalized by Alexandre Dumas in *The Count of Monte Cristo*.

Within seconds she turned down a deserted street fronted on both sides by looming, inhospitable warehouse facades.

Forcing herself not to hurry in case she missed something, she inched down the empty street between the warehouses. Litter was scattered every few feet in piles against the curb.

She pulled her phone off its holder on the car dashboard

and zoomed in on the map, trying to pinpoint exactly where she remembered seeing Nikki's icon.

She pulled the car over and parked, grabbed her phone and left the car, her purse inside it. She ran to the first door she came to. By her calculation, *this* building would qualify as being closest to the vicinity where she had last seen the photo icon. The door was locked tight.

She stepped back and looked around. Half a block down she saw a metal ladder attached to the side of the building. If she could get to the roof, she might be able to find access there.

This is madness!

She got a mental image of herself attempting to climb the ladder—the bottom rung was a good six inches over her head —and make her way across the roof before she turned back to her phone. With trembling fingers she opened up her text messages app and typed and sent a text.

<Im here u might as well let me in>

The bubbles floated beneath her text, indicating Danon was either composing a reply or thinking about it.

Then the bubbles stopped.

Shivering with nausea threatening to overwhelm her, Maggie began to type in another message.

<I know the truth so let me in or I will go to >

She never finished writing it. The door buzzed loudly, making her jump.

She grabbed the handle and pulled it open.

61

Maggie moved quickly into the interior.

A sharp odor of bleach and diesel combined with mold and dry rot filled the dank air. Boxes and paint cans lined the hallway leading to the center of the warehouse.

She could almost smell the fear. It rebounded off the walls like a living thing. She wasn't sure it wasn't her own fear she was sensing or a residue from those who'd spent their last hours on Earth in this terrible place.

She used her cell phone light to show the way. The warehouse space was different from the one where she'd found Gaston's body. This one was full of shelves of industrial bags and kegs filled with God knew what.

"Just a little bit further," a voice called to her.

Danon.

Maggie couldn't move too quickly without tripping over debris on the ground. There was water on the floor too, at least a half-inch, mixed with oil and grease.

Her heart felt like it would explode in her chest any moment.

"Where is she, Danon?" Maggie called out.

"Aunt Maggie!" Nicole screamed from across the space.

The words seared into Maggie's soul yet heartened her knowing Nikki was at least alive. Within seconds Maggie saw her and Danon in the dim light.

They were against the far wall of the cavernous warehouse space. Nikki was seated, with her hands tied in front of her. Her phone lay in shards on the floor.

Maggie began to run to her.

"Not so fast," Danon said as he stepped in front of her.

She couldn't see whether he had a weapon. She cursed the fact that she hadn't brought at least a knife.

Danon looked like he hadn't slept in a while. His eyes were red and blinking desperately, his beard scraggly and greasy looking.

He held a piece of rebar at his side.

So, not unarmed.

"Empty your pockets," he said.

"I have nothing except my phone."

Danon snorted. "There's no reception in here but I'll take it anyway." He held out his hand.

Maggie looked past him to Nikki as Danon snatched her phone from her. Nikki appeared to be in shock. Her eyes were big and watery and she was staring at Maggie with a stunned look on her face.

"Are you okay, Nikki?"

Danon tossed Maggie's phone onto the floor with Nikki's and smashed it with the rebar.

The phone had been useless in here anyway and the fact that Danon was only swinging a piece of metal around told Maggie he was improvising as he went along.

She could work with that.

She went to Nikki and put her arms around her and felt the girl tremble violently.

"You can stop now," she said to Danon, "You haven't gone too far. It isn't the end of the world yet."

"Oh, no? I don't know how they do things in America but over here, two murders are fairly damning," Danon said with a bitter laugh.

"A good lawyer can see you through both of those," Maggie lied. "But not if you add two American nationals to the tally."

"Are you saying that two Americans are worth more than two Frenchmen?"

"When one of them is a no-good neo-Nazi bastard? Yes, I'll go out on a limb here and say yes."

Danon stared at her for a moment and then gave a half laugh. He leaned against the table as Maggie rubbed Nikki's arms to try to warm her up.

"Want to tell me how we all ended up here?" Maggie said.

"If I do then I'll have to kill you." He laughed. "That's a joke. Except not really."

"How did you know Nikki? You saw her at the airport that day, didn't you?"

"We did, as it happened," he said glancing at Nikki who was still staring straight ahead as if in a trance. "I came back for my bag. Well, let me start at the beginning, shall I? The good thing about getting all this off my chest is that I get to confess but I don't have to worry about going to prison for it."

Maggie patted Nikki's arm. It worried her that the girl wouldn't look at her. Was she in shock?

"I was returning from London," Danon said, "and waiting at baggage claim for my bag when who should I happen to see but Leon on his way to the car park? I had no idea he'd been out of town. I stopped him and said 'what the hell, Leon?' and I guess we had words. And we basically had words all the way to the car park where we stopped having words."

Danon chewed on a fingernail and looked off into space as he relived his last moments with Leon Boucher.

"We went to his car. Things escalated as they always did with Leon. I'd put my Botox syringe in my jacket pocket to give myself a touch up in the airport bathroom and right in the middle of our argument I just pulled it out and stabbed him."

"It wasn't planned. After that things went seriously ass-wise. He'd already put his keys in the ignition and had gotten out to continue arguing with me when I stabbed him. As soon as he shut the driver's side door it automatically locked. So now I'm outside and the keys are inside the car. And now Leon is just dead weight on the ground. I saw you drive up. I could see your trunk was open. I waited. You left. I put him inside."

"And then you went back to baggage claim."

"Yes, well, I hadn't gotten my bag, had I? So I ran back to the baggage claim to get my bag. And I have to admit I was pretty upset. I mean, wouldn't you be? And I accidentally knocked into your pretty little niece. We had words and well, I guess you could say I made an impression. Not what one wants to do when one has just killed a man."

Maggie remembered going to the gate—bypassing Nicole who was waiting at baggage claim—too embroiled in her own thoughts to notice her phone was blowing up with incoming texts from Nicole. Maggie glanced at Nicole who was blinking and licking her lips.

Maggie chose to take that as a good sign.

"So then," Danon said, "I grabbed my bag and I followed her and you to the car park and I saw her get in the very car I'd just stuffed Leon's body into! What are the odds? After that it was easy. Your name was listed in the newspaper as the one who discovered the body so it was just a couple of steps after that I knew where you lived."

He grinned at Maggie and tapped the rebar against his boot.

"Then you came to speak to me—thanks for that, by the way, very helpful—and told me everything I needed to know about little Nicole here. It was especially helpful when you told me how upset she was and how she was always on her laptop. It was just a quick step from there and I knew how to reach her. I reached out to her as soon as I left the café where you and I met."

Nikki's eyes flickered at that and Maggie squeezed her hand hoping to give her encouragement.

"I actually hung out around your house for most of last week hoping to catch her alone," Danon continued. "I had a couple of near misses where I nearly got her but in the end, we connected, didn't we, *chérie*?" He nodded to Nikki.

"What about Gaston?" Maggie asked. "Why did you kill him?"

"Well, you're going to laugh when you hear," Danon said, tapping the rebar against the table as testing it for strength. "Gaston and I actually got together for a few drinks the day after I met with you. We got to talking and I thought we really connected. I guess I was more emotional than I realized. I mean, I did just lose the love of my life."

Maggie looked at him to see if he was joking but he didn't appear to be.

"So anyway in the throes of emotion and way too much *pastis*, I sort of confessed."

"You confessed to killing Leon? To his son?"

"Stupid, I know. Alcohol is the devil's handmaiden."

"So you lured Gaston to an abandoned warehouse and killed him. How?"

"Same as with Leon. Botox overdose. I liked the symmetry of it."

"And I assume you then used Olivier's phone to send me those messages to meet Olivier there so I would discover the body?"

"That is correct. It was amusing watching Mohammed stumble all over himself trying to say it wasn't him. The cops brought him in for questioning last night. Did you know that?"

Maggie shook her head.

"Plus I thought you discovering Gaston's body might make the cops look at you for Leon's murder. Kind of suspicious discovering two bodies in one week. It never occurred to me you wouldn't report it! Just when I thought I could count on you."

"Go to hell."

"Yes, well. You first." Danon stood up and smacked the rebar rod against his palm.

Maggie stood too and pulled Nikki to her feet.

"You can leave her there," he said. "She's not going anywhere. Neither are you."

"We *are* leaving here," Maggie said to him and then turned to Nikki. "Don't make me slap you, sweetie. Snap out of it."

"I'm fine," Nikki mumbled.

Maggie shook her arm. "Look at me."

Nikki tore her eyes away from the space she'd been lost in and connected with Maggie's eyes.

"Both of you, sit back down," Danon said as he lay the iron bar down on the table well out of reach and began fishing in his shirt pocket. "I swear this won't hurt. Just a tiny prick and then sweet dreams."

Maggie didn't take her eyes off Nikki's face.

"I'm fine," Nikki said again a little more convincingly.

Maggie dug out her car keys and placed them in Nikki's hands.

"The car is right outside and so are the police. I need you to get in the car and start driving."

"She's not doing that!" Danon said. "And the police are not outside."

Maggie turned to him. "Yes, Danon. They are. I called 9-9-9 before I came in. The dispatcher was not at all surprised to hear that another murder had occurred in this area. It's not very nice real estate you know."

"You're lying!" he said, rocking in one place and turning to look in the direction of where the door was.

"Nikki, go!" Maggie shouted, shoving her away.

Out of the corner of her eye Maggie saw Danon move toward Nikki. Maggie swiveled around and launched herself at him.

He batted at her and then grabbed for one of her arms but Maggie lashed out an outstretched hand and jabbed him hard in the eyes. He screamed and jerked backward. But he didn't let go of her.

"Bitch!" he howled.

He twisted Maggie around in his arms and she felt his arm hard as iron wrap around her throat. She felt a terrible pressure building up inside her. Darkness flickered in her vision peppered with sparks and then died away as she felt her strength fail.

That's when she felt the needle.

Sharp with a stinging pain. It pushed through her sweater into the yielding flesh of her throat.

And then she felt nothing at all.

62

The cold cement floor jumped up and slammed into Maggie's face as she fell. A screeching cacophony of noises and vibrations reverberated in her skull.

"Aunt Maggie! Aunt Maggie, open your eyes! Over here! Hurry!"

Nicole's voice came in and out of Maggie's dark dreams. She licked her parched lips.

"It didn't go all the way in," Nicole said to someone. "I hit him on the head before he could push the plunger I think."

Maggie felt strong hands lifting her up and a light exploded in her eyes until she groaned and turned her head away.

"Do you have water?" she heard Nikki ask. "She's thirsty. Aunt Maggie, can you look at me?"

Maggie opened her eyes a fraction and saw Nikki in front of her, peering into her face.

"You're going to be okay," Nikki said. "I'm pretty sure you're going to be okay."

Maggie looked around and saw she was no longer on the floor but lying on a stretcher, still in the warehouse. A warm blanket was draped over her.

"What? Where?"

"I hit him on the head," Nikki said, pressing her lips into a firm line. "I ran off and he thought I was gone and I picked up this massive mother of a shovel that was just lying there with all this other junk and I came back and knocked the holy crap out of him."

Three uniformed policemen stood writing on clipboards and talking into their cellphones. One glanced over at Maggie. She didn't see anyone else there who looked like a detective. She didn't see Jean-Baptiste.

Maggie struggled to sit up and looked over at Nikki. She shook her head thinking that would help clear it. It made the pain worse.

"He...he didn't inject me?"

"He stuck you," Nikki said. "And the EMT guys aren't sure the needle is too clean so there's that. But no poison got in you we're almost positive."

Maggie put her hand to her throat and one of the EMTs came over and took her pulse. She realized what she had felt must not have been the effects of a toxic drug in her system— but of being nearly strangled to death.

"The police were out front just like you said," Nikki said. "Thank God you called them."

"You didn't leave," Maggie said, reaching for the water bottle Nikki handed her. "I told you to run."

"I couldn't, could I?" Nikki said and sat down next to Maggie on the stretcher and pulled the blanket so it wrapped around both of them.

"Where is he?"

"They took him to the hospital. I really brained him, Aunt Maggie. I mean, seriously."

"Good girl." Maggie said absently and put a trembling hand to her head. It hurt a little less than it had.

"I saw him at baggage claim," Nikki said. "The day I landed."

Maggie squeezed the girl's hand. "What happened?"

Nikki fought not to give in to the tears that were threatening. "He tripped over my bag and cussed me out. That was it."

"Except it wasn't."

Tears streaking down Nikki's cheek. "His...aftershave stuck with me. It was so...memorable. I only spent maybe ten seconds with him. But he scared me. I didn't even understand his words to me. But it was horrible. I don't know why he affected me the way he did."

"He'd just murdered a man," Maggie said softly. "I don't wonder he made an impression."

"I think he was afraid I'd tell someone I'd seen him."

"All it would take was for you to see his photo in the paper or online. And he'd have been finished."

"Do you think our hearing his confession will count?"

"I do. That and the partial fingerprint on the car trunk. Once they match it to him, he's pretty much done."

"I should have told you that he contacted me."

"It's okay."

"No, I should have. I don't know why I didn't."

"I didn't make it easy for you to tell me much of anything. I wanted you to love France so much that I didn't listen to what you were trying to say to me."

"Luc will be happy to see me tonight. Is Uncle Laurent going to be cross with you, do you think?"

Maggie laughed and put her arm around Nikki and squeezed her.

"He'll forgive me. He always does."

63

One week later

Maggie squinted against the sinking sun to watch Laurent and the boys as they monitored the grill in the garden at *Dormir*.

Surrounded by hardscape pavers and a low stone wall, the grill emitted a scent of the cooking meat—burgers, lamb chops and chicken—that lifted tantalizingly up into the early evening air.

"I would die to live here full time, truly!" Bambi Johnson gushed as she watched Laurent where he stood, his hands on his hips as he watched the meat on the grill.

Bambi was staying at *Dormir* with her husband who, as best as Maggie could tell, had yet to say a word his entire visit.

She and Bambi were sitting in lawn chairs that Luc and Jemmy had set up off the courtyard. The sun was still hovering over the horizon although it was past seven in the evening.

Maggie stretched out her legs, enjoying the feel of a chilled glass of rosé in her hand.

"I mean just the pastries alone. Am I right?" Bambi said. "What do you do to keep the weight off? I'd be as big as a water buffalo if I ate like this all the time!"

Since Bambi was sinewy bone and muscle—testimony to the tennis league she was president of back home in Tulsa— Maggie seriously doubted a few pastries would alter her physique.

"Well, we do a lot of walking," Maggie said, her eyes closing and only half paying attention to the woman.

Danielle was in the kitchen with Zouzou and Mila preparing the *gâteau aux pommes* for later while Grace was inside trying to get Philippe to go to sleep for the night. Maggie knew she should probably go in and offer to help except every time she tried, Grace insisted it was a one-person job.

"Your husband is seriously dishy," Bambi murmured, openly ogling Laurent as he moved around the grill, instructing the boys or throwing more wood into the firebox.

With the sun dropping behind the trees, it was already getting cool, even in late August. Just then Maggie's phone vibrated. She pulled it out of her jacket pocket.

It was Ben.

"Excuse me," Maggie said to Bambi and got up and walked away.

Nikki had been home a week and had called twice to check in, which pleased Maggie very much—and Luc even more who'd spoken to her every day since she'd left.

But this was the first time Maggie had spoken with Ben. She'd been waiting for his call. Nikki had told her last night that she was finally going to get around to telling him about her not being related to Elise. Maggie had offered to tell him for her but she had to admit it would be better coming from Nikki.

"Hey, Ben. How's the weather there in Atlanta?"

"Nikki told me what you and Laurent did," Ben said without bothering with a greeting.

"Which part?"

"*Which part*? The part where the two of you kidnap a French kid and don't tell anyone in the family for thirteen years!"

Maggie breathed a sigh of relief. It seemed Nikki still didn't believe any good could come from telling her uncle about being held hostage by a murderer in an abandoned warehouse before she flew home.

Maggie was almost positive that was for the best.

"Are you saying you're less interested in playing the doting uncle now that you know you're not really related to her?"

"Don't be offensive! And that's not the point. You kept this from the family. From all of us!"

"I'm sorry, Ben. At the time it felt right."

"Do you have any idea how this is affecting Nikki? Now that she knows she's not blood-related to us?"

"Well, yes, since she found out while she was here."

"Did you *ever* intend to tell her? Or Mom and Dad?"

"What would be the point? I still don't think Mom needs to know but of course, we were always going to tell Nikki one day."

There was a moment of sputtered silence before Ben spoke again.

"Sometimes, Maggie, I feel like I don't even know you."

"That's interesting that you should say that, Ben, because I've always felt that way about you."

There was another brief silence on the line and Maggie felt a surprising shiver of sadness that she and Ben, now her only living sibling, should always be so distant.

"Is it at all possible we might get along? For Nikki's sake?"

"I would like that. Seriously, Ben. And not just for Nikki's sake."

"Fine," he said gruffly. "Well, you'll be happy to know she's decided to register for some classes at Perimeter College in the fall."

Maggie felt a surge of warmth radiate through her.

"Oh, Ben, that's great! I'm so glad."

"Yeah, well. She wanted me to be the one to tell you. Not sure why."

But Maggie knew why. Nikki was trying to tell her that living with Ben, living in Atlanta, living with the knowledge of who she was—it was going to be fine.

She was going to be fine.

Not surprisingly, dinner was amazing.

The annoying Bambi and her somnolent husband went back to their cottage as soon as dessert was served without waiting for cheese or coffee, which suited everyone else quite well.

Danielle finally sat down and Maggie and Grace refused to allow her to get back up to attend to one more thing until morning. Laurent set Luc and Jemmy to cleaning up around the grill and piling the grates and pans in the kitchen sink where Laurent would wash them before leaving tonight.

But for now, they all sat around the dining table, votive lights flickering down the center, dessert and cheese dishes scattered amongst the glasses and bottles of dessert wine, port and brandy.

The children were playing hide and seek in the adjoining lawn and the adults could hear their laughter and voices.

"It's a perfect summer night," Maggie said. "Just perfect."

"It is, isn't it?" Grace said, sipping her glass of Calvados. "Thanks to good friends." She smiled at Danielle who was still drinking coffee. Maggie often wondered how Danielle could sleep after drinking it so late but Laurent didn't have any trouble with caffeine either.

"Did I hear that you spoke to Ben?" Grace asked Maggie as Laurent got up to have a smoke.

"I did. Nikki told him about her not being Elise's child."

"How did that go down?"

Maggie shrugged. "He was snotty about it of course but he'd already had some time to process it. He wasn't too bad."

"Nicole is a lovely girl," Danielle said. "She should come back to France."

Maggie smiled at Danielle just as Zouzou wandered over to drink from a tall glass of Perrier on the table.

"On the good news front," Maggie said, "Nikki is going to register for community college in the fall."

"Oh, well done, Nikki!" Grace said.

Zouzou frowned. "What's community college?"

"A start," Maggie said, smiling at her.

An hour later, all the children were in the house watching television, Laurent was washing dishes and Danielle had retired for the night.

Maggie and Grace were sitting on the back terrace, just the two of them enjoying the quiet of the evening.

"I overheard Luc talking about the upcoming harvest," Grace said. "He seemed pretty excited."

"He's made a turnaround. Pretty dramatically."

"Something Laurent said?"

"I don't know. Laurent is a man of few words as you know. But it was definitely as a result of a message he gave Luc. I'm sure of that."

"Luc really acted like he was fully family tonight. Did you feel it, too?"

"I did."

All week Luc had been talking about the harvest with Laurent and even reading books about grape harvesting. His enthusiasm wasn't just youthful exuberance, Maggie knew. She could tell he was taking a personal pride in the vineyard—not merely as a seasonal worker as he'd been up to now, but as a part of the family.

"He even asked Laurent about the possibility of changing his name to Dernier."

"Oh my. I'm sure that made Laurent happy."

"Pretty much."

"You've had a busy summer," Grace said as she poured the last of the apple brandy in both their glasses.

"That's for sure. What with Luc and Nikki and the murder at the airport and, oh!—did you know Laurent punched out one of the monks last week?"

"Are you serious? That's surprising even for Laurent. Who?"

"He wasn't there long enough for me to get his name. He came, pissed off Laurent, got socked and the way I heard it from Madame Augustin at the *boulangerie* got his marching orders."

"Dear Laurent," Grace said shaking her head. "He really does run this province like his own private fiefdom, doesn't he?"

"Now that you mention it."

"When is Frère Jean returning to the monastery?"

"Any day now."

"A new man, presumably?"

"Until next time anyway."

They were silent for a moment listening to the singing of the crickets in the garden.

"Is Nikki happy to be home, do you think?"

"I do," Maggie said with a sigh. "I'm honestly not sure we'll ever get her to come back. Especially not after what happened last week on her way to the airport."

"I'm not sure I ever heard the full details of how it was that Danon got her in the back seat of his car in the first place."

Maggie took a long swallow of her brandy.

"Just thinking about it makes my skin crawl. But basically it was my fault."

"Your fault?"

"When I first interviewed Danon I told him I was using Ubers to get around because my car was impounded. He'd already been hanging around Domaine St-Buvard trying to see if he could get Nikki by herself and when he saw her standing in the driveway with Luc that morning, he figured he'd take the chance that she was waiting for an Uber."

"So he just drove up and said he was her ride?"

"Pretty much. He first spoke to Luc who had no reason to think he wasn't the Uber driver."

"Dear God."

"And Nikki had put her cell phone in her carry-on which Luc had set in the front seat so she wasn't able to get to it. Danon locked the car doors and drove her to the warehouse. It's a miracle she's normal after all that."

"How in the world did you figure it was him?"

"It always bothered me that Nikki was so cross with us—from the moment I picked her up at baggage claim. But I didn't make the connection fast enough that something must have happened to make her act so hatefully. When I finally did, I did a process of elimination which led me straight to Danon."

"You mean because Nikki had bumped into him at baggage claim?"

"Yes. And then he followed her—and me—back to the car park and saw that it was actually Nikki's car that he'd stuffed Leon's body in!"

"So now he had a girl who could recognize him and place him at the airport."

"Exactly. Once he knew my name—thank you *La Provence*—he began hanging out around St-Buvard trying to get Nikki alone."

"Okay, so back to the process of elimination."

"Right, well, I figured I had seven suspects for Leon's murder."

"Goodness."

"Yeah, that's a lot. But I was able to eliminate Marie-France who had a disability and couldn't have done it, and both Mohammed and Cayenne Olivier who had confirmable alibis although not each other's, which just left Angeline Sauvage, Joelle Mercier and Danon. All of them had motives. But because the killer had texted me on Olivier's phone to lure me to the place where he'd killed Gaston, I had to ask myself which of the three could have gotten their hands on Olivier's phone *and* didn't have an alibi for Leon's death? Really, only Danon. Then I remembered that Nikki was upset about all Frenchmen and well, Danon was the only one who fit."

"Why didn't Nikki just tell you some guy was ugly to her at the airport?"

"I don't know, Grace. I guess, being a teenager, it was just easier to be mad at me than to tell me some random guy was hateful to her."

"But then he contacted her through Facebook?"

Maggie nodded. "He was trying to threaten her, but he wasn't at the point where he felt he needed to kill her. Nikki was already scared out of her wits and I think he was afraid she might go to the police."

"So what made him decide to try to kill her after all?"

"Oh, that's the interesting part. Danon started getting recognized news sources approaching him asking for interviews about his connection to Leon and he desperately wanted to be semi-famous and agree to interviews, but he was terrified of being seen on TV by Nikki. He knew if she saw his picture in the paper or online she would remember she saw him at the airport the day Leon died. He wasn't on the cops' radar at this point—but whatever alibi he later dreamed up, Nikki would have destroyed it as soon as she opened her mouth."

"And why did he kill Leon?"

"From what Jean-Baptiste told me, he thought Leon was coming back from a lover's tryst in Paris."

"So jealousy?"

"Basically."

"Does this mean you and Jean-Baptiste are back together again?"

Maggie snorted. "If by back together you mean is he taking all the credit and being a horse's ass in the process, then yes, we're back together."

"What about Laurent?"

"Laurent is not amused by any of it. In fact, there was a moment or two after the cops called him to come collect me and Nikki from yet another abandoned warehouse that I would have to say he was downright furious. I don't think I've ever seen him so mad."

"Does he know you at all? You've been doing this for years. Why doesn't he just give up?"

"I know, right?"

And the two old friends laughed and laughed until tears streamed down their faces and they had to fight to catch their breath.

Later that night, back at Domaine St-Buvard, the kids stumbled their way to bed while Laurent let the dogs out and had one last smoke as he looked past the terrace pavers and wrought iron furniture to his grape fields.

Maggie watched him from the kitchen before turning and pouring two glasses of wine and bringing them upstairs to their bedroom. It felt later than it was and because she'd spent most of the day outdoors, she felt all the sunlight and weariness of the day seep into her shoulders and neck.

By the time she'd showered and dressed for bed, Laurent was just coming into the house. She sat up in bed and eased onto her pillow, enjoying a sip of the wine. It was one of last year's Domaine St-Buvard wines and she honestly felt she could taste the summer in it.

Laurent came in, gave the wine glass by his bedside an arched eyebrow, then pulled off his shirt and went to shower.

Maggie listened to the running water and thought she could even hear Laurent humming. She found herself thinking back to the moment after their Sunday lunch when Nikki had asked them both to tell her everything. At the time Maggie wasn't sure Nikki hadn't felt worse afterward.

It's a bitter thing to realize you're truly motherless when before you thought you at least had a dead one.

And while they'd talked a little bit since then about the possibility of looking for Nikki's "real" mother, Maggie knew there was little to no chance of her finding out who she really was or where she really came from.

That was compliments of the decision she and Laurent had made thirteen years ago. Again, it had felt like the right decision at the time.

I would do the exact same thing again.

When Laurent came into the bedroom toweling his wet hair, he sat on the bed and picked up his wine glass.

"I've been thinking a lot of Roger this week," Maggie said.

Laurent turned to look at her and she saw the tension in his shoulders relax.

"*Moi aussi.*"

She couldn't help thinking of Roger, rolling over and over in her mind the memory of his face—kindly and perpetually bemused—and his words as he led her down the path that would eventually bring her to this very room in this *mas* with this man. Roger had been at the heart of everything that had happened that cataclysmic week thirteen years ago.

He'd put Laurent in her life. And also Nikki. He'd brought with him a bonhomie and a capriciousness of spirit that Maggie had never found in anyone else since.

And now, tonight, even more than the week when she and Laurent had traveled to London to say a final goodbye at Roger's funeral, Maggie was feeling the loss of him in the world.

"He was one in a million," she said.

"That he was."

Laurent slipped under the covers and leaned back against the headboard, holding his wine glass.

Maggie had spent a lot of time recently wondering if she would ever have tried to handle things the way she had—or made the life-altering decisions she had—if not for Roger. She supposed it didn't matter now. Things were the way they were.

And in the end she was immensely grateful for that.

"I still can't believe Nikki finally knows the truth," Maggie said. "It's a terrific weight lifted, you know? After all these years."

Laurent set his wine glass down.

"That was very clever of you to tell Nikki that your father knew the truth."

"I think it helped settle her," Maggie said putting her own wine glass down and snuggling against him. He felt broad and solid beside her.

"Lies often do," Laurent said, lifting a tendril of hair from the nape of her neck.

"Well, I guess that's one thing I've learned from you, Laurent. Not everything good has to be the truth."

"Ah, you are using my own words against me, *chérie* and that I cannot allow."

He flipped her on her back on the bed and leaned teasingly over her.

"So I guess now there's only the one secret left," Maggie said, stretching luxuriantly beneath him, her arms over her head.

"If you're referring to Luc," Laurent said, nuzzling her neck, "that is *not* the only secret left."

She stopped him from what he was doing and cocked an eyebrow at him.

"Okay, now you really do have my attention."

"And that, *chérie,* is of course my intention," Laurent said, his eyes glittering with love but also purpose.

To follow more of Maggie's sleuthing and adventures in Provence, order **Murder in St-Rémy,** *Book 15 of the Maggie Newberry Mysteries!*

RECIPE FOR BOUILLABAISSE

There's one meal which Laurent takes particular pride in and that's his bouillabaisse. But you don't have to run into one of the Marseille fish markets where he shops to make this iconic dish--one for the memory books. Just follow the steps, use the best freshest ingredients you can find...and bon appétit!

Makes 6 servings

You'll need for the bouillon:
- 2 lbs whole firm-grained fish, cleaned
- ¾ cups olive oil
- 4-6 large ripe tomatoes, roughly chopped
- 2 large yellow onions, finely chopped
- 2 cloves garlic, peeled
- 1 leek, thinly sliced
- 2 bay leaves
- 1 orange peel
- 3-4 dried fennel stalks
- 1 tsp thyme
- 1 tsp rosemary
- ½-1 tsp saffron

2-3 hot red peppers

For the bouillabaisse you'll need:

4-½ lbs firm-grained fish filets (Dorade, porgy (sea bream), sea bass, monkfish, or similar)

18-24 small potatoes, peeled and sliced into ¼ slices

several garlic cloves, peeled

1-½ cup grated Gruyere cheese

1 day-old stale baguette

Into a large heat-proof casserole, sauté the finely chopped onions in ¾ cup olive oil. Once the onions are transparent, add the chopped tomatoes, 2 cloves garlic, leek, bay leaves, thyme, and rosemary, and simmer until the onions, garlic and leek are browned. Next add 16 cups of water. Salt the water generously and add the bay leaves, orange peel, fennel stalks, thyme, rosemary, saffron and hot red peppers. Add first 2 lbs of cleaned fish. Bring everything to a boil, then lower heat and simmer for 30 minutes. Remove the mixture from the heat and strain through a fine sieve into a clean casserole. (Use a wooden spoon to press the juices out of the fish, vegetables and herbs.)

To make croutons, cut the baguette into ½ inch slices. Drizzle each with olive oil and put in oven until toasted. Rub one side of each bread slice with garlic. Set aside.

To begin cooking the bouillabaisse, add the sliced potatoes to the bouillon in the casserole. Add the 4-½ lbs of fish, and bring the casserole to a boil over high heat. Cook until the fish and potatoes are tender. Put the potatoes in one serving dish and the fish in another.

You are now ready to serve up the bouillabaisse. Place two or three croutons in the bottom of each soup plate, topping each with freshly grated Gruyère cheese. Next ladle in the steaming hot fish bouillon. Finally, add potato slices and fish.

ABOUT THE AUTHOR

USA TODAY Bestselling Author Susan Kiernan-Lewis is the author of *The Maggie Newberry Mysteries,* the post-apocalyptic thriller series *The Irish End Games, The Mia Kazmaroff Mysteries, The Stranded in Provence Mysteries,* and *An American in Paris Mysteries.*

Visit www.susankiernanlewis.com or follow Author Susan Kiernan-Lewis on Facebook.

Made in the USA
Coppell, TX
23 August 2021

61005603R10208